Milk

by

emily hammond

THE PERMANENT PRESS
SAG HARBOR, NY 11963

Library of Congress Cataloging-in-Publication Data

Hammond, Emily
    Milk: a novel /by Emily Hammond
      p. cm.
    ISBN 1-57962-034-5 (alk paper)
    1. Separated people--Fiction. 2. Mothers--Death--Fiction.
    3. Suicide victims--Fiction. 4. Pregnant women--Fiction.
    5. Young women--Fiction. 6. California--Fiction. I. Title

    PS3558.A44892 M55 2001
    813'.54--dc21   00-064251
                                     CIP

THE PERMANENT PRESS
4170 Noyac Road
Sag Harbor, NY 11963

For my father

and

In memory of my mother

Acknowledgements

My gratitude to those friends who offered me a place to write, read drafts, inquired and generally listened to me fret for the ten years this novel was with me: Bitte and Kevin Colby, Leslie Johnson, Gary and Deanna Ludwin, Ann Miner, Susan Moore, Liza Nelligan, Antonya Nelson, Terrie Sandelin, Laura Swauger, Kathryn Symmes, my agent Kit Ward, as well as the writing community of Fort Collins, Colorado. Special thanks to Diana K. Maehlum.

To my brothers Joe and Jim, and to Aunt Nancy and Uncle Bill—my appreciation for your constancy and support.

As for my father, you deserve a star for being such a wealth of information.

Above all, I thank my family for their patience and love: our son Zach, our daughter Elena, and Steven, whose heart and instincts as an editor and husband are unparalleled.

I reconstruct my childhood because that's the spring that seems to be flowing at the moment, something else gushing from the hole, which in one of its manifestations is a fountain.

Richard Rhodes, *A Hole in the World*

Part One:
The Alta Vista

ONE

I wake up and remember. A rushing sound, leaves being chased. Wind, and moaning. It's the middle of the night at the Alta Vista, the residential hotel I mistook for a bed-and-breakfast. No couples making love here. People in pain, crying in their sleep. At the end of the hall lives an old man attached to an oxygen tank; he watches TV, watches me whenever I pass by, nodding and letting his breathing mask slip a little, like a gentleman tipping his hat.

I remember my dream: the girl. She strolled by my bed, the sash of her dress brushing my face. Sometimes it's a woman kneeling in shame or in prayer, my mother come to me in the middle of the night. Or so I believe. They're not quite dreams but hallucinations—my eyes are open. The wind woke me, too, trees lashing back and forth; a hot, mean wind.

Come morning, I know how things will look. Palm fronds wrenched off like dislocated shoulders, lying in the streets which otherwise have a bare, scoured look. The air will be cleaner at least.

I see this place like a series of photographs: How it looks after a windstorm. How it looks after a winter rainstorm—rinsed, brilliant; retreating black clouds, sun. Myself as a child again playing tether ball on a morning after such a storm, in a red parka, the hard black shoes chosen by my mother . . . my hair slicked back like a boy's, except it's in a ponytail with a taut red ribbon. In the background are the San Gabriel Mountains, flashes of light and green and shadow.

This wind. I nearly run my tongue above my lip to check for dust or grit. I could be in a ghost town, the sort we visited when I was a child. We'd look through the windows, able to make out green-blue bottles, shoes, yellowed newspapers.

I can't sleep, worries about whether I've done the right thing. I sit cross-legged on the bed and start a letter to Jackson, my husband. I ask him to join me, then rip up the letter. I start another, writing in the near dark, the letter illuminated by moonlight and the palsied shadows of eucalyptus. I tell him I'm going to be here a while, visiting family and . . . *I don't know what I want anymore,* I write. *I don't know who I am, but with each day I'm surer the future may not include you.* I rip up this letter too.

In neither letter do I mention that I think I'm pregnant.

Early next morning I prepare to visit my father's office, a surprise visit: neither he nor my brother know I'm in town yet. I rinse my face with cold water that smells of rust. This is after contemplating the shower—a soiled athletic sock over the showerhead, like a funnel, the toe cut off and the filthy thing tied on with string. For what purpose I can't figure out, unless it's to control the spray.

I settle for washing my face, with water that slowly heats up.

Driving to my father's office, the new one, I go too far west on Huntington Drive and have to turn around. No parking lot that I can see, so I end up parking across the street at Ralph's Supermarket.

This office is in a building without an elevator, only narrow stairs. Each year for the past three my father has moved offices, to one that is invariably smaller and cheaper, so it is with some trepidation that I knock on his door.

"Come in!" His voice is cheery, businesslike, muffled.

"Dad?"

Abruptly he stands up, hitting his head on a lamp. "Theo?"

"Are you all right, Dad?"

We look at each other, alarmed. Though I saw him just last year he seems thinner, his neck papery as a dried cornstalk, and, in contrast, his pate shining with age spots and strands of white silk. He's dressed in a suit, tie, and stiff black wing tips. It isn't like my father to dress casually.

"Theo, what are you doing here?"

"Dad," I say approaching his desk, "there aren't any windows here." Just walls and fluorescent fixtures that buzz and cast a tallow light.

"Why are you here, Theo? Are you visiting? Are you here on business?" He kisses me on the cheek. We hug. His brown eyes seem unduly moist; their darkness, their depth, their sadness have always astounded me. They are eyes that don't hide anything, although everything else about his behavior does.

"Oh, sort of here on business." My kind of business I can do anywhere, so it's not exactly a lie.

Surrounding my father's desk, the same stained walnut one he has owned for decades, are three tensor lamps and two floor lamps, one I recognize from his house.

"Won't you sit down?" he says, offering his office chair since apparently there aren't any others.

"No, Dad, I—"

"Please." In that tone of voice: *Please, it would make me so happy.*

I sit, all the lamps directly in my eyes as though I were brought here for questioning. Indeed, my father grills me about my flight yesterday—was it on time, was it bumpy over the Rockies, did I like the service, was lunch provided?—the particulars of airline travel is one of his favorite subjects.

"Will Jackson be joining you?"

"Well, Dad, no."

"No?"

"Dad, that's one of the reasons I'm here. We're separating." I visualize the yolk and white of an egg.

"What?"

"We're separating. I left him. Dad, you sit here. I feel like I'm being cross-examined, all these lights. Why do you have all these lights?"

"Would you like me to move the chair?"

"Actually, I don't feel much like sitting." I stand up and wander around the room, picking up things and putting them down. Stapler. Paperweight. Box of paper clips.

"Did you and Jackson have a fight?" my father is saying. "I didn't even know you were having trouble. I had no idea. When did you decide this?"

"Day before yesterday, but I've been thinking about it a long time."

He waits for me to say more. I don't. "I'll tell you more in a couple of days, Dad. When I feel more like talking, okay?" In my hands I'm holding the most cherished of all my father's office things: a box he made in shop class as a boy, the lid of which fits loosely. On the top it says in handwritten letters, JEWELRY. It was for his mother.

"I'm sorry," my father says. "I feel just awful about this."

Though I'm plenty upset, at the moment I feel more upset for him: the way he shakes his head in disbelief and shock, what it must be like for a father when his daughter announces her marriage has failed. "I'm just curious, Dad, changing the subject. Why didn't you rent an office that has windows?"

"Didn't think I needed them," he says primly. It's a rule of his that my brother Corb and I are never to contradict him on matters of money, he who has plenty of it and an inability to spend any on himself.

"But Dad, couldn't you do better than this? It's depressing here, no windows, shabby paint job, not to mention poor lighting, since apparently you had to bring in all these lamps."

"I like it here," he says.

He probably does.

"I'm still in shock about this news of yours," he says. "I had no idea you and Jackson—" He sees my face. "All right, we won't talk about it now. But what are you going to do?"

"Maybe I'll move back here."

"You can't do that!"

"Why not? Don't you want me here?" My tears rise, then halt, stinging. I'm thinking about the baby, if there is a baby.

"Sure I want you here, but—your life is there. You can't just up and leave it. Marriage is . . . marriage is . . . You can't just leave your husband!"

"I have left him, Dad. That's what I'm trying to tell you."

"For good?"

"I think so. I'm not sure yet."

Since I won't sit, he won't either. He paces, he opens drawers, jots down something on a scrap of paper. On his desk is a magnifying glass, which I've never seen before but it's the perfect detail, comforting and somehow seafaring; it goes along with my father's ancient adding machine and what must be one of the world's first Xerox machines that prints brownish illegible copies on strange slick paper. Next to that is my father's safe, big and square as an old icebox, with an enormous dial. What does he keep in that thing? my brother Corb and I used to wonder. Stock certificates, prehistoric files, a diary? Our mother's suicide note, though we never wondered aloud about this, not to each other. There wasn't a suicide note, was there?

"Theo," Dad says. "About Jackson. I just feel—"

"Can't we change the subject, Dad? Please?"

He purses his lips. "All right," he says, putting pens away in his desk drawer one by one. "Well, then. How do you like your chariot?"

My car, he means. Rental cars: another of Dad's pet subjects, along with airline travel and hotel rooms (thank God we haven't gotten to the subject of the Alta Vista yet). "What'd they give you?" he says. "Did you go with Hertz this time? I'm finished with Budget. Did I tell you what they did?" I've spent entire visits discussing rental cars with my father. "I'd stick with the majors if I were you. Did you get their insurance? Your own insurance should cover it, but I'd get extra liability if I were you."

Extra liability. I need a lot more than that right now. In the parking lot of Ralph's, I can't even find my rental car. I have a headache besides, a particular kind of headache I associate with this place, a smog headache: my eyes burn, the front of my head pounds. Never mind that there is no smog today, last night's wind blew it away.

Which car is mine? I have to think back to the airport; was I assigned a red car, a blue car, a Dodge, a Chevrolet? I can't think, familiar as I am with rental cars. I've driven fifteen years worth in all my visits to Pasadena. Compact cars, Fords, Pontiacs, two-doors, four-doors, convertibles.

Examining my keys, I see I've rented from National this time, a company my father detests. I just walked to the car rental area and stood in the shortest line, a practice my father abhors. He calls ahead, makes reservations, compares rates, reconsiders past wrongs on the part of the company, forgives or holds grudges. "National?" he would say if he knew. "You rented from *them?*"

On the National-provided key chain there are letters and numbers, the license plate number, no doubt. I look for a description of the car; there is none. I begin my search, estimating there must be a least ten rows I'll have to walk. I try to think logically: where would I be most likely to park? Was it this crowded when I first arrived, row upon row of cars glaring in the sun?

I don't remember. All I can think about is my headache and my stomach. I'm starving.

Across the street at Twohey's, I'm stuffing a hog dog into my mouth, disgusted with myself. Hot dogs! Fat, meat (or so one hopes), sodium nitrate—but it's all I want, no bun even, just lots of ketchup. For a moment I wish my brother Corb were here, *he'd* find this funny. Twohey's, home of the Little Stinko—onion rings—only I'm not eating in the restaurant but in my car, a white Chevy Cavalier, it turns out, that was parked between two other Chevy Cavaliers.

After my hot dog I continue east on Huntington Drive, not ready to return to the Alta Vista yet; what would I do there anyway? I can't even bring myself to sit in the overstuffed chair in my room—God knows what little beasts the upholstery harbors. (My father's response when I finally told him I was staying at the Alta Vista? Stricken, as though cockroaches were about to emerge from my pockets. I tried to explain. "I thought it was a bed-and-breakfast, Dad. 'Quaint.' 'Character.' 'Restored.' That's what the ad in the Yellow Pages said.")

I've crossed into San Marino now, where technically I grew up, although I tend to label the whole area as Pasadena—it's habit: as teenagers we'd lie about where we were from, San Marino having certain connotations.

I park in front of the Huntington Pharmacy; if nothing else, they have good face creams in San Marino and I left mine behind in Colorado. I recall parking in this same spot on my way to countless errands: having my hair cut at *Charles*, by Charles himself; being taken to buy my first bra at Shephard's (long gone) where pajamas and white cotton underwear could also be purchased—Spanky pants, we called them. Green linoleum floors and big-bosomed old lady clerks who, whenever you had to try anything on, clasped their hands at their stomachs as though waiting for bad news.

The Huntington Pharmacy is more or less the same, aside from having undergone various small remodelings. It's the people who are different, not in behavior but in looks. More than half the town is Asian now, I'm told. A fact that for some reason makes me giddy with relief: it's no longer the town I grew up in but an artifact, a curiosity. As if the past, my past, doesn't exist. As for the Huntington Pharmacy, its atmosphere still resembles a bank's or a library's. Customers talk in hushed tones. Children are well behaved. Women discreetly spray on colognes, sample lipsticks; personal hygiene products and contraceptives are stowed out of sight. Toward the back of the store is the pharmacy, once upon a time a somber darkened area with a small window for consulting with the pharmacist; I think of my mother long ago, in sunglasses, pretending to be someone else.

I leave on my own sunglasses in case anybody recognizes me, not that anyone would. The face creams, the costly, youth-preserving kind I need, are behind glass. I'll have to ask for help but instead I wander around the store: all the years of wandering this store, my father dropping me off as a pre-teen to buy things, female things, me not knowing what to buy. "Please charge this to Harold Mapes." A candy bar, a magazine, Right Guard deodorant . . . same brand as my father and brother, what were girls supposed to buy?

I wander much as a ghost would in a former habitat: I'm invisible, no one speaks to me. Perhaps because I look shoddy, ill-groomed. My hair's wild—couldn't get a brush through it this morning—and I'm wearing one of the three pairs of jeans I threw into my suitcase, this pair a fashionable though frayed black, and my old suede boots that just this morning I noticed have on them a dried dollop of spaghetti sauce, from dinner on the plane—so I'm thinking of this when an Asian woman goes by in crisp white Keds that haven't a smudge on them. Two thoughts occur to me. One, I should get a pair of those, even though I hate Keds; it's just that hers look so clean, so new. The other thought is really habit. I look not at her, but at her clothes, mentally writing catalog copy, which is what I do for a living. *Striped tee, navy blue cardigan, gold buttons for a classic, nautical look that's never out of style, never out of season.*

I find the counter with the face creams: they're like jewels behind glass. I buy one that's terribly expensive and, on an impulse, a special pregnancy cream. "For the belly," the saleswoman says. She must be seventy-five, with an Old World accent. "It's *von*-derful. So soothing. No stretch marks." She gestures toward the area below her cinched-in belt.

Back in the car. To my true destination: east on Huntington, farther and farther, past Rosemead, past the Santa Anita Race-track, until I reach Arcadia Methodist Hospital, where my mother endured many hospitalizations and where she officially died, and where she was brought by ambulance that last time to be resuscitated, too late.

Where did she draw her last breath? My father never said but I always believed it was in the hospital, the moment they brought her in on the gurney.

As a child I thought this hospital existed on an island of sorts: Huntington Drive splits up when it reaches the hospital, one-way traffic on either side, cars rushing by, while on the grounds swayed great lonely pine trees, black and silhouetted: whenever we drove past, I knew my mother had died there and would wave.

I'm not ready yet to go inside and request her records, not today.

In my room at the Alta Vista, I scan the *Star News* that I found in the lobby. Headlines, obituaries, which lately I can't pass up. I check them the way other people check for the winning lottery number: dead people over sixty-five, it'll be a good day. Under fifty, a bad day. I'm nagged by why the younger ones die. Why they die so young. Heart attack, cancer, AIDS, car accident, violence, suicide—speculation on my part although occasionally there are hints, if you read between the lines.

Nobody under seventy today, so I move on to the classifieds, for apartments or rooms to let, if I were to move here, say, instead of returning to Colorado; anyway I've got to get out of the Alta Vista. I can't even go to the bathroom without tiptoeing as though I might step on something wet and slimy. Stupidly, I lost my pen somewhere so there's nothing to circle the ads with, not to mention a phone in my room. Only a pay phone at the Alta Vista and it's not even in the lobby. It's outside.

So I lie down on the bed, training my thoughts away from Jackson. At Stonewall Creek, where we live, where we *lived*, the rocks are red—minarets and pyramids and castles of red sandstone that loom over bluffs of prairie grass and twisted juniper.

This is why I'm afraid to remove my wedding band. It would mean I'm not going back there.

Eagles, snakes, coyote, mule deer, mountain lion. The Arabian horses that grazed, woolly in winter, friendly as dogs, following us on our walks. Licking our cars for the salt, rubbing their teeth against the paint. Peering in the windows of our house while Jackson and I made love.

I should write Jackson a letter and mail it this time. Tell him the truth. Tell him about the baby. Yes, a baby. My period's three weeks late, what else can this be? I try to see Jackson's face as he reads the letter, the profile of his broad, unadorned features, the small stab of the mole on his clean-shaven cheek, the mole that I've always loved. On his face is anger. No, sorrow. He doesn't understand me, never has. *I* don't understand me; why would I leave a perfectly fine marriage?

But it wasn't, it hasn't been.

I have the moral life of a child—no, children have a better sense of right and wrong. One day it seemed a good idea to get married, like playing dress-up. A part of me has never grown up. Entire segments of me have never been exposed to light—they collapsed inside me somewhere, a black hole; no therapist has been able to dig them out. They all want to, especially when they hear those magic words about my mother committing suicide when I was seven, and the infant sister who had died earlier, when I was three, almost four. "Oh?" they'll say, sitting up, suddenly paying attention, taking a lot of notes. It's a weird sense of power, a case a therapist can sink his or her teeth into. I'm the safe they want to crack.

Night-time at the phone booth just outside the front door of the Alta Vista. There's somebody ahead of me, an elderly woman in a pale, thin gown. "They give me tumblers of bourbon or they drug me," she says into the receiver. "Um-hmm. Or I'm shot up with something, a truth serum sometimes. There might be a group of us strapped to one of those circular laundry lines and we're forced to march round and round, like donkeys bringing up water from a well. We're to walk until somebody slips. Darling, somebody always slips. Some of us have already slipped and are on crutches, some of us have lost our minds. There are nooses around our necks. Nooses rigged with razor blades."

She hangs up the phone, walks blithely past me. Maybe my father is right about this place.

"Can I do something? Help you back to your room?" I offer.

"Darling, I'm fine."

I fumble through the phone book—I've got to look up old friends, *somebody*, I've got to talk to somebody other than the residents at the Alta Vista. Maggie Devoe—no listing. Of course, she's probably married now, might have taken her husband's name. Technically, she is a cousin of mine, the relationship so distant it went unacknowledged by both our families. I picture Maggie's face, sarcastic, smirking—a face twenty years younger. I have no idea what she looks like now but I keep picturing cut-offs, T-shirt, hoop earrings. What we wore in high school. Thumbs out, hitchhiking to or from our latest adventure; squished smokes in our back pockets.

I could call Maggie's parents, still listed on Lorraine, I see, but I won't. Anymore than she'd call my father.

I move on to old boyfriends. Gregg, the one I most want to call. To see, to sleep with. A voice in me says: call him, quick, before you get any bigger. Call him before you chicken out. Call him. Call him.

Feeding quarters into the pay phone, I try number after number; the one listed in the phone book leads to another and another. ("That number has been changed. *Please* make a note of it," says a recorded female voice that ever so slightly hinges on irritation.)

This is what desperate women do when they're drunk and it's late at night—they call old boyfriends.

Only I don't have the excuse of drunkenness, just plain old loneliness. As I dial the last number, pigeons coo in the palm trees overhead, not like the racket they make during the day. Gregg's phone rings. Panic: what if he's married? Surely he is by now, even Gregg. The phone rings and rings and I'm about to hang up gladly, when I get a machine.

It's his voice, music in the background. "Gregg?" (My voice comes out like a squeak.) "This is Theo. I'm in town." A pause. Help, I'm pausing too long—what if he picks up? Or his wife does? "Um, I'll call back. There's no phone where I'm staying. Ciao."

Ciao. I never say that. An attempt at sounding continental? I'll call again tomorrow. I'll never call again. If I see him, another part of me is planning already, get rid of the wedding band. Or maybe I should leave it on as a challenge. Or a deterrent.

I dial my brother's number.

"This is Corb," he answers.

"Why do you always answer the phone like that?" I say. "Don't you realize how off-putting it is? Why don't you just say 'hello'?"

"Dad told me you're in town."

"Did he tell you why?"

"Yes." He sighs. "I'm sorry, Theo."

My turn to say something. I can't.

"I hear you're staying at a residence hotel. Dad's all caught up about that too, never mind why you're here. 'She's staying at the Alta Vista!' he said. He wanted me to offer you a place to stay."

"So offer."

"Would you like to stay here?"

I think of nooses rigged with razor blades; I think of my room at the Alta Vista, of the sock dangling from the showerhead. "No," I say. "No thank you."

"Well, I offered."

"Yes, you did. That's over with. Phew, close call, huh?" An old joke between us. None of us have stayed under the same roof in more than fifteen years.

Corb invites me for lunch the next day, a Saturday, and when I let myself in—the front door is unlocked—he and his wife, Diane, are rinsing vegetables at the sink.

"Theo!" Diane wipes her hands on her apron first, but Corb just reaches out for me, hugging me with wet hands.

"Hi, you guys."

"We're so sorry," Diane breathes into my ear, "about you and Jackson."

I break away. "Where are the boys?" Gabe and Bruce, their eleven- and twelve-year-old sons. My nephews.

"Playing Nintendo in the basement," Diane answers. "Let me look at you." She turns me this way and that. "You look fabulous. Did you get a haircut?"

She always asks me that. Maybe she thinks I need one.

"No."

"It's so beautiful, your hair," Diane says, then gestures at her own straight brown hair cut at the shoulders, slightly turned under. What I think of as an adult haircut. "If I want curls, I have to pay for them."

"Come on, now." Corb takes my elbow and steers me out of the kitchen. "I want to show you the new baby."

"The new baby," I say. "I can't wait."

It could be a computer or an addition to the house, or a new animal, which qualifies as a sort of baby, I guess. Corb leads me downstairs to the basement, in something of a hurry. We pass the boys, eyes glazed from Nintendo. By their feet, motionless, is a lop-eared rabbit I've never seen before. "Hi, boys," I say.

Gabe, the younger one, squints at me (glasses that always seem too large for his face) but doesn't answer, in mid-thought about the game he's playing. "Blow it up," Bruce says to him. "Blow it up, Gabe!" Gabe touches a button and the TV screen emits an atomic sound, followed by cartoon smoke and exploding colors. The rabbit's nose quivers slightly. "Hi Aunt Theo," Bruce says, in the same inflectionless way he answers the phone. *This is the Mapes' residence. This is Bruce speaking. May I ask who's calling?*

"Come on," Corb says, pulling me along. Apparently, the rabbit isn't the new baby.

"Where are we going?"

"You'll see." He's like a kid, the most excited I ever see him, whenever he's about to show me the 'new baby,' whatever it may be. For a second I think of my new baby—when do I tell him about that?

"Ready?" Corb ushers me into the storage room.

The new baby is a hydroponic lettuce growing kit. You plant seeds in sand and pour in water, and, with the help of grow lights, *voilà*.

21

The salad at lunch features this lettuce—pale, tender, embryonic.

I can't help asking. "Why don't you just grow the lettuce outside?"

"He likes it because it's a kit," Diane says, "because it's new."

My foot kicks something soft under the table. I look. It's the rabbit.

"Gabe, Bruce—is this your rabbit?"

"Yeah," they answer in unison, absorbed in their second helpings. A far cry from when they were seven or eight and couldn't sit still—they played soccer with cherry tomatoes, made gullies and rivers out of mashed potatoes and gravy; they stuffed their mouths with food, gulped milk, and fled from the table out the back door. Back then they chattered to me nonstop about sports, Legos, their pals, the science projects they dreamed up themselves involving ice cubes and dental floss, cardboard tubes and plastic soldiers.

"So how are we going to convince Dad to have this operation sooner?" Corb says.

I stop mid-bite. "Operation for what?"

"For his cataract. Come on, you're kidding," he says when he sees my face. "You know about this. He's had it for a year."

"He's never said anything about it. I swear to God. Not a word." I shouldn't be surprised—I was the last to know about his high blood pressure, too, though he managed to keep it from Corb for nearly as long. "How serious is it?" I picture old people with bandaged eyes, in wraparound dark glasses.

Diane serves herself more salad. "Well, it needs to be fixed. Not such a big deal anymore these days. It's outpatient. As for how he's doing, he says it's like looking through waxed paper. He can't see to drive."

"He can't drive? How does he get to the office? The grocery store?"

"He says he walks, but Diane drives him half the time," Corb says.

"I can't believe he hasn't said anything to me! How does he read, how does he do his paperwork?"

"Magnifying glass."

"Oh." The magnifying glass I saw on his desk that I found so comforting, not to mention all those lamps.

After dinner Corb and I walk the dogs around the block, at Diane's insistence—the dogs are getting fat, she says. They have just two dogs now, a golden retriever and a collie; their spaniel died last year, hit by a car. I'm never sure of their dogs' names, or the names of any of their pets, each in turn gotten from the animal shelter and fussed over for approximately six months, at which point the new baby becomes simply one of the dogs or cats. Or the rabbit. Iguana. Hamster.

The real reason Diane insisted on this walk has nothing to do with the dogs, of course. She thinks I'm going to unburden myself to Corb, about Jackson. She should know better. At best we cover factual information.

"Why did you leave him?" Corb asks.

"His drinking." There. I've said it. It's both the truth and not the full truth.

Corb nods uncomfortably. My brother avoids personal confidences—mine, his, anyone's. A legacy of our childhood, I've come to believe.

He makes another well-meaning stab at it. "So what will you do?" His complexion is dark, like our mother's was, hollows under deep-set eyes that might be ironic, might be tragic.

"I don't know," I say. "Live here maybe."

Simultaneously we notice where we are and stop—exactly across the street from the house we grew up in. Which is bound to happen if you're at Corb's house and you go on a walk around the block. A walk the two of us have managed to avoid in all the years Corb has lived here.

"Don't you find it strange," I say, "that you wound up living so close to this house?"

Dangerous territory for Corb. I know he won't answer. As if on cue both dogs sit down, the golden retriever holding the leash in his mouth.

"Remember riding down this street in inner tubes?" Corb says.

I chuckle, but only a little. "Yeah." Any mention of the past makes us nervous, leery of each other.

"The water seemed so deep."

"It was," I say to him. "We were children."

The water was up to our waists. Whenever it poured, the street flooded; the gutters became rivers of dirty brown rainwater. Kids ran from their houses screaming, throwing down inner tubes and riding them to the end of the block.

We weren't raised as our father was (at least until the Depression), in a grand house with a pet goat and a dog cart and servants; no, our house—this house we're across the street from now—is a one-story ranch, its flat roof strewn with chips of dolomite, which was the style after World War II. Ours was the first house to be built in the orange grove; this was to be a premier neighborhood. It never quite reached its potential, however, and for a time it was downright seedy by San Marino standards, bordering on a so-so section of Pasadena and containing a few too many vacant lots— nobody wanted to build here. And when eventually that changed and houses were built, they were either peculiar or atrocious: with towering doors reminiscent of cathedrals, or pagoda-like roofs, or golf course landscaping—all lawn, no shrubs or trees (to better display the house, presumably). Or all bonsai trees and hedges trimmed so that they resembled poodles, barbells, or flat top mesas.

Now the neighborhood is toney enough, but then everything in San Marino is, any garage converted to a house, any square foot of land. There are no vacant lots.

Our house, though, the house we grew up in, remains down-cast-looking and sad, the ivy fences brown and dying, trees pruned awkwardly.

At one time, a Japanese blind shaded our front windows, a freestanding object of papery wood held in place by a frame. The blind fell down years ago, never to be replaced by the various owners that followed, and now, all that remains is the frame itself, set out before the house like a picture frame missing its picture.

You'd never know this house was featured in the newspaper once for being "modern," with its cork floors and children's bedrooms that opened into a playroom and Japanese/Mediterranean-influenced landscaping. All our mother's doing, her designs, her wrangling with contractors and interior decorators, her always wanting more—a swimming pool, an enclosed patio—our father insisting they couldn't afford it, she insisting they could, *she* could, she had her own money. My father saying no, enough; her saying no, never enough.

But it's not a remarkable house. Only remarkable in what went on inside, that neither Corb nor I can recall. It's a blank. "What else do you remember?" I've asked him over the years. All he ever mentions are things like riding down the street in inner tubes, or playing kick-the-can—things outside the house. I ask him again now as we walk the dogs: "What else do you remember?"

He won't meet my eyes. "Not much."

"You were older than me."

"Hardly anything."

This house with its missing Japanese blind appears surprised, exposed, caught in the act. Naked: a person rudely shorn of hair and other adornments—jewelry, makeup, eyebrows, lashes. Humiliated and ashamed.

"How come I never believe you?" I ask.

"I don't remember anything, Theo. Do you?"

"It's a very short list, what I remember."

"Well?"

"Well what?" I know he doesn't mean for me to tell him: the rule is that we don't exchange memories, memories from inside the house, even though I always ask.

"You don't remember either," he says. He seems glad of it, almost gloating.

"Tell me one thing. One."

"There isn't anything to tell, Theo. She wore braces on her teeth."

"Braces?" It's like falling or stepping off a carousel, disorienting. "Why braces?" I say.

"The shock treatments. They put in the mouthpiece wrong. She had to wear braces after that."

"Braces." I can see them before me, floating, just braces and teeth. Metal, no lips or face. "What else do you remember? What about Charlotte?"

He flinches, doesn't like to hear her name. In fact, I'm not sure we've ever said her name out loud. Charlotte was our sister who had died in her sleep as an infant. SIDS, they call it now.

"But you were old enough to remember her. Did you hold her? Did she smile at you?"

He walks faster, the dogs trotting ahead of him. "I'm not stonewalling you, Theo. I really don't remember."

"But you remembered the braces."

"That just happened. Forget it, Theo. There isn't anything there. It happened a long time ago; it's gone."

He always says that when I press him. And then we drop the subject for years.

Two

Inventory

I have exactly nine memories of my mother:

1. Her brushing my teeth with Nivea cream instead of toothpaste once, holding me so tight I couldn't escape or tell her she'd grabbed the wrong tube.

2. Spanking me with a hairbrush bristle side down. A hot, spreading, burning sensation.

3. Putting my hair up in pin curls, digging in the bobby pins crossways, my pin curls hard and sticky with clear green hair spray she kept in a spray bottle.

4. A friend is over for the afternoon when I soil my underpants. I must be four or five, too old to have made such a mistake. My mother scoops the mess out with a spoon into the toilet, the bathroom door not closed all the way so that my friend witnesses my humiliation.

5. My mother sitting in a chair filing her nails, a towel across her knees.

6. Holding her hand at Charlotte's funeral. The warmth of her white glove, how her hand trembles.

7. The middle of the afternoon; we're alone. A tumbler of crème de menthe left on an end table. She's gone to answer the phone in the next room. I try a sip.

8. Her wearing a light blue dress with strawberries on it.

9. With Corb, finding her the morning of her death. Being the ones to discover her. Drawing back the curtains, calling her name, shaking her. Our father is in the kitchen fixing us breakfast.

She'd overdosed, though we had no way of knowing that. All we knew was that her face was bluish, still.

Other memories are not specifically of her, but of a time when she was still alive, as in the afternoon with the crème de menthe: she is in another room or in another place, yet in this dimension.

1. Me at the dinner table forced to sit there until I finish my vegetables; occasionally Corb floats by to tell me to make believe they're candy.

2. The dinners she prepared: lamb croquettes, parsnips, twice-baked potatoes. Crab, the white flesh tinged with red. Foods that make me blanch still, except for the cottage cheese sprinkled with sugar—a treat or an apology? Or a bribe?

3. Going to the hospital where my mother is a patient.

4. Being made to sit in the basement among the cans of food.

5. A long hallway in our house that could be closed off with doors, until it was pitch black, a place I called *the woods*, and avoided.

6. Scuffing up and down the hallway in my mother's castoff high heels.

7. My dollhouse.

8. Waking up screaming so loud the neighbors could hear me.

9. A recurring nightmare from that time: I'm in my room, the curtains are closed, everything appears as it is in real life. Then suddenly the lights switch on and off, on and off, the curtains open and shut madly, whipping back and forth as if in a wind; things go upside down, become cartoons flying in my face.

10. I twist up a corner of the dress I am wearing and suck on it.

11. Nap time in my room. The curtains are closed. I have to go to the bathroom but am afraid to leave my bed. Afraid of *the woods*. I squeeze my legs together, imagining what it would be like to pee into my toy pots and pans.

12. I do not sleep during naps. I watch the door. Sometimes I play "here is the church, here is the steeple" with my hands, making a convolution of my fingers until I can't remember where they connect to my body. I choose one finger to stare and stare at, willing this finger into numbness. Is this before or after Charlotte died? I might ask this of every memory.

Some memories are ones given to me by others, ones I don't recall myself but have sought out. The hospital, for instance.

When we went to visit her—just once—she didn't know who we were, her memory blighted by shock treatments (my father).

The most recent: the braces on her teeth. A result of a shock treatment improperly done, the mouthpiece the wrong size (Corb).

The eight to ten hard drinks a day she consumed, in addition to the tranquilizers and sleeping pills she ingested (Evan, my mother's nurse who stayed on after she died).

How, if a doctor wouldn't give her a prescription, she'd drive all over town until she found one who would (also Evan).

Her suicide was the last of three attempts. In the first, she saved up pills in the hospital, then took them all at once. In the second, at home, she slit her wrists, then got into bed. My father found her early the next morning, drenched in blood. An ambulance was called, we children told nothing, her bedroom cleaned while we were at school (Evan again). I remember getting dressed for Brownies that day, long after the ambulance left. I remember the ambulance arriving, the medics having trouble getting the stretcher around the corners of the hallway. Go back to bed, my father said, everything's fine.

Also not my own memories, but ones I've collected, are the things people said about her, anecdotes, facts.

When she was a baby, she spit peas all over the walls of the kitchen. This is the only memory her sister, Aunt Lyla, has told me. I knew nothing about their parents, my grandparents, only that my grandmother died before I was born and my grandfather later on, when I was four or five. We didn't see him much, only on occasion. There were no pictures of these grandparents displayed, nor were there any of my mother and Aunt Lyla together as girls, although I believe some existed once upon a time.

Other things people said about my mother:

She was afraid of horses.

She was beautiful. Smart, talented. They mentioned her skill in Japanese flower arrangements, her lovely thank-you notes.

She was president of the women students at Stanford and graduated magna cum laude.

She rolled bandages for the Red Cross. She volunteered as a docent at the Henry E. Huntington Library.

Her table manners were flawless.

Then, there were the things left behind when she died, which themselves seem like memories. Items sorted through by my father, some kept, others discarded—no particular logic to what was saved or not. A few dresses in the closet, some shoes: flats in different colors, with a T-strap over the instep. Specially made for her, my father said; she had difficulties with her feet.

Costume jewelry. Chunky beads, clip-on earrings, pins. An empty striped hatbox. A notebook on Japanese flower arranging, from a class she took once, plus a few black metal trays, heavy as skillets, affixed with sharp metal combs onto which I would sometimes, in an attempt to reach my mother, impale a few select flowers, anchored by dark green modeling clay and smooth black stones.

Her recipe box. Her linens, an array of tablecloths, placemats, napkins, guest towels, all folded and starched into packages with cardboard on the back, clear plastic in front, a slip of paper with the contents listed neatly in her handwriting. The linens, her crystal and silver, went to me since I was her daughter. I used to pore over the stuff as a child, trying to find clues about her, occasionally coming across a slip of paper I hadn't seen before that might say, in her own handwriting, "silver melon pitcher."

Two cabinets, each with a delicate brass lock. One is the liquor cabinet; the other, a cabinet in the bathroom, well stocked with bottles of prescriptions long gone bad.

This last item exists because of her death: a package of condolence letters sent to my father, tied with string and kept in the bottom drawer of a chest standing in our living room. As a child, each time I read the letters—a secret project, my father didn't know—I had to redo the string so that in the end it became tangled and knotted.

30

THREE

St. Nicholas . . .

It's morning and I'm at my Powerbook, a whole day ahead of me, trying to get caught up with work before meeting Gregg for dinner tonight. "You pick the restaurant," he said when I got up my nerve and called him again. "The Peppermill," I said. Did it even exist anymore? The sort of place boys take their prom dates.

St. Nick winks . . .

My mother's braces. I keep seeing them. It's like this whenever I hear something new about her, something I didn't know before. As if she's here again, walking the earth, close to me—as close as I'll get.

St. Nick is a jolly old . . .

Here is my least favorite catalog, Meadowlark, with insipid rhyming verse at the top of each page. Verse that I make up. About Christmas, spring or summer. Flowers, sailboats, the wonders of grandma and grandpa; the advertising director fed-exes me a list of subjects to write about, along with photos, layouts, product information. I fax or fed-ex back to them the copy I've written; it no longer pays to do it in-house, companies say. Not enough work for one person in-house, so they contract with me or other freelancers, many of whom have their specialties now that catalogs are so endemic. Gadgets, housewares and bedding, books, gardening. I specialize in children's clothing and toys, although I still do some women's clothing and another catalog that sells safety products.

Of all my catalogs, Meadowlark is the most frou-frou. No playclothes here—only elaborate dresses for girls, matching rompers for their baby sisters, with maybe a sailor suit or a nerdy jacket and bow tie for the one or two boys who appear in Meadowlark's pages.

Santa Claus, his nose like a cherry . . .

Screw S.C. I attempt product descriptions instead, paging through the file folder of photographs the advertising director has sent, along with the accompanying list of product information, details that today swim before my eyes: shirred waists and ecru lace collars and triple choir collars, enamel buttons, grosgrain ribbons, jewel necklines and pink satin rosebuds, eyelet flounce hems and memory hats.

I pause at a photo of a girl in a velvet dress, but it's not her dress that stops me (venise lace collar, basque waist, taffeta under-skirt)—it's her braces; braces again, my mother's braces floating before me.

"What?" I say aloud, irritated. "What is it now?"

As though I'm talking to *her*. Something I haven't done since childhood when I used to pray to her instead of God.

I look at the photograph again, unusual in that I've never seen a girl model with braces, certainly not in Meadowlark which is far from progressive, *i.e.*, nothing but the most Aryan of children. This must be their idea of using a challenged child, when most catalogs nowadays will show a child in a wheelchair.

Luxurious emerald velvet, I begin. Didn't I write this about a similar dress last year? No way to check since my file of old catalogs is back in Colorado. I flip down the lid of my Powerbook, considering the list of adjectives I keep there, taped on. *Vintage, charming, classic, sporty, jaunty, romantic, lavish, fresh, crisp, dainty, whimsical, sweet, delectable, timeless—*

I tap in *Timeless emerald velvet.* No. *Timeless velvet—? Velvet is timeless. . . . A dress of emerald velvet is timeless, a holiday classic.*

Try again.

Destined to be a treasured heirloom, this holiday dress of emerald velvet features a venise lace collar, basque waist and scalloped taffeta underskirt.

There. I'm too exhausted to write about the back of the dress, for now. Usually I can write this stuff in my sleep. It doesn't help that I left my thesaurus in Colorado and I'll have to buy another here. Damn it. I go up to the menu and under File, I hit Save, then Quit.

A drive, a little drive is what I need.

The residents of the Alta Vista crowd the window to watch me put the car in reverse.

I drive to my father's house, down the Arroyo Parkway, cutting over to Garfield (with the same old Speed Checked by Radar sign—as I child I believed planes flew overhead, that as long as there wasn't a plane overhead, you could speed).

A modest ranch of dour color with a finicky dicondra lawn, this house is worth, ironically, half a million dollars now just because it's in San Marino. It was Dorinne's house originally. Over the years I persisted in thinking of it as hers, my father as a kind of lodger there. Once she died several years ago he decided to stay—it was near the Y, he reasoned, so he could swim and use the weight room. Actually, he swims at the Valley Hunt Club—the pool at the Y, he says, is not very clean, not very *nice*, my father's most serviceable word. The real reason Dad stayed in Dorinne's house, I believe, is that moving frightened him. Moving houses, that is; offices are different. In fact, he's acquired a taste for moving offices, studying the classifieds for a deal, the smallest, cheapest office possible. But moving houses? He hasn't had much practice: he moved straight from his mother's house to the one he and my mother built, then, more than twenty years later, on to Dorinne's.

I ring the doorbell. I don't have a key and never have had one, even during my brief uncomfortable stays here (the term 'stay of execution' comes to mind), when I was a teen.

No answer. I fight back ivy and shrubs to peer in his windows. No sign of Dad, he must be at his office. Probably walked there, something he wouldn't dream of doing before the cataract. I get back in my car and drive the route my father would walk and sure enough, there he is on the west side of Garfield, in navy blue canvas tennis shoes and a business suit.

I roll down the window. "Dad!" I call. I honk. "Dad! DAD! DAD!"

No choice but to tail him to his office. His stride is that of a diligent schoolboy's—he actually looks right and left at every driveway—and I wonder, as I always do, what he thinks about. Death? He does seem unusually concerned about it—all the letters he's sent Corb and me in the last year, for example, about his own death someday. "I have a living will (copy enclosed), so when the time comes, pull the plug." "A salesman came in here the other day to try and sell me death taxes. I said I have them already, thank you very much." "As for arrangements, do what you want, but no funerals!" I've always found this amusing, as if he anticipated having several. He's a stickler on the point of funerals. "They're a waste of money and a lot of people you don't even know show up." If other people have difficulty discussing old age, terminal illness and death, it's the one subject my father can be open about. "I want to be cremated and, please, no fancy containers for the ashes. A box will do. Frankly, I don't even care if you save them, you can throw them away for all I care, but I suppose you need to put something under the marker." It's the details of death he can discuss, the "arrangements"—estate taxes, wills, burial plots, headstones, letters of condolence—not the meaning of death or the emotional implications.

Finally I catch up to him, heading up the stairs to his office. "Dad? Dad!"

"Oh—what?" He has such a bright, happy, glazed expression, dewy-eyed. He can't really be thinking about death, estate taxes, can he? "Theo!"

"Dad, I've been driving after you for blocks hollering. Didn't you hear me?" I find myself talking loudly in case he is hard of hearing.

"No, no. I didn't. What is it, is something wrong?" he says.

"Nothing's wrong, Dad." Nothing more wrong than it was the other day when I saw him, that is—failed marriage, no place to live, about to embark on an adulterous relationship, my period suspiciously late. My baby, if I am to have a baby, folded inside me like a traveling cup. "Dad, why didn't you tell me about your cataract?"

"I thought I did tell you."

"You didn't, Dad. It's like when you had high blood pressure. You didn't tell me about that either."

We've reached the door of his office. "Won't you come in?" he asks. He turns on the lights, all of them, including the fluorescents overhead.

"Is that why you brought in all these lamps?" I count six of them.

"Yes."

"Corb says you're considering an operation."

"Yes." As though this is extremely hush-hush information.

"When are you planning on doing that?"

"It's outpatient now, you know."

"So Corb explained. Why are you waiting?"

"I can walk to the store," he says defensively. "I can walk to the office."

"Have you set a date for the operation, Dad?"

"Not yet."

"Will you now that I'm in town? Dad, I'm doing nothing here. I can help you. I can drive you. I can take care of you after the operation."

Fear crosses his face. "That's not necessary, it's outpatient—"

"I know that."

"Only a couple of days of recovery."

"I know."

"I'll give it some thought," he says.

"Will you call and make an appointment with the doctor so we can get this thing rolling?"

He gazes at the wall, as though contemplating the view out a window—if there were windows here.

"Are you afraid, Dad?" I say.

"Me? No."

But he is. For all his detailed plans about death, he's afraid of it, not afraid of death perhaps, but of what precedes it, helplessness and degeneration.

"I just don't understand why you don't get this taken care of, Dad. Especially now that I'm here."

"Won't you sit down?" He's bringing around his office chair, evidently for that purpose. "I have something I want to talk to you about, too, since you're here."

The chair stays empty. I cross my arms.

"Jackson called me last night," he says.

"Oh."

"He said he didn't know where you were and did I happen to know?"

I don't say anything.

He raises his voice. "Do you mean to tell me you didn't let your husband know you were coming out here?"

"My husband," I say. "My *estranged* husband."

"Nonetheless. He sounded so worried, Theo. He said he called all your friends and nobody knew where you were. He even called the police!"

"He knew I was leaving. He saw me walk out the door."

"He didn't know you were leaving the state!"

I try to imagine Jackson on the phone to the police. About me. It's almost comic for some reason, Jackson, the very picture of reason, upset on the phone, maybe even hysterical.

"Well, are you planning on calling him?"

I fling up my hands. "I guess. Sometime. He knows I'm here, Dad, he knows I'm okay."

"But he wants to talk to you, Theo, not me."

"I know."

"You need to talk to your husband."

"I said I *know*."

"What in the world happened between you two that you can't even talk to him?"

I shrug.

"I see you're still unwilling to discuss this," he says.

I nod, a bare flicker of a nod.

He opens a drawer for no apparent purpose and shuts it carefully. "Well," he says, "I haven't anything else." His way of saying our visit is over for now. He waits for me to go through the motions of leaving. I can't. Too close to tears.

"Shouldn't you be getting on?" he says.

"If you call about your cataract, I'll call Jackson."

He compresses his lips, as if considering how to trump me in bridge. "All right," he says.

FOUR

Jackson and I met at a dairy farm in France five years ago. It was an old, yellow, moldering set of buildings that centuries ago had been a monastery, now housing a family and their dairy farm on one side and a Chambre d'Hôte on the other. Rooms for rent. Rooms that overlooked the pasture where the family—a man, woman and two children—all wearing rubber boots, drove the cows back and forth several times a day with sticks and the help of a dog. Idyllically beautiful, this farm, wildflowers, green grass you just knew made for sweet milk, and the monastery itself, mystical and eerie, creaking with history, although this didn't seem to faze the family much. Like all Europeans they were used to living right alongside history, as they clumped around in their rubber boots and smiled at the silly, fawning Americans—secretly laughing at us, no doubt, as we stepped around cow paddies trying to take pictures.

The dairy farm had its less romantic aspects. It stank and there were an abundance of flies; the rooms of the monastery fairly crumbled with dust and mildew.

There were two rooms for rent. I had the lower floor room, Jackson the upper, and we shared a bathroom, midway between our rooms on a circular, medieval stone stairway, dank and unlit. This is where we met: we bumped into one another in the middle of the night, each of us trying to find the bathroom.

"I didn't know anybody else was staying here," he said once we finished yelling and untangling ourselves. He'd arrived earlier in the day, he explained, but had stayed in his room till now.

"I'm getting over a cold," he added.

"Oh." I still couldn't see him and for some reason we didn't think to turn on the bathroom light.

"Well," he said, "goodnight."

And we parted, without getting so much as a glimpse of each other.

The next morning took care of that. He saw me, all right—through the tall, gaping, curtainless windows of the bathroom as he hung his wash outside. He couldn't help but look: the laundry line afforded a perfect view, especially if somebody happened to be emerging from the bathtub, as I happened to be doing at that moment.

Not that he looked away.

Grabbing for my towel, I knew it was him. Who else could it be?

From there we became walking companions around the district, through other dairy farms and chicken farms, past timbered Norman houses falling apart, down dirt roads and paths, stopping in town for wine and a loaf of bread and cheese. This was one of the first things we found we had in common; neither of us could stomach French food. We wouldn't admit it—we simply pretended to be full. "No, no, I love tripe." "So do I!" "I'm just not as hungry as I thought." "Me either." Admitting you don't like French food is a little like admitting that you're big and stupid. A heathen. It's like being from Los Angeles. You tell people, they think you're kidding at first. Then they look at you differently; they never look at you the same again. They decide you're vapid, rich and blond (even if you're not even close to blond, like me). Or they say, "You don't seem like you're from L.A."

That's what Jackson said. A compliment, I guess.

He's from the Midwest, originally, and had his own set of embarrassments to worry about. But to me being from the Midwest signaled stability, honesty. As reliable as meat and potatoes; Jackson's feet were on the ground, and large, solid feet they were. He was handsome in a burly, straightforward way, with dark blue eyes and brown hair, lots of it waving around his head.

For me, who grew up in the land of blondes, brown hair and blue eyes is exotic. Midwesterners are exotic, kind of.

Jackson came from the Midwest but lived in the West. Colorado, more West than California, in spirit. He owned a small ranch, but didn't raise cattle, only leased the land out for somebody else's horses. He warned me: it's not like the Colorado you're thinking of. There are bluffs, not mountains, more rocks than trees. But red rock, *red*. It's wild, he said, it's a wild place.

He didn't make much money, just enough to live on. He taught a few classes at the university. I'm a history instructor, he said, not a professor.

All this he told me in France, as we walked around Normandy.

Before Europe:

I had lived everywhere, it seemed—Vermont, Seattle, Eugene, Oregon, and San Francisco. New England, the West, the coast, the desert. I changed jobs, towns, boyfriends, therapists, insurance plans, apartments, cars, colleges—all through my twenties. Finally, I got my undergraduate degree in Boston, where I settled for a while, writing ad copy and believing that, at last, I'd fallen in love. Mistakenly, as it turned out. At twenty-nine I moved to Tucson. At thirty I bought a condominium. Then I left for Europe.

Jackson and I married two months after meeting in France; our families—sparse in his case, an uncle, a couple of distant cousins—met at the wedding. It was so sudden that people assumed 1) I was pregnant, and 2) it wouldn't last. None of my other relationships had, so why should this? Though people never said as much. They delicately asked, How did you decide to marry him? How did you *know*? (After all those men, they meant.) I just knew, I told the friends I'd collected through all my moves. I knew he was the one. I'd also know if he weren't, I told them. I'd realize it on my walk down the aisle—and I'd turn around and walk the other way.

Since we got married outdoors, there wasn't an aisle anyway. There wasn't a wedding march. My father didn't give me away. No bridesmaids or ushers; we were attended only by a friend's five-year-old daughter, who handed out flowers from a basket beforehand, while a lone saxophonist played.

Jackson and I entered the garden together. Afterward, people joked that we'd walked toward the minister so fast, they didn't have time to focus their cameras.

Later I had to wonder if it was the wedding I'd wanted. There was no doubt about Jackson (at the time), or about our vows—for that's what I remember best, the two of us facing each other in the red desert sunset, whispering our vows, holding hands, kissing. No, it was everything else—that I'd refused to let my father give me away or have any part, not that he'd asked; that I'd had no attendants, no one to help me get dressed beforehand, no one to keep me company. Not friends, not Aunt Lyla, and certainly not Dorinne, who wanted nothing to do with me anyway, a feeling that by then was mutual (her motto: I married your father, not his family). No, I'd done everything myself, all the planning, reserving, ordering, the writing-out of invitations; I refused even Jackson's help.

Later on I questioned why I did things the way I did. Why I'd refused everyone's help. Why I wore a pale pink silk and not white. Why I felt uncomfortable at the reception, as though I were a Greek statue on wheels. Jackson could've pulled me along by a string. "You look lovely," guests said. "Beautiful. Splendid wedding."

"Thank you," I said. "So glad you could attend." Jackson would take my elbow: time to roll me along to the next grouping of guests.

Finally we escaped and went out to an all-night restaurant for breakfast—we were starved. Everybody at the reception had talked about the wonderful food (the other topic besides my looks), but we'd eaten nothing.

Our honeymoon was perfect, romantic—cystitis aside. "Tell him to leave you alone," the doctor counseled.

It became our joke, the doctor thinking Jackson was pestering me for sex, when if anything it was the other way around.

Nonetheless, we had to settle for strolls on the beach the last couple of days. Rather, Jackson strolled while I dozed on a blanket.

It was after the honeymoon that I began to worry about details I'd had no interest in before: why, for instance, we hadn't had a receiving line.

A receiving line? Jackson had said. It wasn't that kind of wedding.

We didn't put RSVP on the invitations, I said.

We forgot, he said.

We? *I* forgot, I said. You didn't do invitations.

You wouldn't let me.

I know.

It would be the middle of the night and I'd sit straight up in bed, waking up Jackson: During the toast, I'd say, we didn't intertwine wrists like you're supposed to.

So? I didn't even have champagne in my glass.

What did you have?

Beer.

Beer? Jackson, I'd say, we didn't cut the cake right.

There's a special way to cut the cake?

Your hand over mine. We just cut it. And you didn't feed me cake. I didn't feed you cake.

Don't you think that's a little corny? Personally I'm glad we didn't feed each other cake. You're crying, he would say. Why?

At Stonewall Creek, where Jackson and I lived after the wedding, tiny barrel cactus lay hidden in the prairie grass like eggs, blooming pale pink, yellow and white flowers in June.

Our house was a modern-day log cabin set down on softest red dirt, vermilion dust, like powder in a woman's compact.

There was a particular bluff I liked, of mottled, pot-holed pink and gray rock; where I'd go after rainstorms, to listen to the water seep into rock and gravel and into the roots of the rabbit brush— the sound of everything drinking.

In the potholes birds would bathe.

A sensation of feathers on the bottoms of my feet; I could run forever.

Indeed, Indians had lived there once. Jackson said Stonewall Creek gave him a sense of history he couldn't get from his own family. Both his parents had died in his late teens, his mother of ovarian cancer, his father in a car accident. No siblings. Jackson's being an orphan appealed to me at first. We understood each other. We would strike out into the world unencumbered, together. We would be everything to each other. Although I had a smattering of family, I felt like an orphan myself, and acted the part: I saw my father and brother infrequently, and Aunt Lyla not at all. As for my mother, I'd lived more than three-quarters of my life without her. The place where she should be was blank. So I understood Jackson very well, I thought.

He'd moved to Colorado in his twenties to go to school and find himself, he liked to joke, but instead he found Stonewall Creek which he bought for cheap in the 80's, when Colorado went bust. If he couldn't have family, he used to tell me, he'd have land, this land, where the Arapahos had camped during the hunt. Everywhere there were spearheads, the rubble of ancient jugs, bison bones. After the Arapahos came the horse thieves and cattle rustlers, who drove livestock into the gorge of Stonewall Creek, further made inescapable by crude walls built of rock piled upon red rock.

I felt like a prisoner myself in that gorge, imprisoned in a place I loved, with a person I loved.

Stonewall Creek itself ran high in late spring, so high the sod of the creek bed rolled up in places, like carpets thrown back, baring root systems and the flat, pale rock underneath.

In the creek bed grew reeds and Russian thistle, yucca, some cottonwood trees, though not tall ones, and patches of willow. Everything grew up to your waist so that you couldn't see your feet as you walked, just a thicket of green pulling and scratching at your legs.

In the fall everything laid down and died, grass and reeds flattened as though felled by a sickle, and in these boughs of dead plant material, almost like nests, we'd find the carcasses of deer, two or three a season, killed by mountain lions: we'd know we were about to come upon one by the smell of rotting flesh.

So died my feelings for Jackson, worn down season after season. It's hard to say exactly when they began to change. From the very start I wanted to run from him, hide. I didn't want to talk about myself, my family, least of all what had happened to my mother, though I'd had enough therapy by that point to appear at least willing to broach the subject. But I never really did. Like my brother Corb, I suppose, I shared only the facts. I told Jackson I'd been seven. She'd been sick for several years, in and out of mental hospitals. Corb and I had found her.

"That's about it," I would tell Jackson.

"That's it, huh?" He eyed me.

"Yes," I said coolly. "That's it."

He would stare at me some more.

"Well," I said, "quit staring and ask me some questions. What do you want, a prepared speech?"

"Ask you some questions."

"Yes!"

"All right. How did it feel, you and Corb being the ones to find your mother?"

"Bad. Awful."

"This is not talking about it, Theo." He would turn away, get busy on some sort of household task, weather-stripping, caulking windows.

"Oh, shit, Jackson. What do you want me to say? Listen—" Here I would turn the tables, go on the attack, "—we never talk about *your* parents."

He couldn't even stand the word 'parents.' He would actually withdraw physically, eyes darkening, shoulders rounding, chin pulling inward like a sea anemone that retreats into itself when you lightly touch it.

If you didn't know him (and the subject of his parents didn't come up), Jackson appeared to be stolid and Midwestern, a burgher, dutiful and thick-muscled. Inwardly, however, he was sensitive, curious, and intense, the very qualities that drew me to him in the first place. He pounced on every topic (except personal ones) like a predator, no subject too trivial. Even when we were talking about buying new tires for the car, he turned it into a different subject altogether, rhapsodizing about the history of the automobile, how cars had changed us from people forced to plod across the land, "touching the land with our feet," as he would say, into a people lacking dermic contact with anything—land, animals, horses, each other. He had a point, of course, but it was all for the sake of argument, and it meant nothing to him personally. He loved Stonewall Creek but he wasn't an environmentalist, he wasn't that devoted to the land, and he still bought tires for the car and he drove the car a lot.

I never knew what he was getting at with these lectures. Clearly he was building a case—history of the automobile, the effects of using a stylus when voting, the overabundance of dairy products in our society—but why? Sometimes I would venture an opinion. "But dairy products are the easiest way for most people to absorb calcium."

"Not the only way," he would say dismissively. "Almonds, sesame seeds, broccoli, kale, tofu, carrot juice."

"Wait a minute, Jackson. You have milk on your cereal every day. You put cheese on everything. Yesterday you bought a gallon of ice cream. Are you trying to tell me you're planning to change your diet?"

"No, Theo. Don't you get it?"

"No!"

We'd both storm out of the room only to run into each other in the hallway; the house had a circular design, almost like a hogan.

I'd halt in front of him.

"Are these little talks supposed to make us closer?" I would ask. "Because I don't feel closer to you. You're like a stranger when you talk this way. Why don't you talk about *you?*"

"What about me?"

"You never say much about your childhood, for instance."

"You know the facts, Theo. Middle-class upbringing. Worse than middle-class. My mother boiled the beef before she cooked it. She boiled canned vegetables, for God's sake."

"So it was a very sterile environment," I would say.

"Not a germ or a microbe anywhere."

"I meant the emotional environment, Jackson."

He was difficult to live with, no doubt about it. He contended that *I* was difficult to live with. Moody, opinionated, not very well organized. In his view, somehow, if it weren't for him, our house would fall down around us, we'd contract encephalitis, the Cold War would resume, and we'd starve to death. Disaster would strike, all because of some oversight on my part. I hadn't filled the car with gas. I hadn't paid the phone bill. I left the coffee pot on. I couldn't balance a checkbook.

"If you want the job done right . . ." he murmured once, removing the checkbook and calculator from me.

"Do it yourself." I completed the sentence for him. "Jackson, it's just a checkbook! How am I ever going to learn to balance it if you won't give me a chance?"

"I have to know," he said, "what our finances are."

"We're solvent. Isn't that enough? Is it because both your parents died that the world feels so insecure to you?"

He could play the role of the poor orphaned I-don't-need-anybody child, artfully. Even I was convinced. But at times it would get annoying, how much he believed he didn't need other people—and how other people let him down on a regular basis.

"The world is no more insecure to me than it is to you," he'd say. "If I have that problem, you must have it tenfold. Losing your mother as a child."

Whenever he brought it up, I felt myself deadening inside, eviscerating.

Still, all might have been fine in the long run had it not been for Jackson's drinking. Might have been fine, though I suppose our problems went deeper. But it was Jackson's drinking that I could see, objectify, quantify, and it was enough to make me run from the marriage finally.

It got so I couldn't stand the pop of a beer can being opened; I could *hear* it going down Jackson's throat. Could hear beer bottles rubbing their cold shoulders together in the refrigerator. He'd go through one six-pack, and start in on another. He was never mean when he drank, just absent. He was there in the house, but not there.

Occasionally he'd try to stop, but he made it clear that it was on my behalf; *he* didn't have a problem. I did. Then I'd find beer cans in our Blazer, stashed in paper bags. I kept count. I couldn't stop counting. Whenever he left the house, I counted, lifting beer cans and bottles gritty with coffee grounds from the trash, lining them up on the kitchen counter two by two like school children, two, four, six, eight, ten, twelve.

I tried Al-Anon and hated it. Secretly, I despised my sponsor who had lived with her still-imbibing alcoholic husband for over forty years. In her lined face and gray hair I was supposed to see the serenity we all sought. What I saw was a doormat. What was I sticking around for, what was I doing with Jackson? What bound me to him?

Finally, Jackson went into another phase—last month, December, after his classes had ended—a kind of bender maybe, except he didn't leave the house. He didn't leave the couch. He didn't turn off the TV, nor did he watch it. He stared out the window day and night.

"What is the matter?" I asked.

He didn't answer. I'd seen him do this kind of thing before for a day or two, a black mood combined with drinking, but this stretched into a week, then another week. He seemed deeply depressed, even angry, but at whom I didn't know. Me? Had he guessed about my near-miss of an affair with Gregg four years ago? Had *he* had an affair? On top of everything else, I began to suspect I was pregnant.

"Jackson, what if we were to have a baby?" I ventured one afternoon, attempting to make room for myself on the couch where he lay. He barely moved his feet aside. "Would you still fall into these moods?"

"I don't want to talk about this now." He fingered the remote, gazed past me out the window.

"Fine," I said. "What sort of father would you be anyway?"

I was hoping to goad a response out of him, pick a fight if necessary. Anything but this lifelessness.

"What has set you off like this?" I said. "You won't leave the couch, you won't stop popping open beer after beer. Should I call a doctor? Do you need to go to the hospital? Please talk to me!"

"It's my vacation," he said.

"Yes, that's true." The college was out for a month, winter break. "What kind of vacation is this?" I said.

He shrugged.

That same night I left Jackson, though I hadn't planned on it. I only went to the store, to get out of the house, away from Jackson, but I found I couldn't buy anything. I pushed the empty cart around: the fluorescent lighting made everything look dim and yellow, pasty and intestinal, churning. I felt the beginnings of nausea. I couldn't think of what we needed at the house—there didn't seem to be a *we* anymore. I left the cart in the middle of an aisle and drove home in the dark. It was only six in the evening, but black and tunneled as the middle of the night. What kept me from veering off the road was this idea of leaving, returning to California—*I'm pregnant,* I kept thinking. *Oh, my God.* I pushed away thoughts of Jackson. He wouldn't get up from the couch. And he didn't, not when I packed my suitcase that night, not when I walked out the door. *I'm pregnant and this is the course I must take. My mother . . .* I felt the unwanted chromosomal link snaking around inside me, connecting me to my dead mother like a poisoned umbilical cord.

FIVE

Still, I don't call Jackson. Instead, I get ready to go out to dinner with Gregg. What do I mean by that? There's nothing to get ready—all I brought from Colorado were jeans. I try on different tops, fiddle with my hair. Hopeless.

I run down the stairs two at a time, my purse slapping against my thigh. I stop, remembering: slip off my wedding band. Run back upstairs to rub foundation on the spot, to get rid of the tan line.

Downstairs, I tell the balding man at the front desk, "I'm on my way out. I'll need the key."

As usual he's reluctant to hand it over. "You sure?"

"Yes," I say emphatically, "I'm going to be late. If you're so concerned about not having enough keys, why don't you make copies?"

"Not enough demand. Who goes out here?"

"Since obviously I'm the only one who does, why not just give me the key?"

"I only have the one."

"Fine. I'll take it."

"For tonight only, remember."

I always mean to have a copy made while I'm out, but I never seem to find a locksmith open.

Twenty of seven, I'm clattering up the stairs of Bullocks, where my Aunt Lyla used to take me shopping. Clothes my mother would have approved of, clothes my father had to approve, since he was paying. I would model for him first one outfit, then another, while Aunt Lyla smoked cigarettes angrily. Didn't he think she knew enough to select clothes Marian would have liked? Conservative color-coordinated outfits: red sweaters, bobby socks, kilts. Dirndls, white blouses, dresses with peter pan collars.

Aunt Lyla, my mother's sister, from whom our entire family became distant. I envision her throwing back her gold-dyed hair, laughing nervously, lighting a cigarette. Aunt Lyla never liked my father, blaming him for my mother's death, and she found other reasons over the years to disassociate herself from him bit by bit, a slight here, a lapse there, until it's been maybe ten years since they've communicated. But why should they, when you think about it? Connected only by my dead mother, their lives spun off in different directions, Dad eventually remarrying Dorinne and further antagonizing Lyla—so this was her sister's replacement! (Not that others didn't share her dismay; Dorinne was difficult). Slowly the distance between my father and Aunt Lyla spread to us, me and Corb. Not surprising in my own case since my relationship with her had always been fraught with stiffness and misunderstanding. She adored Corb, however, although ultimately she was willing to sacrifice him as well, for reasons none of us ever understood.

For years it was Aunt Lyla's job to take me shopping, and we always shopped at Bullocks. It wasn't my kind of store then, nor is it now, but I'm afraid the Peppermill won't let me in dressed like this, and I can't think of another store right offhand, and there isn't time to dash across the parking lot to I. Magnins, so—

Quickly I find a baggy pair of black pants. Baggy except for the waist and stomach which are meant to fit tight, and do. Tighter on me: it's starting already, I'm losing my shape. Bullocks doesn't have the next size up, so I camouflage with a blouson top, remembering suddenly how Maggie and I didn't like it when boys put their arms around our waists, how we had to stand up straighter or reposition their arms to our shoulders for fear their hands might discover a roll of fat.

I was hoping, since I'd last seen him four years ago, that Gregg might've grown fat or sloped or stooped, that he'd be wearing polyester—it'd make this easier. But he hasn't even lost any hair. Only his complexion has changed, gradually, from the pale sleepy warm tint of our college days to a more olive cast. All due to living here. You can't help but turn a shade or two darker just walking down the street; even Gregg, a musician, who never rises before noon.

I watch him from my car, watch him go inside, without following. In case I want to change my mind.

It's just dinner, I tell myself. He's an old friend. Perfectly innocent. Never mind what happened the last time we got together—what almost happened.

Now he's standing outside the Peppermill again. I wave, honk. My heart's pounding and I swear, I feel a pounding, almost like a pulse, in my belly, as if the baby knows what I'm up to and doesn't approve. *That isn't my father you're honking at.*

Gregg strolls over and points to my window. "Roll it down," he says. I do and our fingers touch, the beginning of a handshake (already I'm checking for a wedding band, don't see one). I roll down the window further and he leans in, catching me on the cheek with a kiss. Technically innocent, though let's not deny it, the kiss landed a little close to my mouth.

"Gregg . . ." Now I'm out of the car and we're hugging. Well, isn't that what old friends do when they haven't seen each other in years? So why is his leg almost between mine? He's turned sideways, ah, that's why. I back off.

"I'm starved," I say. "Let's go eat." A line females have used for years in this parking lot, no doubt: it's one of those restaurants. Red leather booths, white linen tablecloths, candles so dim they're about to drown in wax. The place is dripping with false romance.

"Follow me," the host says, a man with a handlebar mustache I seem to remember from twenty years ago, the last time I was here.

He loads us into a booth, hands us oversized menus.

"What made you pick this place?" Gregg asks.

We burst out laughing.

Six

Bay of Pigs. Pigs drowning, heads bashed together in the waves, bodies slick with brains and blood. Not pigs, you dummy, says Corb, four years older than me; soldiers, boats, Commies. Cuba. We're sitting on the wood stairs in our basement, knees to our chests; beneath the stairs are spider webs, dust, curled-up worm larvae, maybe worse, who knows . . . we once found a dead cat in our basement, must've gotten in through a grate and died, been there for days, stinking and bloated.

Our mother is making us sit here, amid cans and cans of food stacked up everywhere: according to my fragments, the memories I've sewn together. She is somewhere else in the house. I'm not sure why we're sitting here. Something to do with Cuba or bombs; or is it that Corb and I are being punished? Cans of food with red, green, and yellow labels—pictures of beans, tomatoes, beets, and yams. Smaller cans of tuna, minced ham, spiced beef. Huge cans of juice and bottled water. Towels. Blankets. *Nobody played war better than me* click-click *gun to my head, somebody wants me dead* click-click.

I'm eating cottage cheese sprinkled with sugar at the kitchen table, alone. No, *she* is there, my mother, in the room somewhere, but I'm alone. Or I'm scuffing up and down the hallway in her cast-off high heels. Again, she's around somewhere, but not with me. Possibly standing in my bedroom doorway watching me play with my dollhouse, but she is a distant, punishing presence. When she is watching, I play one way, nicely. The dolls sit in the living room, the house is immaculate. They don't know what to do with themselves. Phone rings, somebody answers, "Hello? Just a minute, please." The dolls stare at each other politely, warily.

My mother leaves the room. The dolls destroy the house, rip the tiny sheets off the beds. Throw towels, food, little china plates and tea sets, vases. Throw whole tables, chairs, lamps across the room. Hit each other with the vacuum cleaner, the phone, alarm clocks. Stuff each other's heads down the toilet. One doll has hard black high-heeled shoes—she kicks the doll whose hair is missing, whose job it always is to clean the house.

Sometimes when my mother leaves the room, I shut the doll-house doors, lock the dolls inside. I rock the house side to side, faster and faster. Worried I'll break something, I can't stop, I shake the house until I can't anymore. Then I open it up, look for bodies in the rubble, dig out the doll whose hair is missing and make her clean the mess.

My mother is dead. Days and days of a fuzzy white space. Some nights I wake up staring at a wall in my room. I'm sitting straight up in bed with the light on and I can't remember how I got there.

All skin is tender when nicked by a razor. So my mother said in my dreams, after she died. She talked like that, never saying exactly what she meant, her face shaded by a straw gardening hat.

She wore white. A white dress with a sash—as though we lived at the turn of the century. And she floated around the garden with small, exact pruning shears.

Sometimes in my dreams she came back for a day and we went on a picnic, my mother, Dad, Corb and me, her in her white dress, us in regular clothes. She carried a wicker bassinet: Charlotte, whom my mother kept hidden under a blanket.

In other dreams she came at me with a knife. Smiling. *I've got a surprise for you.* The knife behind her back. My wrists itched and bled, from them grew knobs of wood, outside there was a field of corn. . . .

No one plays war better than me click click. My made-up nursery rhyme. *No one plays war better than me* click-click. *On my belly in the dirt, toy rifle in my hands* click-click, click-click. *A war, somebody wants me dead.*

Consumed by fear, I don't tell anyone. Every time we have a drill at school, either for earthquakes in which we crawl under our desks, or for civil defense in which we all troop to the auditorium single file, I panic. My heart rocks against the walls of my chest, I can hardly breathe. Outwardly, I look the same as all the other kids, crouching under my desk with my skirt clutched against my thighs so the boys can't see my underwear, or in the auditorium, acting bored and restless along with everyone else, glancing casually at my brother Corb as I would a stranger. Inside of me, panic. Can't remember my name or address, can't distinguish my right hand from my left. I remember that my mother is dead, a refrain: my mother's dead, Charlotte's dead . . . but I can't remember anything about them. Nobody talks about them, not my father or my aunt or uncle or cousins, or my teachers, not even my brother. Nobody says suicide. My mother's dead, Charlotte's dead, mother's dead, Charlotte's dead. . . .

SEVEN

I wake up sneezing, as I always do at the Alta Vista. Sneeze and sneeze again, dust motes swirling in the sunlight. I'm nauseated, too, so I reach for my saltines on the nightstand—I keep the box double-wrapped in plastic bags, old-lady-style. Fear of cockroaches and mice, though I have yet to see either here.

Half reclining, I eat saltines, a tip I got out of my one book on pregnancy so far, bought at Thrifty's. "Eat the saltines *before* getting out of bed; this will stabilize the stomach acids." A book that's about twenty years out of date, even if this particular piece of advice seems to work. The rest of the book is about not gaining very much weight; disguising the weight you do gain; losing weight after the baby's born. Pictures of slim, smiling mothers holding infants so teeny they could fit inside the curl of their mothers' flip hairdos.

I bought the book, along with a standard paperback thesaurus, when I bought the sheets for this bed. I figured if I had to be here even one more night, it would be worth a new set of sheets. The existing sheets were threadbare and smelled of old people, ancient sex, body odor; the new set smells of air wicks, scented toilet paper. A floral print—the sheets have a white background, orange and blue and prune-colored flowers.

Throwing back the sheets, I run to the toilet. Dry heaves. Pregnancy, or guilt over last night? The baby's punishment for dining with a man other than the baby's father. But nothing happened, or so I tell the baby. Nothing really.

We kissed a long time in the car. I prevented Gregg's hands, and mine, from traveling any further. I said "no" a few times. "This is it, Gregg, for old time's sake. No more."

"Why not?" he asked.

"Well, I'm married, for one thing."

He wrenched away from me.

"I wasn't going to tell you," I say. All during dinner I kept my left hand in my lap like a well-mannered person, the foundation I dabbed on my finger a poor disguise. It was sort of a relief to tell him. "I'm thirty-five," I said. "Did you think I'd been alone all these years?" I didn't bother mentioning I was married the last time I saw him, four years ago. "Anyway, I'm separated."

"Since when?"

"A week."

"One week?"

I nodded.

We began making out again. What else was there to do?

"I almost got married," Gregg said suddenly, disengaging himself again.

"When?"

"Two years ago."

"Since then, what?"

Exchanging romantic résumés, reluctantly, resentfully. You'd think we might've covered this during dinner, but instead I strung Gregg along with stories about my job. Funny stuff. Not the writing part—boring—but the photo shoots I travel to several times a year. The boxes and hangers and bags full of clothes, the little girls in makeup made to look like they aren't wearing any, the confusion and chaos, babies pooping at critical moments. Stage mothers. The hot white lights and the backdrops, the occasional lamb or puppy brought in as a prop, and the sounds: big voices instructing little people, big voices trying not to yell, little voices whimpering so as not to burst into tears. While I spoke, I tried very hard not to get lost in Gregg's face and eyes. His eyebrows, though, have always gotten to me the most, arched and quizzical, as though he's engaged in solving an endless sexual riddle. In comparison, Jackson's face is grainy, dry, lined, what people called rugged. It wasn't always so. Too many years at Stonewall Creek, he would say, sun, wind, erosion. I know: it's happening to my face too.

"Gregg, so what about after your engagement?" I'd had to do that periodically through the night, prompt him. Was he hard of hearing from playing too many clubs, or merely preoccupied?

"Since my engagement," Gregg said. "Not much, some dates here and there. It's been pretty lonely." He fitted his arms around my waist. "You're free now, Theo."

"Not quite." I left it at that. My belly gurgled, as if to underscore the point.

So much for the saltines. My eyes run. I fight the heaves, the gagging. *No one played war better than me* click-click *when I was a child. On my belly in the dirt, toy rifle in my hands,* click-click, click-click, *a war, somebody wants me dead.* I kneel before the toilet, lift the seat; I haven't vomited in years. Over and over again goes my made-up nursery rhyme: *No one played war better than me* click-click, a not-unfamiliar sensation of my head being pushed down toward the toilet bowl by an unseen hand. . . .

My mother. I remember what today is: the anniversary of her death, her suicide. The day I dread each year because I feel so keenly the echo of her suicide, a small death inside myself, as though every year a portion of me turns black and dies—a finger, a toe, part of an arm or leg.

But it's time to think differently now. The baby, if there is a baby, is counting on me, as I once counted on *her.* I need to see a doctor.

Dr. Grimes is a man's man. Solid mass in a white coat, hairy hands, with a style that's meant to inspire men onward in battle. Dr. Grimes—what an appalling name for an obstetrician; maybe it keeps patients away. In any case he is able to fit me into his schedule today, whereas the wait at every other doctor's office is weeks.

I'm swathed in white sheets. A nurse stands at attention.

On go the rubber gloves, *snap!*

His fingers up me, I try to get away—as much as one can when one's feet are in stirrups.

"Settle down, now, settle down." He softens his manner, like a dairy farmer soothing a cow, fingers twisting this way and that. "Hold on there, no reason to jump off the table."

He withdraws his fingers, tears off the gloves, palpates my abdomen as though searching for lumps in a pillow.

"Ow!"

"Know what, missy?"

"What," I say wearily.

"As your urine test indicates, I'd say there's a bun in the oven."

"Really? You can feel it?" So he speaks in clichés. So what? I forgive everything. "How far along am I?"

"Eight weeks or so. Of course, we'd have to do an ultrasound to be exact. No need for that—you seem healthy and strapping." Back to cow talk.

I'm allowed to sit up.

"When's my due date?" Due date: that such words even refer to me, to a *baby* . . .

"Late September." Dr. Grimes checks a round sort of calendar with a dial on it. "How's the twenty-fifth suit you?"

"That'd be fine. Great!" As if the date is for brunch, a social engagement.

"See you in a month, Mrs. Mapes."

I'm too thrilled to correct him.

"Maybe next time we'll get a heartbeat," he adds.

"Pardon?"

"The baby's heartbeat."

"You can hear it?"

"You bet." He offers a hairy hand—for me to shake, I realize a moment too late. He claps me on the back instead, vigorously. "Congratulations," he says.

I'm half-expecting cigars to be produced, passed all around. Big fat stogies. Then I remember all the men I've slept with. "Before you go, Dr. Grimes, I was wondering."

"Yes?"

I swallow. "Do you do HIV tests here?"

"Sure, Missy." He's so casual, you'd think I'd asked for a tongue depressor as a souvenir.

"Just in case," I joke to the nurse as she draws my blood.

She doesn't smile, as if my requesting this test makes a positive result more likely.

"I mean, I would hate . . . I just couldn't . . . It's not that I think I . . . but what if?" God, I sound like my father, stammering away about some point of etiquette. "I just couldn't live with myself," I say. "Doing that to a baby."

"We get more requests than you think," she says, tight-lipped. "And we're starting to insist on it ourselves. Standard procedure. Hold this, please." A cotton ball.

I bend my arm at the elbow to keep the cotton in place, trying to imagine cradling a baby in my arms. Have I ever even held one before? I keep picturing a doll, or a swaddle of blankets with nothing inside, only air.

I wish Jackson were here. Not Jackson; Gregg. Somebody. Who? My mother?

I'm shuttled into a different room where another one of Dr. Grime's nurses carries in an armload of booklets and charts. "Now," she says. She's delicate, pale, girlish—speaks with a touch of a lisp. "This is the diet Dr. Grimes wants you to follow."

She passes it to me across the table.

"Aa-nn-d," (she draws this out with a little flourish), "your prescription for maternal vitamins as well as iron pills. And this is a chart you might like. It shows the fetus at different stages, see? Here's eight weeks, where you are now."

I feel rather queasy. "Kind of resembles escargot, don't you think?"

She gives me a strange look.

"Things do seem to improve from there," I add, studying the chart.

Now that pregnancy is a certainty, I feel sicker than ever, my womb and bloodstream and breasts pulsing with hormones. Pain between my legs and in my uterus, as if already it's expanding; pin-like shooting pains up and down my limbs, leaving me too warm, then chilled—is this normal?

To celebrate, I go out for a late breakfast, nearly gagging at the sight of anyone else's yellow-bellied soft-boiled eggs sopped up by white toast, parsley on the side. I'd wanted a diner with homemade blueberry muffins, bowls of Special K in whole milk, sausage, but Denny's is all I could find, smelling of eggs and paper napkins.

I order a mixture of side dishes, going over the menu aloud with the waitress. "Potatoes? No. No. But I will have an English muffin, no butter. Wait. Butter on the side. And an egg, but hard-boiled—do you have any that are cold? No orange juice. Do you have strawberries? Plain, not mixed in with other fruits. Never mind, then, I'll have melon, but cantaloupe, not honeydew. And ice water, please. No, no tea. *No* coffee."

I used to adore coffee, as recently as last week.

After breakfast I feel so much better, luscious in fact, juicy and full. My breasts are about to burst from my bra, and I want to tear off my clothes and lie on a bed naked; make love. Gregg comes to mind, not the father of this child, dimming my lust for a moment. Ah, my body says, who cares. Copulate with everyone. Offer your breasts to everyone and, really, I'd like to: unbutton my blouse and bare them to passersby, men, women, children. As if the milk is flowing already.

EIGHT

I hate to think of myself as one of those people who holds up a dusty old relationship to the light and, fantastically, unrealistically, deems it the best. But I am. It was. I think. Anyway, here I am in this club at Gregg's invitation, watching his band play; a romantic fool to the end, silly old groupie, sipping my seltzer made to look like a cocktail: ice cubes, fizz, lime.

When I first saw Gregg some sixteen years ago, he was standing in line at freshman orientation, tall and slim, dark hair down to his shoulders, parted in the middle, wire-rimmed glasses.

I didn't go up to him. But I decided right then and there I would meet him, be with him in some forever sense.

It was months before we did meet, though. Smoking dope in somebody's room, we sat on the floor together—for some reason people never sat on chairs or beds—the two of us dealing out Tarot cards and not talking, just laughing and laughing.

He walked me back to my dorm and while we didn't kiss, our hands brushed, our elbows bumped, and something had been decided.

Now between sets, Gregg lights up a cigarette and I nearly gag. Me? Gagging at the smell of smoke? Pregnancy: how quickly this baby has set up housekeeping inside me, all my vices swept away. Baby's rules, not mine.

"You still smoke?" I say to Gregg, trying to keep my voice light, even. He didn't smoke last night.

The reek of this bar; how did I ever, ever hang out in such places?

Seeing my face, green and probably glowing in the dark, Gregg immediately crushes out his cigarette. Like Aunt Lyla used to do. Puff, puff. Put it out. Exonerated. "There," Gregg says, half yelling the way people do in bars. "Enough. I only smoke when I'm playing, a couple of drags between sets."

"Yeah," I say, yelling back.

"When did you quit?" He sounds disappointed.

"After I saw you last."

We had met at a restaurant, the smoking section. To be with a man who smoked! It was heaven to me, after Jackson's nagging.

"I quit after that," I yell. "Allergies."

"That's why you quit?"

"Part of the reason. Not my allergies," I mutter, glad for the din of this place, so he won't hear me. It was Jackson who had the allergies, sneezing and wheezing whenever I lit up, even when I smoked outside. He said he could smell it on my clothes, my hair. I quit for him, penance for spending the afternoon in Gregg's bed. After our lunch. That we didn't go all the way was small compensation. I figured I owed Jackson something if not total fidelity, so why not quit smoking? After all, he'd begged me the entire first year of our marriage and I'd resisted, afraid I'd get fat. Which I did. Voluptuous, Jackson said. Luscious. Fat, I said and turned to coffee instead, drinking so much some days that my hands shook. My stomach ached. Finally I grew to resent him. All those afternoons I spent snapping a rubber band on my wrist, which is how I quit cigarettes. A tight rubber band, like my mother's hand on me, I used to think. Not that I could recall such a thing. I couldn't remember anything about her. But whenever I thought of smoking, I snapped the rubber band hard, for some reason thinking of her. Maybe because she had smoked. Anyway, it ended up with me blaming Jackson; I gave up cigarettes for him. Couldn't he quit beer for me?

"Why else did you quit smoking?" Gregg asks, toying with a straw.

"My marriage."

His eyes flicker off, on, coldly. He doesn't like to hear about this; wouldn't he just love to hear about the fruit of that union? Then he's not toying with the straw anymore but staring at me—calculating, I realize.

"What year did you get married?"

"Five years ago. I was married when I saw you last—I know that's what you're trying to figure out. Jackson and I had been married about a year. We were having problems at the time." At the time? When didn't we have problems?

"I gotta go," Gregg says, standing. The other band members are milling around on stage, waiting for him. Time for the next set.

In any case his piano playing has the usual mesmerizing effect on me—electric piano tonight—this band, one of many he's in, being of a jazz-fusion strain, as far as I can tell. Maybe because I'm not a musician and know so little about music, it's never mattered to me what kind of music Gregg plays. It's *his* playing I like, his soul. I drink it in like a cocktail, an espresso. A drug, a cigarette. I watch his hands, his mouth . . . I think about what we might do later tonight, if things aren't sabotaged beyond repair, that is. As Gregg said last night, I really am free. Little does he know I don't even have to worry about birth control, although somehow this isn't a cheering thought.

The set's over and I don't leave. The bar empties out, and still I don't leave. Last call, I order another seltzer. Gregg and the band are breaking down equipment, carrying it out to their cars; he keeps looking at me over his shoulder.

A late bloomer, Gregg always called himself.

In college he did two things well: play music and make love. I could never figure out how Gregg, who couldn't change a tire, who couldn't catch a football or even a pillow if you handed it to him, who couldn't dance, who couldn't talk to people except other musicians, who couldn't pour a cup of coffee without spilling—how someone so lacking in normal everyday skills and most social graces could know so instinctively how to please a woman. And it wasn't that he'd had a lot of experience, like me. He was practically a virgin. He *was* a virgin, he finally admitted to me our first time together, as if it were something to be ashamed of.

"Things," he said, "didn't work out the other times." I gathered he meant his erection, which looked fine to me, all the better once he admitted his virginity.

If I was a first for him, he was for me, too. The first man with whom I'd had an orgasm. Which made me a virgin of a different sort, I liked to think.

In college, aside from playing music or making love, everything else Gregg did was a mild ongoing seizure, nerve-wracking to watch. He fidgeted, he grimaced, he smiled, he frowned; he ran a hand through his hair, then on down his spine until an audible crack was heard; he burped, he sighed; he lit one cigarette to another; he pushed his glasses back up onto his nose; he squinted; wrenched his shoulders up and down. He crossed his arms, his legs, his ankles, his feet, simultaneously, twisting them in and out—basket weaving, it looked like.

He was fascinating, embarrassing, annoying. Stoned, I saw him as a god, the Indian god Shiva, the one with all the arms.

Straight, he drove me crazy. "Can't you sit still?"

"What?"

"*Sit still.*"

I disliked being in social situations with him, although others didn't find him irritating—just nervous and rather lovable, and amazing, which he was. I mean, how could he go from knocking over a bowl of dip, stepping in it, and tracking it across the floor—all without noticing—to sitting down at the piano, boom, a complete transformation, every movement sure and smooth, timed and sexual. He loved to perform, but only at the piano. Anything else, except sex, made him uncomfortable. People, conversation, talk, human interaction (unless somehow paired with music), made the parts of his body appear mismatched, clanking and tangling together like a wind chime in a gale.

Never mind. Everybody liked him. Correction—adored him. Women thought he was cute; men admired his piano playing. At parties he always wound up at the keyboard entertaining everyone, the women who could sing hanging all over him like yowling cats in heat, while I stewed in the corner. I couldn't sing or play piano or any instrument, so there was nothing for me to do at these parties besides admire Gregg and drink, or get up a little game of flirtation in the next room.

After the club closes, he's trying to help me find my car. "A block away," I tell him. "I'm just not sure in which direction." My ears ringing, I almost do feel drunk—that feeling you have after leaving a bar late at night, scoured out, cleansed somehow.

We walk another block in the wrong direction before he broaches the subject. "Why didn't you tell me you were married, Theo? You could've just told me."

"You could've asked. You didn't even ask if I had a boyfriend."

"I figured that was your job. To tell me."

"I asked you about you. You didn't ask because you didn't want to know," I say.

He doesn't deny it. One more block in a different direction, down a side street with no palm trees, just concrete and stucco walls of buildings gleaming in the night and the smell of the ocean. Every step we take echoes and again I forget I'm not drunk, that I haven't had a drop.

"I didn't know how to tell you, Gregg." I recall the words stuck in my throat, like dough. The same feeling as now, only different words. How to tell Gregg I'm pregnant?

"I guessed anyway," he says.

"You did? You knew I was married?" For some reason I'm feigning surprise. He guessed I was married and I knew he knew. "How did you guess?"

"The way you breathed, the way you moaned. Like you were acting."

Even though we're arguing or at the least having a 'discussion,' he's kept his hand on my waist all this time, tethering me. I nearly spit it off. "I wasn't acting. I don't act with you." It's something I hate to hear—any insinuation that my passion is simulated.

I can't say why it upsets me so. Acting is what whores do. Is that it? Only a handful of men ever ventured such an opinion; most couldn't tell the difference. And in a sense, it wasn't true. I wasn't acting out my attraction. I wasn't acting out my excitement. I was acting out a specific part, the orgasm part. Helping myself along. Maybe I could act my way into coming, if I got carried away enough. But not with Gregg, not four years ago, not now.

"I wasn't acting," I say again. "And why would my acting make you think I was married anyway?"

I realize we just passed my car and I swivel around to face it, white and spectral. I persist. "Why would acting make you think I was married?"

"Guilt," he says at last. "Forget it, Theo. It's just a theory."

"Maybe we shouldn't see each other, Gregg. It's too complicated."

"You're probably right."

But his hand is on my waist again and when I unlock the door and get in, he gets in beside me.

When we make love, which happens almost immediately—on the drive to his house we're already unbuttoning, unzipping—we don't bother turning on any lights; we barely make it to his bed. Afterwards my belly is still for once, peaceful, as if the baby, too, has reached a decision about our allegiance, or is at least considering the possibility of somebody other than Jackson: is considering Gregg.

Then he turns on the light and ruins everything. His mattress is on the floor, which is no big deal, but the floor is a stained, filthy linoleum that's chewed up in one corner, as though a dog attacked it. On the bureau is the same clock radio he had in college—a miracle the thing still works—a small, round, cut-out picture of John Lennon's head taped to the front. This, if nothing else, makes me feel at home: how many nights I lay there sleepless staring at John Lennon, whose face you could just make out in the clock's glow.

"Last time you were living someplace different," I say. A decent little bungalow in Altadena.

"I was house-sitting."

His room doesn't smell exactly. It does smell, but of Gregg, a sweet-sweaty odor I remember from college. I try to see the charm in this place, as he gives me a tour. More frayed linoleum in the living room that needs scrubbing, a mopping with bleach. A smelly can of cat food on the kitchen counter with the fork still in it. I count exactly seven pieces of furniture (nine including Gregg's mattress and bureau): a dinette, a leather chair mostly robbed of its stuffing, an old TV with a wire hanger for an antenna, the beds of his roommates (musicians also, away on tour, Gregg says), and Gregg's piano, a Yamaha shiny as obsidian, the only thing cared for in this house, a can of Pledge on top of it and next to that two stacks of score sheets, one for the opera he's working on, he says, and the other a stack of various pop songs he's written.

"Will you excuse me?" I say. I go to the bathroom, sit on the john and bend over, holding my stomach, feeling wretched. It isn't that Gregg is poor; poor is okay, I *like* poor, looking back on my choices in men. It's rich men I don't trust. But Gregg is living like a college student still, and he's thirty-six, and I've just slept with him. I'm not simply here for the afternoon as I was four years ago, and this is Gregg, not a quickie one-night stand. This time I've made some kind of commitment, or a mistake; I can't say why this has happened except that I love him. I must. Who understands love? People can change, I tell myself, and it's just a place, a rental, for God's sake, and it's Gregg's character that matters—but what sort of person would live here? I could pretend it's a fixer-upper, although Gregg wouldn't know which end of a hammer to use. But maybe he's changed, maybe he tore up the linoleum himself and plans to refinish what's underneath. Fat chance. What's really different now as opposed to four years ago is that we're four years older, and that I'm pregnant, looking for a nest to have my baby in. Why not admit it?

Some nest.

He seems a little anxious when I return, as though he's guessed what I'm thinking. He's always been sensitive on the subject on financial success or lack thereof. "I thought you were doing something," he said.

"Something?"

"You know. We didn't use anything. Last time you had a diaphragm."

"Not that we needed it." We had changed our minds at the last minute. *I* changed *my* mind, and Gregg isn't the pushy sort. As if doing everything but made me more virtuous. I brought my diaphragm all the way from Colorado, leaving the case for it there, in the medicine cabinet, so Jackson wouldn't suspect. Actually what I did was put my old diaphragm in that case, because I feared he would check, and, being a man, he wouldn't know the difference between the old and new. It's not a happy memory. The sex part, yes, the subterfuge, no. Since I had the diaphragm, I felt compelled to use it—I mean, I wore it out to lunch, every so often catching a whiff of spermicidal jelly wafting up from under the tablecloth.

"I don't use a diaphragm anymore," I say. On the drive over here, I nearly asked Gregg to stop for rubbers, old habit—an awareness I didn't have my diaphragm and we should use *something*—all the years of pregnancy prevention.

"You're on the pill?" he says.

"Can we not talk about this?"

"Or that shot? Or one of those deals they put in your arm?"

"You mean Norplant," I say.

"That's it."

Subject dropped. He thinks I've got Norplant, and I let him.

We circle the room—there's no place to sit, just a piano bench and the leather chair depleted of stuffing—the desire between us like live electrical wires, which I try to ignore, a little ridiculous since we're not wearing any clothes, and when Gregg catches up with me, I give up, he knows I'm ready, and we head for the bedroom again.

"Am I acting now?" I say.

"No."

He leans into me so that over his shoulder I see John Lennon's head, the size of a coin.

NINE

The next three nights I spend at Gregg's, lugging along my Powerbook and all my layouts, hoping to get some work done while Gregg's out playing. But each night instead of working I fidget and wait for him, napping, fantasizing. I almost forget I'm pregnant. I keep going back and forth with this, as if it's negotiable, not quite accepting it. I call Dr. Grimes' office to find out about my HIV test and while I'm on hold awaiting the results, I start counting how many men I've slept with, like other people count sheep, the men jumping over a fence without a backward glance.

"Mrs. Mapes?"

"Ms. Mapes," I correct her.

"Your HIV test is negative."

"Meaning I don't have HIV or AIDS."

"That is correct."

I don't say anything for such a long time that finally she inquires, "Will you be needing anything else, then, Ma'am?"

"No, I'm just—are you sure?"

"Your test results are negative. Would you like to speak with the nurse?"

No thanks, I tell her.

I call my brother. "Where have you been?" he asks. "I keep leaving messages at the Alta Vista."

Next I call Dad who says more or less the same thing. "Just checking in," I tell him brightly.

"Have you called Jackson?"

Jackson. I resist the very thought of him, but now, hearing his name, I can't help wondering what he's doing right now. Leaving the house to go teach? Classes have started up again. I imagine his worn canvas briefcase, if you can call it a briefcase. It's a simple canvas bag with a strap that goes over his shoulder and across his chest—an object for which I've always had a tender, almost sexual attachment. It's what men feel when they think of women's belongings, perhaps—shoes, clothing, lingerie. It makes them weak. That's what Jackson's bag does to me now.

"Theo, have you called Jackson yet?"

"I will, I promise."

"I'm holding you to that."

"Right. Bye, Dad."

I hang up quickly, then call Aunt Lyla, having no idea what I'll say. I'm not sure why I'm calling exactly—something to do with having a baby and Aunt Lyla being my only living female relative, a last link to my mother.

"I'm just in town," I say vaguely.

"Why don't you come over, dear."

"Now?"

"For an early dinner, won't you? It'd be lovely to see you."

As if we'd been in touch all these years.

When I get there the back door's open, the alarm system switched off, as she said it would be. Aunt Lyla isn't in the kitchen, of course. Although she's expecting me, it's mid-afternoon so she must be resting upstairs, or bathing, dressing, preparing for the evening ahead. Meanwhile, dinner simmers, awaiting us, as if prepared by unseen hands. I check: sure enough there's a roast in the oven, a platter of slivered fruit in the fridge, sun tea out on the patio—a simple supper, which is not to say Aunt Lyla hasn't gone to a lot of trouble.

Aunt Lyla always went to a lot of trouble, meanwhile denying it. Parties especially. "We're casual tonight," she would say, gesturing at a sideboard groaning with homemade potato salad and three-bean salad, breads and hoagie rolls gotten from some expensive out-of-the-way baker, various cheeses both common and imported, pâtés, crackers, chips (that somehow didn't resemble or taste like anything else served on the face of the earth); jello that wasn't *Jello* jello—but a gelatin made from scratch, delicate, lightly sweetened (delighting both children and adults alike) with fresh fruit and whipped cream folded in somehow, the whole mold upended and placed, without a dent or mar, on a ceramic cake plate, then marvelously cut into jiggling slices. And she served it to you personally, with a fancy-tined spatula, all the while telling you (again), "We're casual tonight. Just sandwiches and whatnot. Help yourself!" Glasses with the ice already in them, ice, incidentally that never seemed to melt; paper plates, yes, but paper *mâché* plates arranged inside wicker basket holders with little handles. The food tasted so delicious, you'd line up for seconds, even thirds. Aunt Lyla would insist on it. "Oh honestly," she'd say, "it's a party! Don't be such a boy scout." It was as if you'd never tasted a roast beef sandwich before, or salad, or iced tea; who knew it could be so heavenly? Nor would you be able to reproduce this meal on your own, either, although Aunt Lyla was more than glad to give you the recipes, typed out just for you on her own personalized recipe cards.

Holiday parties were the best: massive Easter egg hunts for the kids with the eggs hidden everywhere, anywhere—on the gutters of the roof, at the very tip top of the orange trees (how did she get them up there? . . . it had to be her, Uncle Morgan stayed out of such matters); or at Christmas, a tree that might as well have been in the White House, and Christmas stockings as long as your leg, brimming over with toys (you were never too old for toys!), each one selected with only you in mind. So different from our own father who filled our normal-sized, dull red stockings with practical items like scotch tape and soap and ballpoint pens, the price tags still affixed. This was after our mother died so we were old enough to know by then that it wasn't Santa Claus who packed stockings, but parents. Aunt Lyla was every bit as good as Santa Claus, though, if not better. At Christmas she and Uncle Morgan would even dress up, he as Santa Claus, and she not as Mrs. Claus but a saucy elf in short felt skirt rimmed with white fur (to show off her legs), matching cap, black boots with her trademark stiletto heels. Or maybe she *was* supposed to be Mrs. Claus—a young mod Mrs. Claus.

The deal was, at Christmas—as well as every other holiday— we'd spend the early part of the morning at our house, chomping at the bit to go to Aunt Lyla's. This was only after our mother died. Before she died we seldom went over there, especially not on holidays, and when we did go our father accompanied us. Our mother stayed home. She and Aunt Lyla didn't speak. They simply had little to say. They got on each other's nerves. They weren't close, or so went my father's explanation in later years, what bits he would tell me.

After fifteen minutes of pacing Aunt Lyla's kitchen, peeking in drawers, snitching cookies, I venture upstairs.

"Aunt Lyla?"

She emerges from her bedroom smoothing on hand lotion. "Oh there you are, dear. I was beginning to worry."

She offers me her cheek, as though we saw each other yesterday rather than five years ago at my wedding, and says, "Don't you look fresh! So outdoorsy."

Which means my attire is questionable. I glance down. Same old black jeans, my suede boots again (from which, thank God, I remembered to remove the dollop of spaghetti sauce), a raw silk tee shirt that I thought was hip but now seems faded and wrinkled. Grunge without any fashion sense. How I've always felt around Aunt Lyla. Graceless, orphaned, not at all pretty—older now, is all.

She hasn't aged, not much. As light as my mother was dark, her hair golden—dyed, my father used to claim, shuddering. Aunt Lyla must be close to seventy-three, my mother's older sister by two years, yet she's as petite as a girl, nimble legs and a little pot belly. Her skin is smooth. Face lift, Retin-A or just good skin, which hopefully I'll inherit, although who knows what my mother's skin would've looked like, had she lived; dark, shadowed . . .

"Let's go downstairs where we can visit," she says. I let her precede me, marveling at her stiletto heels. Will she never give those up? Barbie doll shoes, I thought as a child. Like Barbie, she had a million pairs, in every color, along with matching necklaces and earrings.

Not your mother's taste, my father would say pointedly.

It was Aunt Lyla's way of rebelling, I realized, once I grew older. Of the two sisters, she was considered the rebel. A jitter-bugger who secretly bought a car of her own and dropped out of college to marry Uncle Morgan, who was not considered wealthy or accomplished enough at the time.

As a teenager Aunt Lyla had been sent to the Arizona desert for allergies—hay fever, asthma, eczema so severe it left her with scars. There, it was rumored, she had a nervous breakdown over some boy, and developed a taste for drink, a taste she later was able to control and let subside, unlike my mother.

"Can I get you something to drink?" she says now, at the foot of the stairs, swaying a bit. Losing her balance from those heels? Or perhaps it's me who's swaying, pregnant and dizzy.

"A drink?" I hesitate, as I always do here.

"Gin and tonic. Coke. Wine. Coffee. Iced tea? What would you like?" Only five minutes and already she seems a tad impatient with me.

"Nothing, thanks." I imagine my father clearing his throat expectantly. "Thank you," I add. Having said this, I realize I'm actually dying of thirst. Water.

"I'll get it myself."

"Get what, dear?"

"If I need a drink, I can always get it myself," I say.

She rolls her eyes ever so slightly and sighs. "Whatever," she says.

I don't believe Aunt Lyla ever meant to be critical of me, or even that she disliked me. She simply didn't know what to do with me or how to talk to me. I was a foreign, exotic, exasperating species—her sister's daughter. The sister she hadn't been close to; just that fact alone seemed a strike against me. She'd tried to win me over after my mother's death, failed, and lost interest in me. I made her uncomfortable. I was too quiet, nervous, sensitive, secretive; a nut case in the making, perhaps. Or perhaps she resented me. That because my mother had died I expected her, my aunt, my mother's sister, to take her place. Or else it was that ultimately I wouldn't let her. I rejected her—or she rejected me. In any event we rubbed each other the wrong way, and early on a chill set in.

We're here on the living room couch with the iced tea Aunt Lyla insisted on fetching me after all.

"How are Susan and Daniel?" I ask. Her children, my cousins with whom I'd never been close. They were twins, Corb's age, and as straight as the stripes on their Oxford shirts. One lives on the east coast, the other in Chicago.

"Just fine, dear. They were here for the holidays and both brought their children. Charming!" *Charming*—this might mean their visit truly was charming, or it might mean Susan and Daniel and all their kids running all over the house was anything but.

"How's that husband of yours?" Aunt Lyla asks now. We're side by side on the couch where she's brought me to chat. To "catch up," as she says. Already she's gotten up once to check the roast, and another time to answer the phone, clattering away in her high heels, cigarette in her mouth. She still chain-smokes, never an entire cigarette, and empties ashtrays constantly so there's practically no stench. (When I was younger and smoked myself, no sooner would I rest my lit cigarette in the ashtray than Aunt Lyla would sweep it up, throw the contents into the garbage disposal, wash the ashtray and dry it and return it to its location, all the while insisting I have a seat so we could "visit.") "He certainly is handsome," she says.

Aunt Lyla smiles winsomely, as though trying to pry some kind of confession out of me. A confession of what?

"Is he a professor now?" she asks.

A professor is the last thing Jackson would be. He claims to have almost no ambition; I think of his canvas bag again, how it rests against his hip, and I swallow painfully, then reach for my iced tea, grateful for it. The way Aunt Lyla gazes at me, I realize she's waiting for an answer, waiting, in fact, for me to say my husband's name that she can't recall. It's been five years since the wedding, after all, and we've had no contact since.

"Jackson and I are separated, Aunt Lyla."

"Why—" She doesn't appear much surprised. That I ever got married to begin with is the surprise. "Theo! I'm so sorry, dear." She tries to give me a little hug and just as quickly we break apart, by instinct.

"What will you do?" she inquires, lighting another cigarette, fidgeting. I can tell she wants to check the roast again, or empty out the ashtray. "I suppose that's why you're in town, I must admit I wondered."

Not only in town, but here, seeking pity from Aunt Lyla who is glad to serve it up along with dinner and drinks, pity offered from the vaguely smug height of raising children who Turned Out Well, unlike her sister's children, twisted and wretched, blighted, well, what can you expect?—stunted by their mother's act of you-know-what-starts-with-an-S. . . . and damn it, I start to cry in front of her, blubbering on about the night I left Jackson and how the car wouldn't start, but I wouldn't go inside and ask him for help, nor would he offer it—then, finally, the engine turned over and I drove to town, arranged a ride to the airport, and left the Blazer on a side street, which seemed such a cold thing to do, no phone call to Jackson about the car or the fact that I was fleeing to California. How I couldn't stop myself from acting out this role of the injured party. But injured about what? I'm dabbing at my eyes with a tissue; Aunt Lyla doesn't like people to go on too long about their problems.

"Well," Aunt Lyla says, patting my arm, somewhat stiffly, I think, "whatever happened between you two, I'm sure it can be resolved. If the love is there."

"You have no idea," I say. Nor do I. I still can't put into one sentence, or even two or three, what exactly went wrong between us, aside from Jackson's drinking. What my part in it is.

"Have you tried marriage counseling, dear?"

I almost laugh. There is something about the way people who've never been in therapy ask that question—gingerly, as though trying out a brand-new foreign phrase. For I am sure Aunt Lyla has never considered therapy for herself; therapy is for people like me, the lost, the wounded.

"No, Aunt Lyla. No marriage counseling." In fact Jackson was open to the idea, but I wasn't. I'd had enough therapy to last me two lifetimes, and what good had it done?

During dinner I'm struck with how much Aunt Lyla resembles my mother after all, not in specific features but an overall impression, something I can only glimpse for a moment, and when I do, it's like I'm having dinner with *her*, my mother. I tell Aunt Lyla this. My words come out knotted, pained.

"You still think about her, then," she says.

I nod, unable to swallow the food in my mouth.

My aunt survived and my mother didn't. What I'd really like to say is: I wish my mother had had your strength. But there's no need to say it. Aunt Lyla is thinking it and so am I. All through her dinner of paper-thin beef and rolls and wedges of melon we are thinking it—every time we raise our glasses and every time she looks at me, and I look at her; it's my mother between us, sitting at the table toasting us with her glass of blood and bitterness, dust and milk, fear and death, with us as she's always been, shouldering us apart with her presence and her secrets.

Later, when it's time for me to kiss Aunt Lyla goodbye and say "Thank you for dinner," I suddenly realize I've failed to mention my pregnancy.

It was one of my reasons in coming here, my main reason. Aunt Lyla is one of the people I feel I should tell. Like telling my own mother. In fact, I meant also to ask her about my mother.

Direct questions that seem more important now that I'm going to be a mother myself.

"What is it, dear?" At the back door Aunt Lyla is about to lay a hand on my shoulder as though to draw me back inside, but at the last minute she doesn't touch me.

I decide to dive in, right here by the back door by the washer and dryer, the plastic bag of limes she's foisted on me hanging from my wrist. "Aunt Lyla, why did my mother kill herself?" The words creak out of my throat: I shouldn't ask, we don't talk like this. Shouldn't.

"She was unhappy, dear. You know that." She's eyeing the washer.

I'm trying to get her to look at me. "Why was she unhappy?"

"Excuse me, dear, I just have to—" She picks this moment to open the dryer door and clean the lint tray, can't help herself apparently. "None of us will ever know why she did that, Theo."

"You don't know why?" Why do I never believe them, the us she speaks of. "But you were her sister."

"We weren't close."

"What are you hiding?" There. I've said it.

"I'm not." She's folding the lint into her hand, like a blanket. I have a memory of peeling it out of the tray myself as a child, thinking it was a blanket; where was my mother then?

"Why won't you tell me anything?" I say. "How she looked the last time you saw her, what she said—"

"Honestly, Theo. I don't remember." That impatience with me she can barely disguise, especially about this, my mother; isn't this what her impatience stemmed from all along?

"Aunt Lyla, you don't seem to realize. I know nothing about her. Simple things. What her favorite food was, what music she liked, the books she read, what she talked about, the sound of her voice—"

"The sound of her voice. You were a child. How can you expect to remember?"

"Exactly. So I need you to tell me. Don't you understand? There's a hole. It's like I came from nothing. I don't know who my mother is, I don't know who I am! Can't you, in some way, give her back to me?"

"I didn't take her, Theo. I can't bring her back. I can't raise the dead."

As if that's what I'm asking. As if my request can be reduced to this. I'm holding back tears. "I'm asking you to tell me more about her, as much as you can remember."

"It was so long ago, Theo. I really don't remember. Frankly I don't want to. She's dead. She's been dead years. Isn't it time for you to go on with your life?"

She gives me one of her famous searching looks, the sort older, wiser people bestow on the younger and less experienced. My cue. I'm supposed to agree: we've had our little talk, I feel better now, and by golly, she's right; it's time for me to get on with the business of living.

"What are you saying, Aunt Lyla? That you can't remember or you won't?" The bag of limes swings on my wrist.

"Neither one, dear. I'm tired. Can't we call it a night?" A smile that's supposed to appear gentle.

"What about the baby, then? What about Charlotte? How come no one will talk about her either?"

If I'm not supposed to bring up my mother, I'm never, ever to mention Charlotte. A thin white arm, a cry—did she even exist? Aunt Lyla looks furious.

"We don't talk about Charlotte because it's too painful, Theo. You should know that. It destroyed your mother."

"Is that why she killed herself?"

"I keep telling you, I don't know why she killed herself. Charlotte was one reason, absolutely. She was unhappy, Theo, and there was her drinking too, and her pills. Can't you just leave it at that?"

"I can't leave it! It's what's been wrong with me all these years—I can't stay married, I can't settle down, I can't do anything. . . ." And, I'm thinking, I'm going to have a baby now besides. My child, my mother's grandchild. I want to tell this to

Aunt Lyla, scream it at her, but instead I just leave, just walk out the door.

I don't trust her and I don't know why. Telling her about Jackson was a tidbit. I run to the car grateful that I've kept the one thing I care most about a secret. The baby, my baby.

TEN

"Jackson? Did I wake you?"

I'm calling at nine o'clock in the morning and I know just how the winter sun filters in through the windows, backlighting the red butte across the narrow canyon.

"Theo?" Jackson says. The mattress, our mattress, squeaks as he sits up suddenly.

"I did wake you. I'm sorry."

"I'm on a Tuesday-Thursday schedule this semester, so the other days, I . . ."

"Sleep in." Code for hung over. All the little codes we used to have for everything. *Sleeping in* for hung over. *Do you want to keep me company?* he'd say, meaning did I want to get sloshed with him? *Going to the store* roughly translated to no beer in the house, if he said it; no food in the house, if I said it. Not all the codes related to his drinking. *I'm going to go read* meant I wanted to be left alone for an hour or so, after which maybe we'd have sex; *watching TV* meant Jackson wanted to be alone to drink. No sex.

"Why did you wait all this time to call me?" Jackson's voice is husky—how it sounds when he's close to tears—and I realize we've been waiting in silence, each of us, for the other to speak.

"I guess I wasn't ready yet."

"You scared me, Theo. I didn't know where you'd gone, no one knew. You could've been injured, something could've happened to you. I had to call the police, I called your father—"

"So I heard."

Neither of us says anything for a while.

"Would you at least tell me why you left?" he asks.

As if he hasn't a clue. The injured party. The last to know.

"Jackson," I say as tactfully as possible, enunciating my words—or maybe it's that I'm filled with hurt and anger and distrust, incensed that he acts so in the dark. "You knew I was leaving. You saw me get the suitcase out, you just chose not to say or do anything." I'd put in an item and wait. Pair of jeans. Wait. Blouse. Socks. Wait. Toothbrush, toothpaste. Wait some more. Jackson never got off the couch, never said a word.

"All right, you left. I let you go. Huge mistake. Is that why it's over? *Is* it over between us? As for my drinking, I'm quitting."

"Quitting. That's a strange verb tense. Does it mean you're planning to quit or that you have quit already?"

"Ongoing," he says. "In process. Anyway, Theo, it isn't just my drinking that broke us up. You know that."

"I do?"

Another unbearable silence.

"So what now," he says. "You're out there, I'm here. What happens now?"

"I can't answer that for you."

"But you've already answered it for yourself?"

"For now," I say, thinking of Gregg this morning in bed, how he rolled over onto his back in his sleep, baring his pale chest to me, his stomach. His soft parts.

"Theo, I have a question."

"Ask." A fleeting image of Jackson's face in the mornings—in direct contrast to Gregg's soft parts—his beard grown in overnight, the dark bristles shadowing his cheeks, how I used to ask him to put off shaving sometimes, until after we made love.

"Why Pasadena?" he says.

"It's not such an unlikely choice, you know. My father's here, my brother—" *Gregg is here.*

"It just seems peculiar considering you've spent your life avoiding the place. Is there some other reason?"

Defensively, I put my hand on my belly. "No."

"Something to do with your mother?"

"No."

"All right," he says, "changing the subject. Yesterday I hiked down to your favorite part of the creek."

I recognize this as a ploy: Jackson's appealing to my love of Stonewall Creek. He's referring to the place where the creek diverts around a bend of rock. It's hollowed out, the rock, the underside of it eroded by water, producing an echo, like a hidden grotto, and you can't see how far the water spreads, how far back under the rock it goes, if it's a pool or a lake, or just an illusion.

"Did the horses follow you down there?" I ask.

"They seemed to be looking for you. Butting their heads up against me, looking behind as if you might be there after all, hiding." He laughs, then stops short, the way he does, biting it off at the end; today, though, he sucks in air and his laughter merely quits, a somber halt.

"I'm sure the horses have forgotten all about me by now," I say, and in case Jackson takes this as any kind of wistful remark, I add, "I have to get off the phone now. We need to say goodbye."

My next visit to Dr. Grimes yields a surprise: he's at the hospital delivering a baby and can't meet with me today, but I'm told there's a midwife in the office now. How about an appointment with her?

"Dr. Grimes has a midwife working for him?"

"Or if you prefer, we can reschedule you with Dr. Grimes," the receptionist says, as if she doesn't care either way, but I can tell she's uncomfortable with the midwife option. Rather, she thinks I'm uncomfortable.

"A midwife is fine." I suppress a smile, remembering my last visit here: being swathed in white sheets, Dr. Grimes' cow talk, the nurses adorned in those old-fashioned starched caps kept in place with hairpins.

"Have a seat, then. It will be a few minutes."

I sit next to a woman wearing some kind of sling, indeed, with a baby inside.

"How old?" I ask about her infant.

"Six weeks. We're here for our six-week checkup. My checkup, I mean." She laughs. "Everything is *ours*, now."

"A girl or a boy?"

"A baby girl."

She looks like a girl. Pink, a soft stubble of blond hair. The baby begins to fuss a little.

"Hungry," the woman says and adjusts the sling a little, begins to nurse.

"How neat," I say. "The sling. Where'd you get it?"

"From a catalog."

"Really? Which one?" I'm on familiar ground, mentally writing copy. *Close, cuddled, safe. Our sling allows mother's hands to be free, though her heartstrings are tied.* Awful!

"Which catalog," she says. "Hmm. Either Sensational Beginnings or, you know, the other one."

"Which one?"

"They usually keep some copies here. You can check that table over there." She points.

I stay right where I am. "I have a lot to learn. A lot to buy. I don't even know what to get." Alarm: the first time I've thought about this aspect. What I don't have. Diapers, baby clothes, mysterious ointments and balms—can you buy a crib from a catalog? I can write about this stuff, but I know nothing, nothing! What I don't have, and what I'll need to get. What I won't have: a husband. Or I could have one, at a price. Then there's Gregg. Would he like to step into Jackson's shoes? Images collide: young fatherly sort steps into a staged nursery shot, crib, mobile, changing table, bright lights—*One hundred percent cotton, machine washable, sling comes in an array of colors*—his arms held out for a baby with makeup on who screams at the sight of him.

"Plenty of time," the new mother assures me. "We're still pretty unequipped—actually it never seems you're equipped enough. How far along are you?"

"Almost twelve weeks."

"How are you feeling?"

"Nauseous. Starving. It's beginning to seem normal."

She laughs, rises to her feet and rearranges her baby in the sling, having just been summoned for her appointment.

I try to concentrate on the form I'm filling out, one I thought I'd already filled out last time here; evidently I left out a few things. Epilepsy? No. Heart disease? No. Yes, I've had mumps, chicken pox, German measles. Nervous breakdown? Not yet. Baby's father's name? the form politely requests. I leave that blank.

Soon after it's my turn and I follow the nurse down the hall.

"Theo? Is it you?" The midwife—at least I think she's the midwife—hurries into the exam room checking her clipboard, frantic for some reason. Oh great.

"It's me all right."

"Theo, Theo, look at me! Don't you recognize me?"

I stand up suddenly: woman in a white coat, long stringy blond hair, about my age. Then I notice her eyes, blue and iridescent. I always used to think she looked like one of those Nordic Madonnas you'd find in an art museum, from the early Renaissance period—haloed and blond, sapphirine eyes.

"Maggie?"

I'd forgotten about her smile, as dazzling as when we were teenagers.

We fall into each other's arms first, then talk for a while—how Maggie came to be a midwife of all things, and the circumstances of my move back to Pasadena. She asks about my father and I ask about her mother, technically an aunt of mine (or is it cousin?) through my mother's side. "Still alive and drinking," Maggie says. Whatever our familial connection, it's so distant and convoluted as to be absurd. We don't resemble each other in the least.

At last we proceed to the actual exam, gentle as a sponge bath. Maggie places something called a Doppler on my belly; I hear for the first time the whoosh, whoosh, whoosh of my baby's heart.

I don't want to leave.

Is it time for the knitting needles yet, Maggie and I used to say in high school. Code for, Are we pregnant? Knitting needles referring to either booties or abortions, depending on how you looked at it. Is it time for the K.N.'s? we'd say, counting on our fingers since our last periods, and when it—what we kept hoping were isolated incidents of sex—had occurred.

We'd become friends in high school gym class while standing in the furthest reaches of the softball outfield, gloves hanging lethargically from our wrists. We talked while the balls sailed by: "Your turn," I'd say or she'd say, and whoever's turn it was would stroll off after the ball while the pitcher hopped and screamed and cursed.

I broached the subject of our cousinhood first.

"Aren't we cousins or something?"

"Maybe," she said, that ironic smile on her face. "Third cousins twice removed, or is it second cousins thrice removed?"

"Emphasis on removed," I said.

From there we progressed to sharing cigarettes in the parking lot, having found out we smoked the same brand, Larks. Then, we made the leap to sneaking out of our houses at night and meeting at St. Edmund's Chapel (where we'd both been baptized) for more smokes in the pew; and from there, somehow, to hitchhiking all over Pasadena, being sure to stop at Bob's Big Boy for milk shakes, french fries, and more cigarettes, laughing about the fools who'd picked us up, or tried to. We gave them names. Phil and Dan were Feel and Damn; Rich and Steve were Bitch and Heave—Bitch and Heave were painters; Feel and Damn were college-age transients living off their parents, sharing—what else?—a VW van, and listening to—what else?—Neil Young, Damn attempting to mimic him on his out-of-tune guitar and squalling voice while we listened, horrified.

That very night I meet Maggie's boys, at her apartment in Pasadena. Maggie's changed into jeans, a T-shirt, old canvas espadrilles. I already know about her soon-to-be divorce, just as she knows about my separation, territory we covered earlier today.

"This is Willy," Maggie says, her hand on the smaller boy's head. "His brother's name is Dylan. Say hi, Dylan."

"Hi," he says.

"Chucks," says Willy.

"He mean truck," Dylan says. "That how he talk, he just one. *I* two, I talk big boy. Car wash, Mommy." He looks at his mother expectantly and, from beneath the kitchen sink, Maggie pulls out a plastic basket filled with toy cars and trucks, toothbrushes, rags and a couple of spray bottles. She spreads out a towel.

"Chucks," Willy says, dumping out the basket.

"They spend hours doing this," Maggie says as the boys bend over miniature cars and trucks, spraying them and going over them with toothbrushes, wiping them down with rags. "Car wash," Dylan says to himself, singsong, "brushes go round and round."

"They're cute," I say, entranced, reminded of my nephews when they were little. Meeting these boys is a gift, even more reason for coming here, to Maggie's home, to the area where I grew up; to confront the ghost of my mother; to become a mother myself.

I stay for dinner. I help put the boys to bed, I read them stories, I stay the night.

ELEVEN

My father didn't know how to make a lunch, in my opinion. He was never going to learn. Into my lunch sack he seemed to put the ugliest foods possible—black bananas, lunchmeats flecked with little white round things, limp lettuce. Things he wouldn't mind eating. (Years later, I watched him buy peaches from a roadside stand, take them back to the hotel room and cut one open . . . teeming with unborn insect life. He cut out the insects and popped the peach into his mouth.)

My father wasn't a mother any more than my mother had been and I despised him for it. He never knew what I was talking about. "A bruised banana *embarrasses* you at school? Why?"

The only other person at school whose lunch was as weird as mine was Betsy. Her mother believed in organically grown fruits and vegetables, thick brown breads, and animal meats that hadn't been shot up with antibiotics or chemicals; even the family dog ate pure, raw liver, not canned food. Each morning before we walked to school, Betsy would have to swallow a spoonful of cod liver oil.

I thought this very glamorous and sometimes Mrs. Cramer would let me have a spoonful, too. It tasted terrible but I knew it was good for me and all morning long, tasting cod liver in the back of my throat, I felt protected against misery and cold.

Betsy's lunch usually consisted of an ungainly sandwich made with lettuce, tomato, and leftovers from last night's dinner; an apple or orange (no bruised bananas); a slice of heavy brown cake made with honey and no icing. Betsy never complained, although both of us looked longingly at the other kids' lunches: white bread spread with peanut butter and jelly, Ding-Dongs, candy, bologna and cheese.

Betsy's mother didn't approve of processed sugar, of course. It was bad for you. I adored the way she said *bad for you*, her face downturned and sweet, woeful and beatific. I was in love with Mrs. Cramer, though she wasn't really beautiful. Mornings she wore a plain bathrobe and old furry slippers, as she stood at the kitchen counter, making Betsy's lunch. She never sat down in the mornings and in fact there was a period of time she had to march in place because she'd had an operation for varicose veins, thick ace bandages that I thought were lovely wound up and down her legs.

"Don't forget your lunch, Betsy." March, march. "Betsy? Your lunch. Now, girls . . ." March, march. We were halfway out the door. "Cross at the crosswalk, girls, and look both ways, remember." March, march.

I lived to hear her call us *girls*. I felt I belonged to her in some way, if only for a moment. And just as I longed for her to feed me a spoonful of cod liver oil, I fantasized she would cook me breakfast, fix me lunch. I would be glad to eat her strange, clumsy sandwiches and mushy apples and brown honeyed cakes and sticky raisins.

"We have to change what we eat," I insisted to my father.

"Why?"

"Because it's not good for us!"

I told him to call Mrs. Cramer and find out where she shopped, that we should buy the same, that white flour and sugar were bad for us. So were the vegetables and fruit—they were sprayed with insecticides—they were *poisoned*, didn't he get it?

"You know I don't do the shopping, Theo."

"Make Evan shop somewhere else," I said. Evan was our housekeeper who came afternoons to be here when Corb and I got home from school. She cooked our dinner, left it warming on the stove, and disappeared minutes after my father arrived home from work—she had to go home and cook for her own family.

"Well, I'll mention it to her," my father said.

I knew he wouldn't. "You have to make her," I said, pulling on his long, hairy arm. Didn't he understand anything?

"You have to realize," my father said. "Evan has her own way of doing things. I can't tell her what to do."

I didn't see why not. She worked for us, didn't she? Although, I had to admit, it was difficult *making* Evan do anything. I shopped with her myself; I knew. It was my job to push the cart up and down the aisles and put into it what she told me. We always bought the same things. Round beef for Swiss steak. Ground beef for meat loaf. Mushroom soup and chicken for a casserole. Frozen vegetables, iceberg lettuce, tomatoes, fruit. Milk, juice, jello, paper towels, detergent, wax paper, furniture polish, tin foil . . . While I pushed the cart after her, Evan added up items on a little red plastic thing made to look like a miniature cash register. She complained ceaselessly about the prices and told me again and again how important it was that I learn how to go grocery shopping. I was going to need it someday, she said. When I got married. When I was running my own household.

"Evan," I said. "Instead of here—" I gestured at the whole refrigerated white bread mausoleum of Safeway—"Why don't we shop at Healthco?"

"Healthco, what's that?" She paused in front of the canned fruit, put on her reading glasses that hung from a loop around her neck, glanced at her list. "Pineapple, Theo, two four-ounce cans." I tossed them into the cart. "I'm going to make us a pineapple upside-down cake," she said. "How about that?"

"It has sugar in it," I said with disgust. "Can't you make it with honey at least?"

"Recipe calls for sugar," she said.

It was always so embarrassing going places with Evan. First of all, she talked loud and second of all, she talked to everybody. She told them everything, about her operation for hemorrhoids and about her flat feet and that she was allergic to perfumes and deodorant, and that my mother had passed away and so she, Evan, was working for us now and that *I* thought of her as *my* mother. Which was sort of true and not true. Somebody had to act as my mother, and there wasn't anybody but Evan. I didn't have a choice. But did she have to be announcing it all the time? Did she have to carry that big fat white purse that she shined up with shoe polish? Did she have to wear a nurse's uniform? She was entitled,

I guess, she was a nurse; she'd been my mother's nurse originally, that's how she'd come to work for us in the first place. But couldn't she dress like a normal person? Not to mention her hair, a bouffant: teased and colored brown this week, auburn the next . . . she actually wrapped *toilet paper* around it at night, to keep it looking nice, she said. She'd stayed with Corb and me once or twice when our father had gone out of town on business and it was true, a few times around with the toilet roll, topped with a hair net.

"Healthco," I informed her now, "is a health food store. Mrs. Cramer shops there and I think we should, too. They don't use pesticides on their fruits and vegetables, and they have wheat germ bread, and they don't use beef from cows that have been shot up with antibiotics and God knows what." I myself was impressed with how knowledgeable I sounded; how could she not agree with me?

"There isn't anything wrong with the food here, Theo. I'm a nurse." As if I didn't know. She was forever reminding me.

Evan and I were to attend our first mother-daughter tea. For two weeks in advance I prayed she would fall sick or that some last-minute emergency would come up in her large, extended, accident-prone family, as was sometimes the case. We'd get a call at seven in the morning. "This is Evan. We're having a crisis over here." *Cry*-sez was how she pronounced it. Somebody in her family had had a car wreck or a collapsed lung or double pneumonia or had been burglarized or had nearly sawed off their hand, Frankie, Ernie or Arnie—all the males had names that ended in 'ie'—or Ava, Marilyn, April or June—all the females had movie-star names, or were named after a month. In our family we knew the names of everybody in *her* family, though we'd met so few of them.

I'd hoped to attend the mother-daughter tea with Betsy and her mother: Mrs. Cramer in pearl earrings and a soft, pretty, pastel dress, making soft, pleasing conversation, me attached to her somehow, literally holding onto her dress and Betsy's hand.

But no, there was no last minute phone call, no *cry*-sez. All that day at school I worried—what would Evan wear? Her uniform, her white elevator nurse shoes? Worse. "I'll show you what *I'm* wearing," she said when I got home from school. There, on a hanger over a chair, was a dress the color of lime sherbet with a splash of flowers across the front; next to it, a hot pink purse and matching shoes; and on Evan's long, sagging earlobes, daisy earrings the size of silver dollars.

We got dressed together, which was sort of fun—it's what I imagined other girls did with their mothers—Evan buttoning up the back of my dress (fortunately she didn't pick my clothes, Aunt Lyla did that), fussing with my hair, gentle on the tangles, pulling her own dress up over her girdle, and finally, me waiting on the edge of the tub for her while she applied a thick coat of pink lipstick in the mirror. She smacked her lips and blotted them—breaking the spell of my fantasy. This was Evan all right, not my mother. My own mother had been beautiful. All the pictures my father had hidden in drawers confirmed this, even if my memories didn't.

"Let's go," Evan said, sorting through the compartments of her big white purse—wads of Kleenex, coupons rubber-banded together, several combs and brushes, makeup bag, cracked red wallet, stray curled-up pieces of paper used for shopping lists, phone numbers, all of which she crammed into her hot pink purse. "We're gonna be late!" Evan was nervous, misplacing her keys, forgetting her lipstick, searching for the invitation with the address on it. Nervous and excited, eager, *thrilled* to be going to a tea where she could show me off as "her" daughter.

The thing was, she really did love me. When I got sick, she was there, coming to our house the whole day, canceling all else; if I got sick on a weekend, she came to nurse me, refusing to accept money from my father. She told me she loved me, held me when I cried, kissed me hello and goodbye, told me stories, played with me. . . .

We arrived at the tea just as all the other mothers and daughters were filing in, the mother's heels clacking along the sidewalk, their daughters' flat-soled party shoes trying to keep up. Nobody except Evan, I noticed, wore hot pink shoes. No, their shoes were buff or cream-colored, tan or pale yellow. "Hello, hello Mrs. Knight! Mrs. Matley!" Evan cried out, the Mrs. coming out like *messes*. That she called them Mrs. this and Mrs. that and not by their first names was another giveaway that we didn't belong here.

Once inside, Evan pushed her way—and mine—to the refreshment table. "This is Theo," she said to everyone she didn't know, "and I'm Evan. We hurried so much getting here, now I'm HOT." She fanned her face with a napkin and proceeded to tell everyone that when summer rolls around, all she wears is a shift and panties. "I don't wear no bra! And no deodorant either, I'm allergic—"

I squirmed away to find Betsy and Mrs. Cramer. They were socializing with several other mother-daughter pairs, the mothers laughing in bell-like tones, daughters at their sides looking dutiful and solemn. I stood there not sure what to do, then weaved my way back through the perfumed crowd. "I think of her as my own," Evan was saying, while ladies nodded sympathetically—oh God, not again. I turned to leave, but felt Evan's work-worn hand on my shoulder. "Have you met Mrs. Cartwright?"

"How do you do?" I said. Evan beamed, her hot pink lips swelling into a smile. I loved her. I really did in my own squeamish way, and I needed someone to be proud of me, even if it was Evan.

Finally, the daughters were separating from their mothers and going outside. I joined them.

Evan considered it part of her job to educate me in matters of housework. I stripped beds, emptied wastebaskets, dusted, polished furniture and silverware and copper-bottomed saucepans; I cleaned grout with a toothbrush, scraped wax off the floors, washed windows, reorganized closets, sewed on name tags and buttons, planned menus, cooked dinner, ran the vacuum cleaner, ironed my father's shirts.

Corb ironed too, but for different reasons. Evan wanted him to be able to take care of himself when he was a bachelor someday, that is, before he got married and his wife took care of these things for him, so Corb learned how to make an omelet, hamburgers, and stew, how to sew on a button and how to iron a shirt.

Often when I was cleaning house, Corb was outside playing. At first I didn't mind because it gave me time alone with Evan. She'd talk to me, tell me stories about cases she'd worked on, couples she knew who'd gotten divorced, exactly who did what to whom and other salacious tidbits children weren't supposed to hear. It made me feel grownup and somehow it went along with the housework. Sometimes she talked about my mother, although she tended to repeat herself. "She was a lovely person," Evan said, "before she got sick. She used to tell me everything, all her problems. She'd talk and talk, she'd say 'Evan, what should I do?'" Evan said a lot about my mother without revealing anything, and most of her talk centered on herself, Evan; how my mother adored Evan. "She'd tell me all the time, 'Evan, what would I do without you?'" There seemed to be a not-so-subtle message in Evan's reminiscences: if my mother adored Evan, so should I. Evan was wise, Evan was good, Evan knew people, understood them. Yet I often had the feeling she didn't know my mother at all; this person we talked about couldn't be my mother. I tried to picture her as Evan portrayed her, sitting at the kitchen table with her head in her hands, confused, vulnerable. What about her brushing my teeth with Nivea cream? Her spanking me with a hairbrush? I grew to suspect my own memories: "Your mother was a lovely person before she got sick." But Evan had come to work for us *because* my mother had been sick; she hadn't known my mother when she was well. What did 'sick' mean anyway? Evan never said and I seldom asked, and if I did I received hazy answers. "Oh, your mother," Evan said, "you know she wasn't happy." In later years she would be more explicit, but for now it didn't matter to me that Evan was vague, repetitive, or even possibly lying about my mother—she talked about her. No one else did, except to mention how much I resembled my mother, *but*, they added ominously, *don't be like her.* The talks with Evan took on an illicit, mesmerizing quality, her talking, me listening, while we cleaned, polished, cooked. I loved the rhythm and sensuality of housework, the snap of the sheets as we shook them out before laying them on the bed, the milkiness of furniture polish, the whisk of the broom and clatter of the dustpan, the drone of the vacuum, the wringing out of a mop. I loved the praise, the feeling of importance, the pleasure on my father's face when I set dinner in front of him and told him I cooked it myself.

At some point, however, I became resentful. Summers and school vacations, Evan would arrive late and ask me, "What have you done?" Meaning, what housework had I accomplished so far? If I listed several tasks—cleaned the bathroom, emptied trash, stripped the beds—it was never enough. She didn't chastise me; it was the look on her face: *Is that all?* If, on the other hand, I muttered, "Nothing, it's Spring Break," the look was more severe, as if my whole character were now in question.

I began hinting to my father. I couldn't come out and say the truth because, being a child, I didn't know the truth, which was that on some level I was being exploited. And, the truth was never spoken in our house—about my mother or sister or anything— although the idea of truth was highly vaunted. I told my father I didn't like Evan. What did I mean, he wanted to know. Well, I said, I don't like the way she does things. I still don't know what you mean, he said. I opened the hall closet. Look, I said, look at this mess. Blankets and hangers and books and thermoses all mixed in with packages of shoelaces and thumbtacks and cardboard boxes. I pulled out the sewing basket, a tangle of thread and buttons and clothes waiting to be mended. See? I demanded. This is what I mean.

My father's solution was to hire a maid. He asked Evan to find us one. We hired one of her relatives, a young woman named Yvonne who wore heavy eyeliner and a large fake diamond ring on her hand, and a white uniform like Evan's. The two of them sat at our kitchen table gossiping while the TV played reruns. I'd come home from school, go to my room, reappear to fix myself a snack. . . . "What have you done?" "Nothing." That look.

But mostly I did what Evan asked, if a little sullenly—got loads of wash going before school, dusted after school or in the evenings, polished silver, wiped down shelves, put down new liners in the drawers; took showers and cleaned grout at the same time. "That way," Evan said, "you don't track dirt in and out of the tub." I did what she said. I needed her approval; I needed her love.

Sometimes we napped together, if it were summer or if I was home from school for some reason. If Yvonne wasn't around. We'd set the TV up on a chair and squeeze into my tiny bed and watch soap operas, drowsing, Evan waking now and then to give advice to the characters on the screen.

"I love you," she'd say, "as if you were my own girl."

I'd sleep with my arms around her neck.

Sometimes we all cleaned together, Yvonne taking the bathrooms, Evan mopping, and me dragging the vacuum room to room. I felt numb, powerless. I wanted to be outside playing, doing anything but this stupid housework.

My mother makes me clean my room. If I do, cottage cheese with sugar. If I don't? The curtains are closed, I can't see.

"What have you done?" The pressure grew greater the older I got. Too old to play with Betsy, who wasn't even wearing a bra yet, I came straight home after school now except for Wednesdays when I had choral practice. While we cleaned Evan told me about menstruation, hosiery, boys—Yvonne listened in and giggled. "They're going to want you to do things," Evan said. "You're a woman now, something can happen, so watch it." Betsy's mother didn't talk to her like this. They didn't even talk about this stuff, and in any case, Betsy didn't have breasts; she still wore an undershirt. I had to wear a bra. "Sex is a wonderful thing," Evan warned. "But there's a time and place for everything." During my periods, whenever I went to the bathroom, I had to roll my used sanitary pad into a ball, wrap toilet paper around it like some kind of mystery present you'd find at a toy store, put it into a paper bag and carry it outside to the trash, past my father, past Corb, past Yvonne in her heavy eyeliner. Past anyone who happened to be around. "That's the way I always do it," Evan said. "Otherwise they smell up the whole house." Yvonne giggling. Who were these people? Not even my relatives. My father's paid help.

TWELVE

After my father's cataract surgery, his eye is bandaged thickly.

From his kitchen where I am wiping down counters, I watch him in his bedroom trying to get situated. He lies down with his shoes on. Sits up. Re-ties the lace on one shoe. Readjusts the shade of the lamp on the bedside table. "Can I get you anything, Dad?"

"I'm fine, thanks." He abandons the bedroom and settles himself in the family room, on the couch.

I've been here two full days since his cataract operation, going back nights to the Alta Vista. The counters clean, I unzip my Powerbook from its bag and walk around hugging it to my chest looking for the best place to work, an outlet next to a table. I settle for the coffee table, dragging it closer to the wall. I sit on the floor.

"You're going to work there?" my father says.

"Why not? It's the perfect height." I reach for my bag and for the box of graham crackers I brought with me. My latest comfort food, like sweet moist cardboard.

"Theo?"

"Yes, Dad." I know what he's about to say since we just had this conversation half an hour ago.

"You cannot live at the Alta Vista. It's a firetrap! It's a *residence* hotel."

"I know. I'm residing there, for now. Now if you'll excuse me." I study the pictures, the layouts. Blond babies in pumpkin costumes and green stem hats, elastic under their chins. Forty-five dollars a pop. I'm closing in on a deadline, hoping to fed-ex off the disk today. Then in a few days, a business trip to the Bay Area for a photo shoot with a different children's catalog, so I can see the goods in person, rub fabric between my fingers. Get inspired. "Want one?" I say to Dad, inspecting my box of graham crackers.

"You're getting crumbs on the carpet," he says.

I glance around me. "Oh. Sorry. I'll vacuum it, Dad, as soon as I'm finished. I promise." I type in *Harvest delight, chill fall nights—and days.* One hundred percent polar fleece jacket. Double-backed for extra warmth. Snaps, pockets, hood. Comes in pomegranate, cobalt, cherry red, mallard. I lean forward and study the next photo, brushing aside graham cracker crumbs. A toddler in a white cape and a hood like a caul, fangs. How'd they get him to pose like that? Smiling ghoulishly, the boy must be all of two. Polyester blend, machine wash and dry. *Boo!* I write.

My father regards me with his good eye, brown and gleaming. "I have something for you," he says.

He often does. An old yearbook, a first-place ribbon from a long-ago, forgotten contest, stuff he's come across in drawers or closets. What I wish for, but seldom get, is an item connected to my mother, a photograph or a piece of odd silver that somehow eluded storage at Pink's. Sometimes it's a box of books from my childhood—*The Little Lame Prince, Black Beauty, The Courage of Sarah Noble*—although one time there were books belonging to my mother when she was a child, *The Fairy Tales of Charles Perrault,* and a biography of Joan of Arc with an illustration of her burning at the stake that I particularly remember staring at as a girl.

"Let me get it," my father says.

"You stay," I say, rising to my feet. "Where is it? I'll get it."

"Top drawer in the kitchen. The legal pad."

"This? What is it?"

"A record of Jackson's phone calls."

"What?"

"All the times he's called you here or at the office." The entire page is filled.

"I'm stunned," I say. "Doesn't he have anything better to do?"

"You and I had an agreement," my father says, "and you haven't held up your end."

"I have, too! I called him. Didn't he tell you?" I glance at the dates on the log. "I talked to him last week. Must've been after you talked to him."

"And?"

"Dad," I say gently, "I'm sorry. Nothing's changed, you know. I realize you probably had your hopes up, but . . ."

My father's face droops, all the sadder with one bandaged eye.

"Dad, there's something I should tell you."

So that's when I tell him—that I'm pregnant.

"Theo, no. No!" He sounds heartbroken. The white strands of hair from on top of his head have sprung up, despite the generous helpings of hair grease he applies. "A baby? Now you must go back to Jackson, Theo! For the sake of the baby."

"Dad, I can't."

"Why not? All this time and I still don't know what went wrong between you two."

"It's hard to explain."

"Try."

"Well." I think for a moment. "We just don't get along, Dad. I'm not sure we ever really did."

"You mean you fight a lot?"

"That's kind of it."

"But lots of couples disagree," he says. "Why, your mother and I—"

"Yes?"

"Your mother wanted me to do yard work and I just didn't want to."

"*That's* what you argued about?"

"Sure," he says.

It seems so tepid compared to the arguments Jackson and I have had. Arguments of the soul versus arguments over household duties.

"Well, Dad, Jackson and I don't argue over that stuff. It's hard to say what we argue about. Everything, I guess. Jackson's just so moody and difficult, then he accuses *me* of being difficult."

Dad is sitting up now, working on a scratch on the coffee table, licking his finger and rubbing; I've lost his interest or perhaps what I'm saying isn't making much sense, doesn't seem quite dire enough for me to have left my husband.

"There is something else about Jackson," I say.

"What?"

"He drinks too much."

"Oh?" Dad always sounds so scandalized when he says this word.

I nod.

"*I* never saw him drink much," Dad says. "That time we went to that restaurant—you know, out where you are, the Italian restaurant—he didn't touch a drop."

"That was for your benefit."

"Does he drink whiskey?"

This is my father's idea of man who drinks too much, one who swigs Jack Daniels from a leather flask hung off a belt loop.

"No, Dad. Beer."

"Beer?" Said almost joyously, as if there's no problem now, simply a misunderstanding.

"Beer is liquor, Dad. He drinks it like soda pop."

"I suppose you're right." He's brooding, trying to think (I know him so well) how to convince me to return to my husband, despite what I've just told him, because, after all, one shouldn't leave one's husband. He smoothes down his hair, opens his mouth to speak.

"Forget it, Dad. I'm not going back. Even if I weren't pregnant."

"Fine," he begins. "I *do* understand. Still, I just feel—"

"Don't even start."

Gluefoot, his second wife Dorinne used to call him: he could stand in one place and argue, wheedle, nag, haggle, until hell would freeze over.

I know this is just the beginning. He won't say anything more now, won't say a word, but his campaign to convince me will stretch into months, years, whatever it takes. Gluefoot.

In my father's version—so I know without us even discussing it, though we will—there are, or were, two things wrong with my marriage:

1) I went on all those business trips, alone. Not my worst offense but indicative of my overall abandonment of Jackson.

2) I didn't take Jackson's name. I wasn't Mrs. Jackson Zander or, on less formal occasions, Theodora Zander—but Theodora Mapes.

"You can't be truly married," he used to sputter on the phone, "unless you take your husband's name." This was two, three years after the fact.

"Either we stop discussing this," I would say, "or I hang up. This is absurd! You'd think I was the only woman in the world to do this."

"A baby," Dad is murmuring now, shaking his head. "A baby." He says it over and over. "A baby. A baby." No faint smile, no tenderness, no bafflement even. The person who would appreciate this moment the most right now is, of all people, Jackson. How we always used to imagine telling my father this news someday—that it wouldn't be like telling any other prospective grandparent who would be gushing, parading, whooping. Not my father. The only living representative of his generation (Jackson's parents dead, my mother dead), he's not exactly grandfather material; to Bruce and Gabe he's been more like a distant, moneyed uncle. When they were small he would bend slightly from his towering height to greet them: "And how are you, young man? Have you been a good boy? Minding your parents?" Absolutely no idea how to talk to kids. They were foreigners somehow related to him. Children, to my father, represented a kind of celestial bondage—pretty to look at, tied to you by gravitational pull: you couldn't get away from them, their starry eyes, their buoyancy, their needs, and so they must be endured for eternity and remembered generously in one's will.

Telling my father I'm pregnant is like telling myself. Takes all the fun out of it. The mallet of responsibility pounds a stake next to my heart. What if the mallet slips and hits an artery, mine or the baby's? My mother wasn't up to this, what if I'm not either?

After lunch Dad says, "Shouldn't you be getting on?"

Eager as always to shoo me out the door. In fact I do have plans to meet Maggie for coffee, something we've done as often as we can since reconnecting; we call it coffee but Maggie, ever the midwife, insists I order something "hydrating," such as herbal tea or juice.

"What are you going to do once I leave, Dad?"

He answers very deliberately. "I'm going to read."

"Can you do that yet?" I imagine the words swimming before his one good eye. "What are you going to read?"

"I have," he says, in a negotiating tone of voice, "a biography of De Gaulle. I'll read that."

A history book, of course, one I gave him last year, as a matter of fact. A rare birthday present for a man who squirms at the very notion of gifts.

"De Gaulle was very French, I'm afraid," he adds, not elaborating. "Now will you go?" He looks at me pleadingly, as if alarmed by having to spend any more time with me than necessary.

"If that's what you want," I say. I kiss him on the cheek.

Doesn't my father feel any loneliness, fear? Doesn't the man feel anything at all? For him, human feeling is a component that either wasn't built into his system in the first place or was edged out piece by piece over the years. Since his second widowhood, I've tried to imagine a secret life for him. Dime store mysteries and ice cream bars? A flirtation with a widow met in church? No. He dislikes movies, TV, although he enjoys travelogues, going to see them occasionally at the public library. He likes to exercise, too, but that's out for now, as are the classes he often enrolls in— Conversational Spanish, French Literature. Once upon a time he liked to garden, but last year he hired a gardener.

A secret life? My father is the world's last puritan.

His love for me is constrained. At best, it comes across as a dim sort of affection—as one might appreciate a flower or a sunset. The mystery is, he's not a cold man, though he might seem that way. His love runs deeply, unacknowledged even to himself, so that it's inaccessible, like a stream in a undiscovered cave; it may not be found, it may never be tapped. Did I ever believe my having a baby would change him?

I say none of this.

Following "coffee" with Maggie at a juice bar in Old Town Pasadena, I realize, after discussing it with her, that a call to my brother Corb is in order, now that Dad knows I'm pregnant. As I suspected, news has leaked out.

"I knew it!" Diane says. "I just had a feeling."

"You did?"

"How are you feeling? This is so exciting! Maybe you'll have a girl. I always wanted a girl," she says, "although I'm perfectly happy with boys."

Corb isn't as enthusiastic. "You sure didn't waste any time," he says. "Who's the father?"

"Jackson, stupid. Didn't Dad tell you?"

"But you and Jackson are separated."

"Bingo. Why are you being so nasty? You're treating me like some kind of unwed teenaged mother." I stop. If I'm divorced, won't I be an unwed mother? I continue. "There's no shame involved. I'm *happy* about this."

I can hear Diane scolding him though I can't make out the words.

"Sorry," Corb says. "I just—I don't know why I said that. It's your situation. You've got to admit it's not totally happy."

"That's true. But I'm happy. I'm happy! That's what matters." Why do I keep saying this?

All this reminds me I haven't told Gregg the truth; of course I haven't seen much of him lately. A night together here and there, is all. Maggie reminds me often enough, though; Gregg deserves the truth. "You deserve the truth too," she says, which is why she finally escorts me through the unassuming doors of Arcadia Methodist Hospital: so that I may sign the release for my mother's hospital records.

"See?" she says. "Nothing to it."

I can hardly move pen across paper, much less breathe, and I'm relieved when the woman in Records explains it will take several weeks for the hospital to locate the files, which will then be mailed to me.

My father is waiting by the door when I bring him dinner the third night after his operation. Enchiladas from the Acapulco.

"You cannot *live* at the Alta Vista," he says again, in one of his moods. Stewing. "Not with a baby coming. What about the Hilton? Until you can find an apartment, that is. I suppose I could lend you the money to buy—"

"Why shouldn't I live at the Alta Vista?" Absurdly, I can't resist the opportunity to rile him. "What's the matter with it?"

"Well, it's—it's—" He sputters on for a while. "The Alta Vista simply isn't *nice.*"

"Nice!"

"Why do you object to that word so?"

It always comes down to this: the idea of his daughter living in a dive. In one form or another. The not-nice life. A gypsy, a profligate, driving a junker, wearing second-hand clothes—or black jeans and stained suede boots. That his daughter doesn't get her hair done ("Can't you do something with your hair?" "What's the matter with it?" "It's—it's awfully wild." "It's curly."), won't do her nails, or wear a slip.

That his daughter inherited these big boobs from somewhere, to go along with her big hips (certainly not from her mother, who was delicate, tasteful). That his daughter ought to concern herself with reducing the size of those hips, and minimizing her chest through some sleight of hand or a bra of lycra and underwire. Maybe a bra of steel.

Throw in a chastity belt while you're at it.

In my father's eyes I'm a failure in all things that matter.

Point one. I wasn't a virgin when I married. A long story, my virginity: how I was sent away from home at the age of sixteen, the unscrupulous young man who took advantage of (ahem) my purity.

Was I ever a virgin?

Point two. I lived with a man. Men. Several of them. And then there were the others . . . .

Once I got married, of course, my "history" could be forgiven.

History.

High school. I met two guys playing Frisbee at Lacy Park; fell for them both, drove around smoking pot with them in their crate of a car. Brought them home to meet my father, who didn't notice anything amiss—not the fact that they wore torn jeans without underwear (you could tell if you had only the slightest awareness), flip-flops and shirts without buttons. Or the fact that they didn't have jobs, or go to school, or seem to live anywhere but in their car, or that my father's liquor supply diminished exponentially upon their arrival into my life. Who knows what else they stole from him? His daughter, but he didn't notice that either. My father even said, after meeting them the first time, that they appeared to be "nice boys."

Within days I had chosen one of the two "nice boys," Ike, graduate of various reformatories, illiterate, his hair so blond he was practically albino; and within another few days I was sneaking him into my bedroom for the night.

This is probably the place to mention, I suppose, that it was Ike to whom I lost my virginity officially. What I mean is, I couldn't remember being with anyone else in this way, yet there was no blood or pain to speak of.

Each weekend when my father went out with his brand-new "ladyfriend"—as they both referred to her, the infamous Dorinne—Ike and I would get drunk on my father's vodka and screw on the living room couch. My father would return at eleven, curfew time, and shake Ike's hand as he left the house ("seems like a nice boy"), not noticing or wanting to notice the obvious, that we were crocked, we reeked, the house reeked, there was a stain on the couch.

"What did you two do last night?" my father would ask the following morning.

"Watched TV," I'd answer, blushing prettily. "Sat on the glider and held hands." My father turned his back to pour himself another cup of coffee. "Emptied a case of vodka," I'd say softly, "fucked our brains out." Softly but not that softly, he wasn't deaf.

Almost instantly, it seemed, my father and Dorinne became engaged. I knew nothing about her, only that she went to the beauty parlor weekly, always wore dresses, never pants, and had very specific ideas about how children ought to be raised—so my father told me—based on how fabulously her two sons had turned out. One was an accountant, the other in law school; I couldn't tell them apart. My father said they were "nice boys." I thought they were lifeless, especially around Dorinne. "Certainly, Mother," they said. "Can I get you anything, Mother?" They seated her at tables, rose when she entered the room, wrote prompt thank-you notes, dated nice girls.

They reminded me of my father.

Not long after my father's engagement, he caught me with Ike. I was sent to boarding school. There I smoked dope, dropped acid, and wrote in my journal. Lists, how much I weighed, my measurements. "I'm eating too much," I wrote. "Here's my plan. Two hits of speed in the a.m., nothing for lunch. Smoke after school, salad at dinner (this will be the hardest!). Pint of ice cream later as a reward, then Ex-lax." More lists, records: how many guys I'd kissed, fooled around with, or slept with—all in separate categories. I made lists of what I drank the night before. "Half of somebody's screwdriver, four swigs of Wild Turkey, a beer, most of a bottle of wine. It's amazing I didn't get sick." I kept records of how much I spent on ounces of pot, how many pills I swallowed. "Two weren't enough to knock me out, so I took three more. Knock me out, I just want to be knocked out."

Sometimes I worried about following in my mother's footsteps. In a rare conversation with my father during this time, he

*told me that on my mother's death certificate was the word
suicide. He said not to pay any attention to this; it was just a
word, a mistake. Oh yes, he conceded, she'd overdosed on pills—
officially—but . . . What, I asked him, did she really die of, then?*

*"She wasn't well, she, uh. . ." I'd heard this before: she was
nervous, she wasn't happy, hospitals, psychiatrists, etc., etc. My
father repeated the business about the word used on the death
certificate; I was to pay it no mind, he said, but he thought I
should know. It was my right to know.*

After I change my father's eye dressing, we drink tea by the
fire, it actually being a cold enough night to have one.

"Did he drink beer out of the bottle?" my father asks in a
hushed, guarded voice. I know at once he's talking about Jackson,
but I say, nonetheless, *"What?"*

"I know it's beside the point," he says sheepishly.

"I'm relieved to hear that you at least know it's beside the
point, Dad."

"I was just wondering," he says. "Did he?"

There's a note of envy in his tone as we sit here in the flick-
ering glow sipping our tea.

"The answer to that question," I say, "will go with me to the
grave."

He laughs and for a moment I enjoy his company. We could
be old ladies together, at a tea party, and in fact my father is a
wicked gossip, in style if not content, teasing you with what he
knows, pretending he doesn't know a thing. A skill he inherited
from his mother, who died before I was born. His most vivid
memory of her, he has said, is of her wearing a silk dressing
gown, laughing gaily into the phone, "Do you have any *dirt?*"

This question, over the years, has become a kind of joke with
us. "So, Dad," I say now, "do you have any dirt?"

He tells me what he knows, all of it pretty tame stuff, some of
it dated or rehashed: the business about Mrs. Beecham disliking
her daughter-in-law at first because (my father stage-whispers as
though shocked, for effect) *she's Mormon,* I've heard for a couple

of years running now. That and how Mrs. Beecham's son chose
to convert, which just about *killed* Mrs. Beecham, until she got
used to the idea; and do you suppose they—meaning Mrs.
Beecham's son and his wife—do they still wear long underwear?
Mormons, that is. Or is that only before marriage? "But she's a
lovely girl," my father always concludes. "Did I tell you I met
her?"

There are a few divorces to report (he winces at this, remembering no doubt that soon *I'll* be divorced); some houses in the
neighborhood bought and sold, Asians moving in; a handful of
marriages and babies born.

Babies born.

Dad finally asks what he couldn't bring himself to the other
day. "When is—when is your—the—baby due?"

His brown eyes lighten to amber and I think the worst of it is
over, he accepts my situation.

"Late September," I answer.

"September. That's a good month, awfully hot though."

We sit companionably for a while before he goes on with the
dirt: a minister asked to leave for his political views; a financial
scandal involving a bank, rather difficult and boring to follow;
Mr. Marsden's teenage son suspected of—here Dad cups a hand
to his mouth as though whispering into somebody's ear—*selling
drugs.*

Such is my father's gossip. Innocent in content, relatively
lacking in malice, but material *he* thinks of as censorious; and so,
it animates him.

I could listen all night.

THIRTEEN

I don't see him at first, sitting with the old people in the day room of the Alta Vista. My bag holding my Powerbook slung over my shoulder, I start up the stairs toward my room.

"Theo?"

I almost keep going. "What are you doing here, Jackson?"

"I'm here for a conference."

"A conference for *what?*"

"Theo, can we go somewhere?"

"I'm going to my room."

"Can't we just talk?"

He's at the bottom of the stairs. In jeans, what he always wears, and a blue work shirt, which, for a change, is ironed. A half dozen pairs of rheumy eyes peer at us, to see what I'll say or do next.

"Oh all right. Come on." I lead him upstairs to my room, a vague feeling of guilt, sneaking a boy into my room. Not a boy, my husband. My estranged husband.

At my door we're standing very close while I work the key into the lock, so close I could kiss the mole on Jackson's cheek; I can smell the soap on his body.

"How long have you been in town?" I ask, shouldering open the door, which sticks.

"A day and a half."

"And Dad told you where to find me, right?"

He nods, following me inside.

I drop my bag and scurry over to the chair. A place I never sit ordinarily. Jackson stands in the center of the room, glancing around.

"I wish Dad would stop interfering," I say. "Oh well, here you are. There's the bed. If you want to sit."

He hesitates, then does, as I wait for him to say something about this room, the Alta Vista. He doesn't, just keeps looking. His eyes flit from my belly—does he know? did Dad tell him? has he guessed?—to my face. Then I remember Gregg's leather jacket, hung over the back of my chair. I ended up with it after I saw him last, a couple of days ago when I decided I just had to see him. I drove over there at seven a.m., sliding into bed with him, making love all day until he had to work that night.

"Which conference?" I say to Jackson.

"What?"

"You said you were here for a conference." I can't stop smelling Gregg's jacket, the rich leather scent, how it hung on me the other night, too big, comforting—just as you'd expect to feel, wearing your boyfriend's jacket.

"The Organization of American Historians, downtown, at the Bonaventure."

His eyes go from my face to my chair. I know him well enough to know he won't say anything about the jacket, but he's noted it, he's trying to figure it out.

"How did you get to Pasadena?" I ask.

"I rented a car."

"Oh."

The faucet drips in the bathroom, accentuating the starts and stops of our conversation. I've asked at the front desk to have it fixed, to no avail. Nights I muffle it with a washcloth, to soak up the sound.

"All this time and you've only called me once," Jackson says. "Why?"

"I know it was wrong and I can't explain it. I'm sorry."

"So why do I get the feeling there's something you want to tell me?"

"You're right," I say with several deep breaths. "I should've told you this on the phone the other week, but . . . I'm pregnant. I was pregnant when I left. Maybe I left you *because* I was pregnant."

He stands up from the bed—bounces, really. He looks so happy I'm afraid he's going to embrace me. He smiles, frowns, then looks totally dismayed. "Wow. Shit. How far along are you?" he asks.

"Almost to the end of the first trimester."

"Shit. I don't know what to say." Now he's really staring at my belly. "I can see it now, see that your belly is bigger. You look different all over. You look so beautiful. I'm so happy, and so pissed you didn't tell me sooner, and pissed you left me. God damn it, you didn't even tell me where you were going! You wouldn't call, except that once. I slept by the phone waiting . . ." He stops, gazing at me. "This is amazing, amazing news."

"Nothing is different between us, Jackson. My feelings about you haven't changed. I'm not coming back to you." This sounds like such a prepared speech but I say it because he looks too hopeful, as if this—my pregnancy—is the very news he's been waiting for.

"When is it due?" he says.

"September 25th."

"Wow. Would you mind if we went out?"

"Where?"

"Out for some air? Some lunch?" His eyes are on my belly again.

"What would you say if I moved here?" Jackson asks once we're walking up El Molino, under swaying palms. "If, say, I got a job out here."

"You've got a job. In Colorado. You *love* Colorado."

"If I got a different job. Out here. If one of the jobs I'm interviewing for over the next couple of days hired me."

"I'd say you were crazy. Why would you leave Colorado?"

"To be near you. To be near the baby."

I have to smile: Jackson is such a sap. "Did you just come up with this idea? Now that you know I'm pregnant?"

"I've been mulling it over ever since you left."

"But why? You know we're not getting back together."

"Well, then, I'll move out here for the baby."

"My baby."

"Mine too."

"But mostly mine," I say. "I'm carrying it. Listen—are you going to do anything weird? Like hire a lawyer and try to take this baby from me?"

"No. I'm just thinking of moving out here, that's all. If I can get a job."

At Charleyville, several blocks from the Alta Vista, we join a line of business types, women with brick red lipstick and ruddy men who seem to have just this minute finished shaving. It's a cafeteria, but a hip one, and when we get to the cash register there's an awkward moment of Jackson reaching into his pocket for his wallet and me digging through my purse for mine. Dutch treat, our backs turned away from each other.

When we get to our table the first thing I notice is that on Jackson's tray is a beer. At least I think it's a beer. It's a brown bottle facing away from me so that I can't see the label. A beer, what else could it be? Everything in the room suddenly seems too bright, too keen-looking.

"You've hardly touched your sandwich," Jackson says. "Don't you like it?"

"Not really."

"You spent so much time ordering it." He mimics. "'Sourdough bread, toasted light, wait, not toasted. Mayonnaise—no, no mayonnaise. *No mayonnaise.*' Ah, my Theo. Were you always so picky?"

"I'm not your Theo." That he doesn't know me like this, pregnant and picky, only widens the gulf between us: it becomes easier not to think of this baby as his. "As for your seeing the baby when the time comes, I don't know how I feel about that."

"Oh, you don't," he says, glaring at me. The glare turns sad, self-pitying: so misunderstood. His gloomy midwestern look, I used to call it. Dark blue eyes, pale skin, as though internally he's clouding up, raw and cold, about to storm. A storm he will weather stoically, alone.

We sit without speaking for a while, then he excuses himself to use the restroom.

Now the agony.

Do I look at his bottle to verify it's beer? I scan the restaurant for the bathrooms, to see if he's coming, then I tip the bottle toward me. Root beer. God damn it. Great. I'm glad for him and furious with myself for checking up on him—and annoyed with Jackson, incredibly, as if this were *his* fault.

Guiltily, I search the room for him again. I don't want him knowing I gave into this . . . this snooping. No different really than sticking my arm into wet trash and counting up the empties.

"So which schools are you interviewing with?" I ask when Jackson rejoins me at the table, pretending I'm not in any way invested in his answer.

"Orange Coast College, Saddleback College, Santa Ana College, Costa Mesa Junior College."

Jackson's dusty old dissertation that sat in the corner of our living room the first four years of our marriage: now and then he'd take it out, only to pronounce it shit, and kick it back into the corner again. Then last year he suddenly finished it, in a month, on a dare from me.

"Those are all junior colleges," I say.

"Yep."

"You're not interviewing any other places? Any schools up North, say."

"I don't want to live up North, I want to live here."

"But Jackson, why? You know we're not going to get back together."

"I'm not sure I want to be back together," he says.

"You don't?"

"I'll settle for being friends, Theo. We don't even have to be friends. Just let me see the baby now and then. Think you can handle that?"

"Depends."

"On what?"

I shrug, watching him drink his root beer. "Did you really quit drinking?"

"Yes."

I could get lost in those blue eyes of his, and I have; his eyes that have lied to me so many times, not maliciously—he told me what he wished were true, that lies might become the truth. Cheap alchemy. I wonder what it's like to not trust your own eyes when you look in a mirror, what it's like to hate yourself. What did my mother feel, looking in a mirror? I can't say I feel any differently about myself.

I get up to leave and kiss him on the cheek. "Jackson, I'm sorry I tried to dissuade you from moving out here. It's none of my business now anyway, what you do."

Why did I ever think my moving out here would solve anything?

FOURTEEN

The next day I'm at the Burbank airport early, to complete arrangements for buying the Chevy Cavalier I've been driving around, broken air conditioning and all. I need a car and I just can't deal with shopping right now, and on the dashboard is a sticker: "Would you like to buy this car? Call 681-4358."

After I buy the car, it's one foot in front of the other, down the hallway to my gate. Lay suitcase, purse and Powerbook down on the conveyer belt of the x-ray machine, out the gate door to the runway, hot noisy wind. View of the mountains, dry and brown, but clear. Middle of February and it still hasn't rained. Drought. Should be raining cats and dogs, as it did when we were children and couldn't walk to school. Mothers in plastic coats and hats driving carpools, shooing children in and out of doors telling them to hurry, hurry—not my mother; everyone else's. Tropical storms that lasted for days. This February it's desert sunny, eerily pleasant and dry, as it might be, one can't help thinking, after a quick blast of radiation.

Clunk, clunk, clunk, up the metal steps to the plane, then down the aisle to my seat. Sink into seat, close eyes, wait until plane is well in flight before starting up my Powerbook. Open folder for next assignment: Boomer Toys.

Toys we had as kids, or wished we had: maple wood blocks, rowing carts, Lincoln Log trading posts and houses, the original Radio Flyer wagons, pine tables and chairs, maple stoves—most everything is wood. This catalog is done in black and white, some sepia, appealing to customers' secret love of the fifties and early sixties. The same thing my copy is supposed to do: invoke Leave it to Beaver, Dennis the Menace, innocence with a little butch wax, hair ribbons, Keds, the old thermoses with the glass inside. I write: *Remember playing in the twilight up and down the street? You and the gang? Kick-the-Can, Red Rover, Capture the Flag . . . .* Nowadays people are just getting home from work at twilight, after stopping off at daycare first, then the market. Kids are tired, cranky, parents are exhausted, and nobody knows their neighbors anymore. I write copy that sells an idea, the illusion of a lost era.

I scroll through the file and start in on the new products, thumbing through the pictures and product information the advertising director has sent. The original Skittles game, a tumbling mat, a giant floor puzzle, miniature pool table, pogo stick, see-through models of a man and woman.

Like Jackson and myself, only we're not see-through—rather, opaque and hard to decipher. Yesterday, when I said goodbye, I kissed him on the cheek. A sisterly kiss or the kiss of Judas? Part of me hoped never to see him again, part of me saw this was unreasonable, impossible.

. . . educational. Every organ colorful and realistic. Perfect for budding surgeons. I change *surgeons* to *doctors*.

Done.

The plane starts its descent into San Francisco Airport. I'm met at the gate by Meadowlark's advertising director, Bill somebody, forty-five-ish.

"We'll check you into your hotel later," Bill says in the car, followed by questions about how am I liking Southern California and do I intend to stay? Each time I answer, he nods quickly and volleys back a comment. "California's still the land of gold for me, Theo. Never wanted to live any other place." His idea of small talk, then he cuts to the chase. "Wait till you see our seasonal stuff," he says. "Dresses like out of the Czar's Russia."

Nausea races through me; Bill's cologne trapped in my sinuses, as if my nose is buried in the glands of some animal. "Bill? Could we open a window, please?"

"No problemo." Exhaust-tinged air fills the car, a slight improvement. "You have kids, Theo?"

"No, not yet." Just a little fetus.

"You can pick one out to take home," he says.

"Pardon?"

"One of the dresses, Theo. You got a little niece?"

"Nephews."

"Have one of your own someday, eh? A little girl?"

If I do, I think, she won't be dressed like the Czar's Russia. As we continue north on 101, it occurs to me I won't be working for Meadowlark much longer. Once the baby's born, I'll weed out the companies I don't like.

I've only quit one other catalog before, one of the first children's catalogs I joined, a doll company, which is how I got into children's to begin with. Jackson and I shared an office in our house at Stonewall Creek, a situation we didn't always like, but neither of us would move. "You work in the bedroom." "No, you." "But it'd be more difficult for me to move. I have more stuff." "No it wouldn't. I'll help you. Besides, this was your idea." "What?" "Sharing an office." "I thought it'd be romantic." Erratic silence while we attended to our own work, punctuated by my curses as I neared a deadline.

As for the dolls, they were perched around the office, smiling their pink petaled smiles. Jessica and Callie and Laura and Monique, who lived in the French Quarter of New Orleans. Period dolls—Colonial, Victorian, Pioneer, Turn-of-the-Century. I had to write about them as though they were real little girls: Jessica, who lived in Vermont but spent the summer with her cousin Polly in New York, even visiting the fanciest ice cream parlor in the city! Laura, who caught her very own fish! With her very own fishing rod and bait basket (complete with plastic grasshoppers and a frog)!

The dolls had dolls of their own, naturally, and sometimes even those dolls had dolls. And if that weren't enough, you could buy outfits to match your doll's—dresses, nightgowns, shoes—as well as storybooks about the doll's adventures. Which is about the time I quit, when I got promoted to writing books about Jessica, Callie, Laura and Monique, and (I was told excitedly), there were plans for cookbooks, calendars, a magazine.

No thanks, I said.

In this sea of blond girls in party dresses at the Meadowlark shoot, there are the rustle of petticoats and the harsh whispers of mothers commanding their daughters. One girl tiptoes by me, hands clad in white gloves—so she won't dirty her dress? Or are girls' gloves back in style?

Bill, the advertising director, is off talking to someone, so I'm alone with a bagful of swatches to rub between my fingers—for inspiration, Bill said, the Czar's Russia, ha ha.

Suddenly I notice, to my surprise, a couple of little black girls about to be photographed. Maybe Meadowlark has received a few complaints, or maybe the company has caught on to multiculturalism at last. In any case the girls look out of place here; they look real. As if they have real lives, parents who actually take them to playgrounds and let them run in the sprinklers.

It's the blondes who always get to me, their halos of hair, not a freckle on their pale listless arms. Are they drugged? Do they like this? Why do their mothers bring them?

I flee the photo shoot momentarily to check phone messages at home, home being the Alta Vista still, where the man at the front desk protractedly reads one message at a time, one each from Gregg and my father, another from a children's bed and bath catalog, and one more message from, as the balding man at the desk says, "your *Ahhnt Lyla*." He takes great pride in being exact. "'I talked to Corb, dear, and he told me your happy news. Congratulations.' You're to call her." My happy news must be the pregnancy; the real news is that Corb and Aunt Lyla are talking again after all these years. I tell the man thanks, then return to the photo shoot. Klieg lights, props: gilt-armed chairs, fake marble pedestals, brocade curtains. The photographer steps up to the two black girls, in matching floral gabardine dresses, and checks his light meter. I close my eyes as much as I dare, the feathery blur of my eyelashes dimming my vision, a game I played as a child pretending to sleep, watching everything through slitted eyes. I'd test myself in the mirror, tipping my head upward to peer up under the lids—was it convincing, or could you see the shine of my eyes?

The photographer shakes his head. That brocade's too dark, he'll use a flash in addition to the lights.

Back in town, I've arranged to meet Gregg at Denny's. I can still taste Twinkies in the back of my throat. I ate a whole package of them on the way over here, and now, trying to rinse out the memory, I drink my ice water. Even the water at Denny's tastes like Denny's, bland and impersonal.

Gregg isn't here yet. Fine with me; right now I'm fingering the menu, thinking—mashed potatoes, no gravy. Fried chicken. Salad, French dressing. Milk. I nibble a saltine from the basket, so dry it catches in my throat going down. I'm sick, sick, sick of saltines.

There he is at the door. Inwardly I groan. How did I ever think I could hide this from him? Even as long as I could've hidden it, three months, four, five . . .

"Hi," I say glumly. To the waitress I say: "We're ready to order now."

"I haven't even looked at the menu," Gregg says.

"Have the chicken club," I tell him, adding by way of explanation, "I come here all the time."

"You do?"

"Yeah." I stare unapologetically at the orange vinyl seats and the plasticized photos of meals on the wall. Next to us an elderly couple shares a sandwich and a bag of chips; only old people come here, or broke students, or the pregnant population. Pregnancy turns you into a philistine. You'll eat anything.

"Shall I come back?" the waitress asks. She's been standing here all this time, her pad out.

"I know exactly what I want," I say and give her my order.

"Guess I'll have the chicken club," Gregg says. "I hear it's pretty good." After jotting this down, the waitress bustles away, her stockinged thighs rubbing together, an embarrassing sound.

"The problem," I say, "is this."

I don't say anything else. Can't force the words out of my throat.

"Oh, Gregg. Can't you guess what the problem is? Think. *Think.*"

"Why is the fact that you're married a problem exactly? You left him, didn't you?"

I nod my head dumbly, posing the words in my mouth. *I am pregnant. You are not the father but I want to be with you.* Why can't I just say it? Am I so afraid of losing Gregg? Or does the pregnancy seem—still—not real?

"I left my husband," I say. "Yes."

"You're going back to him."

"No."

"You still have feelings for him."

"It's a little more complicated than that. I'm pregnant, Gregg. I'm going to have the baby." I gaze at the half-eaten saltine in my hand, my husband's name on my lips. "The baby isn't yours. It's Jackson's."

I wait for him to ask when did this happen. How far along am I. Something.

"Aren't you going to say anything?"

He stares at me, too stunned to talk. I touch his hand, but he pulls it away.

"I understand how you must feel."

"No," he says, "you don't."

He won't look at me, but the miracle is, he doesn't leave.

When the food arrives, I devour my fried chicken, mashed potatoes, salad, and milk, lots of milk. I lick the mustache off my face. Gregg has pushed his plate in front of me; I finish off his sandwich. We sit closer and closer to one another until his arm is around me, my hand on my belly as if for balance. Wafting from the speakers is a muzak version of "The Cat in the Cradle"—a song I despise for its sentimentality. "The cat in the cradle and a silver spoon, little boy blue and the man on the moon. . . ." Tears are rolling down my cheeks.

FIFTEEN

ARCADIA METHODIST HOSPITAL OF SOUTHERN CALIFORNIA

NAME Marian Greer Mapes _____ HOSP. NO. 61621

SEX F _____ AGE ON ADMISSION 38 ___ CITIZEN, ALIEN, NON-RESIDENT,

SINGLE, MARRIED, WIDOWED, DIVORCED, SEPARATED

DATE OF ADMISSION February 5, 1963

INFORMANT: The informant, Harold Mapes, is the husband of the patient. Mr. Mapes is 38-years-old and is presently a stock analyst. The address is 342 Bonitas St., San Marino, Calif. The informant appears to be an intelligent though nervous man who gives this information willingly and voluntarily. He shows concern but little insight into his wife's condition. The information can be accepted as reliable.

FAMILY HISTORY: The informant is not aware of any previous family history of suicide or suicide attempts, nor is he aware of any history of mental illness in the patient's family. The patient's father is retired, having been an attorney. The patient's mother is a housewife. It is unclear whether they know yet of their daughter's current hospitalization, or of this most recent suicide attempt.

PERSONAL HISTORY: The patient was born in April 1924 in Los Angeles. She has one sister in good health who is 41-years-old at this time. The patient grew up in a stable home, although the informant seems to have little knowledge regarding the childhood and early teenage years of the patient. The patient graduated magna cum laude from Stanford University and edited the school newspaper there, as well as served as President of Women Students. She was very ambitious, yet uncertain around people, possibly withdrawn. The informant and patient got married in 1951, after a six-month courtship, when the patient was 27-years-old. After marrying, the patient quit her job at an advertising agency and stayed home to keep house. According to the informant, the marriage was a happy one, sexually well-adjusted, although there was interference from the patient's parents. The patient bore three children: in 1953, 1956, and late 1960. The last child, a baby girl, died in early 1961, of crib death. The patient's symptoms, according to the inform-ant, began even before the infant's death, sometime after the middle child was born. He notes that he would come home from work to find his wife agitated and crying for no apparent reason. He wondered if she had been drinking. In the past he has found empty liquor bottles in the trash.

PREVIOUS MENTAL ILLNESS: According to the informant, the patient's first mental breakdown occurred in early 1962, following a year-long period of depression probably precipi-tated by the baby's death. The patient was admitted voluntar-ily to Huntington Memorial Hospital for treatment and while there, attempted suicide by an overdose of Thorazine, prescribed by her psychiatrist at the time, Dr. Johnson. Lavage was administered, followed by the patient being transferred to St. Vincent's Hospital in Los Angeles for an extensive course of electroshock treatment. In Fall 1962, after another break-down, another series of electroshock treatments was undertaken at St. Vincent's with the patient allowed to go home for three-week intervals between one-week sessions of electroshock.

ONSET OF PRESENT ILLNESS: Three weeks prior to her admission the patient became agitated and depressed, succumbing to fits of crying, fearing that she would once again suffer a break-down. She expressed suicide ideation on at least two occasions

123

to her husband who reported this to her present psychiatrist, Dr. Robert Gris. This was followed by a period of about one to two weeks when the patient seemed to feel better. Then without warning the patient was found lying unresponsive in bed one morning, having slashed both wrists.

AT ARCADIA METHODIST: The patient was admitted to Arcadia Methodist Hospital on 2/5/63 upon a Involuntary Application by Dr. Mead who stated: "According to the application, completed once patient had regained consciousness, the patient states that she is very depressed and fears she might try to kill herself again. On examination today, this is a 39-year-old brunette Caucasian woman of average height and weight, who appears to be in fair physical health, despite loss of blood. She appears to be depressed and her affect confirms these observations. She is fairly well-oriented for time, place and person, and is aware of the nature of her surroundings."

PHYSICAL EXAMINATION: By Dr. Martin, 2/7/63
Physical findings essentially negative except those regarding patient's recent suicide attempt: weakness, dizziness, possible anemia from blood loss; stitches on both wrists. One wrist appears markedly inflamed.

MENTAL EXAMINATION: By Dr. Martin, 2/7/63
This is a 39-year-old Caucasian female who is markedly depressed, tearful, anxious and tense during the interview. She admitted to being in the Huntington and St. Vincent's last year, receiving electroshock treatments for depression. She is reluctant to discuss suicide attempts, both recent and previous. Her speech is coherent; her associations are well- preserved. She denies hallucinatory experiences and exhibited none. There were no persecutory feelings, no paranoid trends, no hypochrondriacal ideas. Sensorium is clear. Insight and judgment limited.

INITIAL PRESENTATION: By Dr. C.H. Franklin, 2/28/63

This 39-year-old woman has grown up in this area and except for college, lived here all her life. There is no history of suicide in her immediate family, although there may have been a distant cousin who killed himself. There is alcoholism in the family, her father possibly, although she remains vague on this point. She doesn't feel her own drinking is a problem, which is rather hard to believe. She claims a close relationship with her parents in that she sees them frequently, although she faults her father for being overbearing and her mother for being a "mouse." Somewhat contradictorily, she says her parents irritate her greatly, her father in particular, although as a child she worshipped him. She reports her marriage to her husband is satisfactory although she admits to a cessation of sexual relations. She is not sure why, perhaps her husband is no longer attracted to her—or perhaps it results from the death of the baby. She is inconsolable on this latter subject and blames herself extremely. She claims to be a bad mother and when asked why, says she cannot protect her children adequately, although it is unclear what she wishes to protect them from. She says now that the baby is dead, she has little to offer her other children, her daughter in particular. She speaks of this daughter, Theodora, frequently, almost obsessively. But the content of what she says seems to have not much bearing on the actual child—she speaks in generalities about mothers and daughters and the responsibility of mothers to their daughters. The tone of her words approach hysteria on this subject, although the words themselves are lucid and quite sensible. She says she is a poor example to both her children, and an inconstant wife, lost to fits of mental illness, and that all would be better off without her—thus her most recent suicide attempt.

She has been depressed since the death of the baby, maybe even prior to that. She says she has always suffered from periods of depression and anxiety, even when she was a child. She was happiest when she was first married and after the birth of her first child.

She is not presently suicidal. Nor is she hopeful about the future.

The diagnosis here is difficult. This looks like a chronically insecure, schizoid woman with depressive tendencies whose defenses finally gave up. The outlook here seems to be extremely bad. She is too young for menopause although unquestionably she will develop an involutional psychosis when the time comes. At the present time she could be diagnosed as such: Tentative Diagnosis: DEPRESSIVE PSYCHOSIS, DEPRESSIVE TYPE. Recommendations: 1. No final certification (Voluntary). 2. Individual and Group Psychotherapy. 3. Electroshock treatments.

SUBSEQUENT COURSE: After admission the patient was placed on Ward 3 where she was depressed, tearful, and quite seclusive. She was not delusional. She was able to maintain a sensible conversation; was placed on Mellaril 100 mg. t.i.d. and Tofranil 25 mg. t.i.d. During her 2-month stay, the patient received Individual and Group Psychotherapy and Electroshock treatment. However, she showed very little improvement. Most of the time she was preoccupied with herself and mostly sat by herself on the ward. Off and on her depression was diminishing but later on became even worse. At times she had suicidal ideas; other times she had violent thoughts about her father. Patient was approved for Home Visit for four days and has had two successful ones; however, after each of them she was quite depressed on returning to the hospital.

On 2/28, the patient was transferred to the Intensive Treatment Unit where electroshock treatment was approved. Her pre-electroshock treatment EKG revealed an incomplete bundle block on the right side; therefore, patient was checked by Dr. Curtis who okayed electroshock treatments.

DISCUSSION:

Hereditary Factors: There is inconclusive evidence of a family history of suicide. Same for mental illness. Strong family history of alcoholism.

Developmental Factors: The patient suffered bouts of depression and anxiety as a child. She has always feared mental illness, believing that her father had a breakdown a long time ago as a young man that nobody speaks of.

Precipitating Factors: It is felt that in this patient's mental disturbance a great role was played by the loss of her infant daughter, whom she can barely bring herself to discuss. Nor can she discuss sensibly her surviving children, particularly the daughter, without linking them inexorably to the dead child.

DIAGNOSIS: DEPRESSIVE PSYCHOSIS.

CONDITION: SLIGHTLY IMPROVED.

TREATMENT: MELLARIL 100 MG. T.I.D. AND TOFRANIL 25 MG. TO 75 MG. T.I.D., OCCUPATIONAL THERAPY, INDIVIDUAL AND GROUP THERAPY, ELECTROSHOCK TREATMENT.

PROGNOSIS: GUARDED

     Dr. Martin/nen/tfh

MAY 4, 1963: This patient has handed in her notice. Because of the suicidal history she is referred for screening.

DISCHARGE DEFERRED

     Dr. C.H. Franklin: rr/tfh
     Assistant Director

MAY 6, 1963: This case has been screened by Drs. Clardy and Rochlin and also seen by the undersigned. The following observations were made: "This patient was admitted on an Involuntary Application, later a Voluntary Application and has turned in her notice. At the present time she is quite depressed and admits she is still sick, to the point of commenting recently that she may as well throw herself out the window, for all the good this hospital has done her. The patient has also been observed befriending another patient for the purpose of obtaining that patient's medications.

"She has agreed to withdraw her notice and has made a signed statement to this effect on the letter.

"If the patient again turns in her notice and is not well, the question of having her committed should be considered since she is still in a dangerous state."

DISCHARGE DISAPPROVED.

DR. C.H. Franklin: rr/tfh
Assistant Director

PRESENTATION FOR DISCHARGE
BY: DR. IVERSON
JULY 26, 1963

SUBSEQUENT COURSE: The patient has been in the hospital approximately 6 months. She has a past history of recurrent depressions and suicidal tendencies as well as two attempts. In the Intensive Treatment Unit she has improved to the degree where she was able to socialize a bit, able to function fairly well. Her depression lifted so that she was no longer suicidal. Since April 18 she has been going on weekend visits rather regularly. She is on the open ward, has her I.D. card. She now socializes to a degree. She has one or two friends on the ward. She is rather inactive, preferring to read, and had to be coerced into working in the sewing room by threatening to remove her I.D. card. She walks around the ward with a supercilious expression on her face, smiling rather stiffly if at all. She is on a combination of Elavil 25 mg. t.i.d. and Trilafon 4 mg. t.i.d. It is unlikely that she will get much benefit from these medications as her present behavior is probably not the result of her depression but probably represents her longstanding personality. It is felt that she could not benefit from further hospitalization here but would do better outside with the continuation of her psychotherapy with Dr. Robert Gris. It is also felt that the patient at the present time is not a risk to herself or to her family. There is no evidence of suicidal or homicidal tendencies.

PLAN: The plan is to release the patient to the care of her husband, Mr. Harold Mapes, 342 Bonitas St., San Marino, Calif. He has engaged a nurse for her as well as a housekeeper so that she will be under less pressure at home. Arrangements have also been made for the patient to continue treatment with Dr. Gris.

DIAGNOSIS: DEPRESSIVE PSYCHOSIS.

CONDITION: IMPROVED.

RECOMMENDATIONS: RELEASE ACCORDING TO ABOVE PLAN. PATIENT TO CONTINUE WITH ELAVIL 25 MG. T.I.D. AND TRILAFON 4 MG. T.I.D.

PROGNOSIS: GUARDED.

Dr. Iverson/sa/tfh

PRESENTATION FOR DISCHARGE
BY: DR. IVERSON
SEPT. 2, 1963

There is a suicidal history. Referred for screening.

DISCHARGE DEFERRED.

> DR. C. H. FRANKLIN rr/thf
> Assistant Director

PRESENTATION FOR DISCHARGE
BY: DR. BUCHANAN
SEPT. 4, 1963

This patient was today screened by Drs. Rockwood and Winne and was also seen by the undersigned. The following observations were made: "The patient who is here in the hospital on a Voluntary Application has handed in her notice to leave. A plan has been made for her to be seen by Dr. Robert Gris. Her husband apparently wishes her home. At the present time she is in good contact, makes a favorable impression and it is felt has no dangerous tendencies. Discharge is approved."

DIAGNOSIS: DEPRESSIVE PSYCHOSIS.

CONDITION: IMPROVED.

DISCHARGE APPROVED.

DR. C. H. FRANKLIN mgt/tfh
Assistant Director

Sixteen

Diffidently, I finger the nightgown I'm still wearing, though it's one in the afternoon. In the hallway outside my room at the Alta Vista, I hear a person with a walker plunking down the corridor.

Last night's dream after reading my mother's hospital records:

My mother's dead body is being brought into the mortuary and I am waiting for her there. There are tables for the dead people—sort of like a clinic—and I am standing by the one reserved for her. They bring my mother to me in a clear case packed in fluid, her dark hair undulating within, and I think, *That's her.* They remove her from her case and lay her out on the table, naked. I'm to get her ready for burial. She is accompanied by a list of requests, written in her own hand, but her writing is sloppy with many misspellings, provoking a comment from one of the employees at the mortuary. *But that just shows how far her mind was gone,* I want to say; *she was smart, she could write.* I prepare to put her body inside a white tent, along with some of the things she requested— an infant's blanket, a red papier mâché bird. Meanwhile, almost imperceptibly at first, her body starts to move a little here and there, her arms, her hands—the next thing I know, she's sitting up, her rubbery white legs dangling off the table. She's trying to stand and I help her. "Oh no," she says, "I'm a boy." She thinks she has a penis. I look down and check. "No, you're a girl, just swollen from the packing fluid." I mean to ask her about Charlotte, my baby sister, but before I can my mother lets loose with a stream of urine, smiling ecstatically with greenish teeth.

I haven't dreamt of her in years.

As a child I wrote myself postcards, pretending they were from my mother. Postcards I would get in stacks from my father's friends as souvenirs, brand new, not sent through the mail. Post-cards of bears in Bern, Switzerland, beergartens in Germany, the Black Forest; cherry blossoms in Japan, kimonoed girls with fans upheld; the Queen of England, the Tower of London, a village in Wales—I pinned them up on my bulletin board in a mural, but on their backs were the notes I had written. Starting from when I could first write, they were like a child's letters from camp, except they were about heaven or some such place. *"It's nice here. They have haarps." "Weather is fine, no moskitos."* Supposedly, my mother wrote them from heaven, but I feared she was somewhere else, floating and vaporous in the sky or maybe right in my own back yard, behind the azaleas, or in my closet, reflected in a door-knob, in the pantry with the cans of Campbell's soup. She hovered beneath the floor of my room listening to me with a glass and sometimes she was good and sometimes she was bad.

At thirteen I became convinced I could contact her, that she was trying to contact me. From a book I taught myself self-hypnosis (many hours in my bedroom with a candle burning, picturing myself going down a set of stairs backwards: ten, nine, eight, seven, six); I sent away for books about spirits, tried to obtain the *Tibetan Book of the Dead.* I studied Tarot cards, wrapping them in a silk scarf inside one of my mother's old lacquered cigarette boxes.

Every day I hurried home from school to watch "Dark Shadows" and eat mouthfuls of saltines—Evan wasn't there anymore to warn me about my figure—and after sating myself with milk, I'd begin. Forays around the house for an item belonging to my mother: a necklace, a shoe, an old bobbie pin wedged in the crevice of a drawer. I'd hold it in my palm and repeat her name over and over again very fast until I was dizzy, my scalp prickling. Then I'd wait. Nothing. I read Tarot cards by the hour, or I'd meditate on a particular card, the High Priestess or the Hanged Man. Never the Death card. I was too frightened, though I understood perfectly well that it wasn't about death, but rebirth.

I knew by then, of course, that my mother wasn't going to write me postcards. I'd torn them down from the bulletin board and thrown them in the trash. Instead, I attempted automatic writing, hypnotizing myself first. My eyes half-closed, I wrote in shaky letters, *book, no, an, wha,* sort of like doing a Ouija Board; I tried to imagine it was my mother moving the pen, albeit slowly. Each letter from the alphabet took five minutes to form and most were unrecognizable. I tried a different approach and wrote anything that came to me. *I really like Brian, his locker is next to mine no no no my mother my mother what is there to say?* This became my diary, which remained after I'd quit all the other stuff. It said hardly anything about my mother and was mostly about boys.

This left dreams. In preparation each night I would picture her face and say her name, begging her to visit me in my dreams as she did when I was younger, when she'd return for a day and we'd go on a picnic and then she would say goodbye—always the same dream.

Instead, my dreams became sporadic and nightmarish, more like that other dream from childhood in which my mother had smiled, holding a knife behind her back. *I've got a surprise for you.* When I was fourteen, I dreamt my mother took me to a carnival. She grabbed my wrist and squeezed it tight, like a rubber band cutting off my circulation. No longer ageless or beautiful as she'd been in the dreams of old, she was drunk, her hair unkempt. "We're alike," she hissed. "We're exactly alike."

Two hours later, I'm still in my nightgown, embarrassed that I can't get dressed, can't go downstairs and fix myself a cup of tea at least from the ever-present pot of hot water in the Alta Vista's day room.

Everything at this moment seems unreal; rather, nothing is more real right now than my mother's presence, her pain. I don't want to be distracted from it. I want the feeling to stay, however desperate: my mother's hand brushing my cheek. Her hand on my throat. At least she's here, conjured up by a medical report, spread all over my bed at the Alta Vista. I tell myself it's an artifact, a document, a processed lie, not her at all, but there she is laid bare before me, discussed in terms that are at once too general and too specific. My mother with her wrists bound, one inflamed, infected; with this hand she touches me. And Charlotte? Thin white arm, a cry—I mourn her too.

Later, I throw on some clothes to go use the Alta Vista's pay phone outside. First I leave a message on Gregg's phone that I won't be able to see him for a few days. "I've got a lot of work to get caught up on," I lie. "Call you in a few days. Miss you."

Then I call Maggie.

"Theo?" Her voice sounds scratchy, far away. "I've been trying to call you. It's impossible reaching you there, when are you going to move out of that place? Anyway, I wanted to tell you about my mother. She died a couple of nights ago."

"Maggie—"

"While you were out of town."

"What did she die of?"

"Heart attack and a lifetime of drinking. Big surprise, right? You know what she used to do when I was little? She'd stand in the doorway to my room and hang onto the door—probably so she wouldn't fall over, she was so drunk. Just hung on to the door, staring at me, while my father beat the shit out of me."

Maggie's father had died by the time we became friends, but I remember the way her mother used to stare at her, in doorways and elsewhere—with sick longing, as if she couldn't for the life of her figure out why Maggie had rejected her.

"How about if I come over?" I offer. "I'll pick up a movie for the boys, fix you some dinner—"

"Okay." Her voice is low and keen. I can't imagine telling her or anyone else about my mother's hospital records.

SEVENTEEN

Florence S. Devoe, 66, of San Marino, died Tuesday, March 9, 1991, at Huntington Memorial Hospital.

Services will be at 11 a.m. Friday at St. Edmund's Episcopal Church in San Marino. Interment will be at the cemetery of Church of Our Savior in San Gabriel.

Mrs. Devoe was born August 3, 1928 in Los Angeles, the daughter of Henry and Eleanor Greer. She married Wyatt Devoe on June 12, 1946.

She was a homemaker and mother.

Her husband, Wyatt Devoe; preceded her in death. She is survived by a son, David Devoe of Manhattan Beach; a daughter, Margaret Matheson of Arcadia; and two grandsons, Dylan and William Matheson.

Memorial gifts may be made to St. Edmund's Church.

The morning of the funeral, I let my father know I won't be stopping by.

"I've nothing important—" He means I don't need to stop by. Always ready, even eager, for me to throw him over for something else, somebody else. I wonder if he's even aware of my mother's hospital records with their intimations of nervous breakdowns, alcoholism, and my father's own weakness and ineffectuality.

"Don't you want to know why I'm not stopping by, Dad?"

"It's not any of my business."

"Oh, but it is. Remotely. Mrs. Devoe, Maggie's mother, died. Her funeral is this morning at St. Edmund's."

"Oh! Well."

"What do you mean *well?*"

"That's a shame." Naturally he doesn't ask about the cause of her death. If it were someone more conveniently distant, someone not the least bit related to us, he could ask, he could hint, he could gossip. *Was it her drinking?*

"I thought you'd want to know, Dad. About the funeral."

"You mean you're going?" At once scandalized and grateful—if I go, he won't have to.

"Isn't it obvious?" Because of the hospital records, I feel especially irritable today. "They're our relatives, aren't they, Dad? And Maggie's my friend."

"You—still see her?" As if she still might lead me down a dark and forbidden path, although it was always questionable as to who was leading whom.

"As for being related to them," my father quickly changes the subject, "well, yes. It's true but we don't—we haven't—" His stock explanation all the years of my life. "We never really communicated. We're related on your mother's—her father's—side."

"I know how we're related. I just thought you'd want to know, Dad, about the funeral."

"Yes, of course." Back to being the good boy. "Please do convey my condolences."

"I will."

"I suppose I ought to write a note," he adds, with considerably less enthusiasm.

"Whatever, Dad."

After Maggie and I drop the boys at the sitter's—they never knew their grandmother well, Maggie explains; she'd decided it was best to avoid that situation—we drive to St. Edmund's.

"Church or chapel?" I ask as we speed down San Gabriel Boulevard.

"Chapel."

We both smile a little sheepishly, remembering when we used to meet up after sneaking out of our bedroom windows for smokes. We'd smoke where the choir was supposed to sit, pulling up the corner of the carpet to stub out our smokes. If we were feeling guilty, we'd blow away the ashes, stick the butts in our back pockets; if not, we'd line the butts up along the tops of the prayer books and hymnals for the janitor to find. The chapel is also the site of my own mother's funeral, although I'm not sure Maggie knows this. I'm not sure what she knows about my mother or Charlotte, what I've told her. Suicide, crib death—not words one can work into most conversations gracefully. Even Maggie may not know the full truth, it's been so many years since we discussed it, back when we were teenagers.

One thing I'm certain of: Maggie doesn't know that after today, our mothers will be buried in the same place. The cemetery at Church of Our Savior, some miles from St. Edmund's.

This being the first Sunday of the month, we visited the cemetery, beforehand gathering a bouquet of flowers from our yard. Flowers my mother had loved: roses, Siberian iris, camellias, daisies. My father did the job himself, leaning into the shrubs still dressed in the white shirt he wore to church, jacket off now. I heard the snip of shears. He placed each flower into the basket I held; soon I would fill a jar with water at the kitchen sink, while in the next room bombs fell, rockets flared, men shook hands saying goodbye forever, their faces streaked with gunpowder, tears—Corb sprawled in front of the TV watching war movies.

The flowers gathered, we climbed into the car, Corb in back and me in front with the flowers in their glass jar between my knees. "Would you not drive so fast, Daddy?" I complained. "I'm getting water on my dress."

He apologized and drove fast anyway, feather-braking for stop signs, the way he always drove, as though roads were freeways. I'd never known my father to drive slowly, although he believed one should, gratefully accepting every speeding ticket he got. In the back seat Corb hung his elbow out the window, a bored expression on his face, in case we passed anyone he knew—who would never guess where we were going anyway.

The cemetery at Church of Our Savior. Right next door was the church itself, where my mother had been baptized. Also "where your mother and I got married, you know," as our father always pointed out, but just that fact alone, not about the wedding itself. We had the photo album for that, in it my mother beautiful, my father young and smiling; pictures of wedding silver displayed on long tables; my mother in her dressing room surrounded by bridesmaids; my mother in her slip holding a hand mirror—why, she was gorgeous, like a movie star—would I ever look like this?; my mother on her father's arm about to enter the church; the wedded couple leaving the church; then the reception, a sea of hats. Too many pictures of women in hats—my father's complaint. Hats! Festooned with birds, fruit, flowers, seed pearls, netting, ribbons. Driving past the church, I dreamed of hats, my mother's slip.

We proceeded into the cemetery—the only place my father drove slowly, because of the speed bumps—and Corb was out of the car before it even stopped, throwing open my door, grabbing the jar of flowers and striding toward the two flat stones with our mother's and sister's names on them, next to the graves of our grandparents, and our mother's grandparents. Come on, Corb's motions seemed to say, let's get this over with. He wiped the stones with a rag he brought, blew off the grass. I wandered over with our father, pausing to ask dumb questions at the graves of young children who had died at the turn of the century; according to Corb, they were dumb. "Why would a baby die?" Our father gave the same long drawn-out explanation each time, about how children in the olden days weren't as healthy as you kids now—and then he would list the illnesses, diphtheria, scarlet fever, smallpox, influenza, consumption. I always listened for the name of our sister's disease, wondering what she had, why she had died. Only once did I get up the courage to ask: did Charlotte have diphtheria or influenza? No, my father said, looking as solemn as I'd ever seen him. Sometimes babies died, he said. Died in their sleep.

Corb meanwhile dumped dead flowers into the trash, rinsing out the plastic vases that fit into the slots in the ground. He ripped open one of the two packets of sugar we brought to keep the new flowers fresh, pouring the other packet in his mouth when no one was looking. He put most of the flowers in our mother's vase, reserving a few daisies and a rosebud or a pink camellia for Charlotte's.

"Done!" he called.

My father would inspect Corb's work, nodding, murmuring his approval, but this wouldn't be the end. Now we checked on other family gravesites, some maiden aunts as well as our father's parents, in another section of the cemetery. Our paternal grandfather's headstone was cracked nearly in half; he had died a long time ago. I always studied my father's face for any sign of emotion as he gazed at the grave of his father. None that I could see. But his father had died of a sudden heart attack when my father was ten, and as I understood it, he had witnessed this, his father dying in front of him. We had this in common, then, losing a parent at a young age. What did my father feel? What did I feel, standing at my mother's grave?

Dry-eyed caution, like a catch in my throat. Excitement of a sort: so this was where my mother and sister lived, their home now.

Back in the car, we drove through the rest of the graveyard, passing the long pink granite building where people were buried. Their ashes, that is. Small gold plaques all up and down the sides of the building, with tiny vases attached able to hold no more than a single flower. Each like a post office box. Marilyn Monroe, I believed, was buried in such a place, her tiny pile of ashes in, what, a jewel-encrusted box? Or a small metal locked box — that's where I pictured my mother's ashes to be, underground.

Those who burned my mother's body wore gloves on their hands, aprons streaked with soot. Rolling her corpse inside like a loaf of bread they later forgot.

One more stop, or pause rather, as we exited the cemetery at Church of Our Savior. Our father slowed the car. "See over there? By the trees? That's where our plots are."

Not by our mother's or the rest of the family's, because there was no more room there, but off in some corner, and why was he buying funeral plots anyway? Did he expect us not to last either?

Our father explained: maybe we'd want to be buried some place else, with our own families we would have some day, next to a wife or husband. That was fine with him. He'd bought these plots just in case. It wasn't easy, he said with an apologetic laugh, to find a plot in a cemetery these days. It was a little like trying to find a parking space downtown.

During Maggie's mother's funeral, I think of my mother's braces. What happened to them when she was cremated? Were they removed beforehand? Did she wear clothes? I pictured the people who worked there, dressed in white aprons, gloves on their hands—death's bakers. They rolled her in, waited. For how long? Later they scraped her out, into a box. Was the box placed in my father's hands? Was he present when it was buried?

How little I know.

If Charlotte was cremated, for instance: I've had the idea all these years that my parents wouldn't allow it. Couldn't bring themselves to cremate her.

My mother's braces. They float before me, her mouth open, then closed. What, of the human body, burns?

The minister drones on about Maggie's mother: a devoted wife before the tragic loss of her husband; a loving mother. . . . Maggie fixes her gaze at the top of a hymnal and I imagine she pictures stubbing a cigarette out on its pages. Nearby sits her brother, extremely good-looking now. As a boy he was a toad. Jailed last year on a drunk driving conviction, he nearly killed an elderly woman. Now he works in a CD store, Maggie has told me, but he wants to be a pharmaceutical salesman. She doesn't see much of him, nor did she see much of her mother, whom I remember as always wearing shorts. Tanned long legs with pachyderm-like baggy knees. Her blinking, tipsy gaze; her smoker's hack. To think she was my aunt!—a subject that never came up between us, though many a time I examined her features for a trace of family resemblance. The eyes, the nose? She didn't look anything like my mother's side of the family, so the fact of our being distantly related would return to the realm of conjecture, although I knew it was true. No one in our family ever denied it was true. They just didn't discuss it.

The chapel is surprisingly full. Neighbors, friends—people I recognize from years ago. The ongoing drunken party at the Devoe's house. Maggie and I would walk in tripping on acid, watch their drunken faces and the pores of their skin, so pitted, so craterous. We laughed and laughed—we could've peed on the floor, no one would've noticed.

Now I reach for Maggie's hand. We touch fingertips, the fingers of my hand meeting hers, then we press our palms together, something we used to do as teenagers, in a kind of combined prayer, each of us contributing a hand.

My mother's funeral: I'm sitting in the front row crying. Today I can see myself back then, the stiff pointed shoulders of my navy blue dress. My father doesn't cry, my brother doesn't cry. No one but me is crying, it seems, and I am crying loudly. I don't think I'm supposed to cry this loudly. It's the middle of the day but it's dark outside, overcast. I am crying so hard that Aunt Lyla picks me up and carries me from the building, and I sob into her chest, pulling away suddenly. It's as if she knows what I'm thinking. *You're not my mother.* She never forgives me, nor I her. Following the funeral, there is a reception at our house, a party. People smile, then stifle their smiles. Cocktails and a few haphazard bowls of mixed nuts, pretzels, candy. I eat so much I make myself sick. There is no one but my brother to play with, no other children have been allowed to come, and it is he who informs me that our mother is actually dead. No, no, I tell him. She is asleep forever—that's what Daddy said. Sleeping Beauty, that's how she looked on her bed, her skin a delicate shade of blue, like the throat of one of her lilies. Waiting for a kiss. I kissed her, her cool cheek, then shook her hard while Corb ran for our father. I search for him now in the tall gray figures of adults standing about our living room, the trousers of the men like tree trunks, the ladies' stickpins in the design of leaves, flowers, their diamonds like ice, their slender arms branching out to one another.

Of Charlotte's funeral I remember less, I was only four. But what I do remember is very vivid: my mother's white-gloved hand, enclosing my own; that the hand in this glove is warm and trembling.

Later, as Maggie and I drive past the Church of our Savior, I remember my mother's face, as she's about to enter the church to be married, from the photo in the wedding book. Her arm through her father's—what is the look on her face? One of dewy triumph: she is almost free.

I tell Maggie I need to stop at my mother's and Charlotte's graves, since we're a little early. She waits in the car.

It's sunny out, humid for Southern California—like damp silk on my skin. My feet easily find the way, although I haven't visited in years. Part of me is afraid I'll find nothing there, no marker, because you can't see it from a distance, but of course it's still there, plain, flat granite, the letters grayer and darker than the rest.

Marian Greer Mapes
February 13, 1924—May 21, 1964
And beside it:

Charlotte Anne Mapes
January 20, 1959—April 15, 1959

I get to my knees and blow off the grass clippings, wishing I'd brought flowers, that I could go back to our old house and clip some from the shrubs my mother planted. In my head, I say a little prayer. *Send me a sign.*

Of what?

Charlotte is a cipher, a tiny disintegrated skeleton, dust. I try to picture my mother instead, not her ashes or the braces on her teeth scorched to black bits, but her. The Marian of her photographs: hair the color of my own, her glorious smile . . . instead, I feel fear.

"I'm pregnant," I say. I can't call her 'Mother,' not 'Mommy,' though I probably did as a child. I don't know what to call her now. "Marian," I say, "I'm going to have a baby. Your grand-child."

I start to weep. *Come out,* my unspoken prayer goes on. *Show me. Not how to be a mother, you don't know about that. How to survive—you don't know about that either. Show me. Something. You must have something to teach.*

Out of the corner of my eye I see a form kneeling—the way my mother comes to me at night. The shame. Hands over her eyes. "Not that," I whisper, angry, and there really is someone kneeling in the distance, kneeling at a grave as I am now.

"Show me something else. Show me."

The church bell begins to toll. One, two, three, languorous and piercing; my eyes and heart sting, tighten with tears. Four, five, six, seven, my heart cracks and I am hot, sweat on my face and hands. I lick my fingers, salty, expecting blood. I'm twitch-ing, as though being shaken from the outside, a plane or a heli-copter flying low, fuselage breaking open, my heart splitting. The bell tolls on and on—it's noon and I'm fighting with my mother. I'm a woman, not a child. I'm a woman protecting my own child. My mother won't let me go and I don't know what she wants.

Part Two:
The Dollhouse

EIGHTEEN

There are the parrots. A flock of them flies by on a regular basis, pausing at our phone wires to argue and do tricks, hanging by their claws and poking their heads between their legs—sort of a skin-the-cat routine. They used to belong to somebody, I learned from a neighbor, but they escaped and are flourishing in the wild, if a suburb in Arcadia could be called wild. Originally there were four parrots. Now there are almost a dozen.

Maggie found this place for us both after I moved out of the Alta Vista finally, a house for rent in Arcadia with a paved-over pool, neglected for years and then damaged so severely in the last earthquake that the owners decided to get rid of it once and for all.

I live in the former pool house, while Maggie and her sons, Dylan and Willy, live in the main house.

My pool house is one room, two if you count the bathroom, but it's large with a sliding glass door. Overlooking the paved-over pool, of course, and surrounded by overgrown bamboo and banana trees that squeak incessantly, as if communing with unseen beasts and insects.

The birds that really sold me on the place, though, are the peacocks. They come over from the L.A. County Arboretum; how, without being hit by cars, is anybody's guess since they can't fly very well. Descended from Lucky Baldwin's peacocks, brought over from India at the height of his fortunes in silver and real estate, each spring they hop the fence and strut up and down the streets, the males shaking their tail feathers violently while the females pretend to pick at the lawns.

At nights they land on the roofs and scream their heads off. An unnerving sound, but one that I like for some reason.

It's a bizarre neighborhood, architecturally speaking. East meets West: Swiss chalets cut off at the knees, shingled and low to the ground, broad dichondra lawns dry around the edges from drought, and banks of tough green ivy. The streets curve around gently and rather uselessly, as if to steer one's attention away from the area's other famous neighbor besides the Arboretum: the Santa Anita Racetrack. Every day of the week you can hear the races, the mariachi bands, crowds roaring amid tinny bugles and the drone of the announcer.

And in my mind, I can hear the echo of other people at Santa Anita, people long gone. It was a way station for Japanese-Americans on their way to internment camps during World War II, according to Jackson. He told me during one of our short, friendly, civil phone conversations that Japanese-Americans were put up in horse stalls barely hosed down for the occasion. It's those people I think of at the Santa Anita racetrack, clutching whatever belongings and suitcases they were allowed to bring.

I keep in the pocket of whatever I'm wearing (maternity clothes invariably have pockets) a copy of my mother's death certificate. Sent to me by the hospital, attached to my mother's hospital records, this is my last and final record of her:

CERTIFICATE OF DEATH
STATE OF CALIFORNIA
USE BLACK INK ONLY

STATE FILE NUMBER			LOCAL REGISTRATION DISTRICT AND CERTIFICATE NUMBER

DECEDENT PERSONAL DATA

1A. NAME OF DECEDENT—FIRST (Given)	1B. MIDDLE	1C. LAST (Family)	2A. DATE OF DEATH—MO, DAY, YR, HR. HOUR	3. SEX
MARIAN	GREER	MAPES	MAY 21, 1964 6:50	F

4. RACE	5. HISPANIC—SPECIFY	6. DATE OF BIRTH—MO, DAY, YR	7. AGE (LAST BIRTHDAY) YEARS	IF UNDER 1 YEAR MONTHS / DAYS	IF UNDER 24 HOURS HOURS / MINUTES
CAUC.	☐ Yes ☒ No	FEB 13, 1924	39		

8. STATE OF BIRTH	9. CITIZEN OF WHAT COUNTRY	10A. FULL NAME OF FATHER	10B. STATE OF BIRTH	11A. FULL MAIDEN NAME OF MOTHER	11B. STATE OF BIRTH
CA	USA	MORGAN R. GREER	CA	CANDACE HALLOW	CA

12. MILITARY SERVICE?	13. SOCIAL SECURITY NO.	14. MARITAL STATUS	15. NAME OF SURVIVING SPOUSE OR WIFE, ENTER MAIDEN NAME
19___ TO 19___ ☒ NONE	572-30-9867	MARRIED	HAROLD MAPES

16A. USUAL OCCUPATION	16B. USUAL KIND OF BUSINESS OR INDUSTRY	16C. USUAL EMPLOYER	16D. YEARS IN OCCUPATION	17. EDUCATION—YEARS COMPLETED
HOUSEWIFE		OWN HOME	15	B.A.

USUAL RESIDENCE

18A. RESIDENCE—STREET AND NUMBER OR LOCATION			18B. CITY	18C. ZIP CODE
342 BONITAS STREET			LOS ANGELES	

18D. COUNTY	18E. NUMBER OF YEARS IN THIS COUNTY	18F. STATE OR FOREIGN COUNTRY	20. NAME, RELATIONSHIP, MAILING ADDRESS AND ZIP CODE OF INFORMANT
SAN MARINO	39		HAROLD MAPES

PLACE OF DEATH

19A. PLACE OF DEATH	19B. IF HOSPITAL SPECIFY ONE IF: ER/OP, DOA	19C. COUNTY	(HUSBAND) SAME
METHODIST HOSP.		SAN MARINO	

19D. STREET ADDRESS—STREET AND NUMBER OR LOCATION	19E. CITY
300 W. HUNTINGTON DR.	LOS ANGELES

CAUSE OF DEATH

21. DEATH WAS CAUSED BY: (ENTER ONLY ONE CAUSE PER LINE FOR A, B, AND C)		22. WAS BIOPSY PERFORMED?
IMMEDIATE CAUSE (A) ACUTE BARBITUATE POISONING	▶	☐ YES ☒ NO
DUE TO (B)	▶	24A. WAS AUTOPSY PERFORMED?
		☒ YES ☐ NO
DUE TO (C)	▶	24B. WAS IT USED IN DETERMINING CAUSE OF DEATH?
		☐ YES ☐ NO

23. OTHER SIGNIFICANT CONDITIONS CONTRIBUTING TO DEATH BUT NOT RELATED TO CAUSE GIVEN IN 21	25. WAS OPERATION PERFORMED FOR ANY CONDITION IN ITEM 21 OR 23? IF YES, LIST TYPE OF OPERATION AND DATE
NONE KNOWN	

PHYSICIAN'S CERTIFICATION

I CERTIFY THAT TO THE BEST OF MY KNOWLEDGE DEATH OCCURRED AT THE HOUR, DATE AND PLACE STATED FROM THE CAUSES STATED.	27B. SIGNATURE AND DEGREE OR TITLE OF CERTIFIER	27C. CERTIFIER'S LICENSE NUMBER	27D. DATE SIGNED
		NO EMBALMING	

27A. DECEDENT ATTENDED SINCE MONTH, DAY, YEAR	DECEDENT LAST SEEN ALIVE MONTH, DAY, YEAR	27E. TYPE ATTENDING PHYSICIAN'S NAME AND ADDRESS

CORONER'S USE ONLY

I CERTIFY THAT IN MY OPINION DEATH OCCURRED AT THE HOUR, DATE AND PLACE STATED FROM THE CAUSES STATED.	28A. SIGNATURE AND TITLE OF CORONER OR DEPUTY CORONER	28B. DATE SIGNED

29. MANNER OF DEATH	30A. PLACE OF INJURY	30B. INJURY AT WORK	30C. DATE OF INJURY	31. HOUR
	HOME	☐ YES ☒ NO	5/21/64	2:30

32. LOCATION (STREET AND NUMBER OF LOCATION AND CITY)	33. DESCRIBE HOW INJURY OCCURRED (EVENTS WHICH RESULTED IN INJURY)
	PROBABLE SUICIDE

FUNERAL DIRECTOR AND LOCAL REGISTRAR

34A. DISPOSITION(S)	34B. 10 400 OR FIELD, DESTINATION—NAME AND ADDRESS	34C. DATE MO, DAY, YEAR	34A. SIGNATURE OF EMBALMER	35B. LICENSE NUMBER

36A. NAME OF FUNERAL DIRECTOR (OR PERSON ACTING AS SUCH)	36B. LICENSE NO.	37. SIGNATURE OF LOCAL REGISTRAR	38. REGISTRATION DATE

STATE REGISTRAR

A.	B.	C.	D.	E.	F.	CENSUS TRACT

VS-11 (REV. 1-90) — MAKE NO ERASURES, WHITEOUTS, OR OTHER ALTERATIONS — 01-9-1-712

Maggie and I spend a lot of time at the kitchen table talking about pregnancy, kids, dead mothers—a subject I am mostly silent about. For comic relief Maggie tells me about working in Dr. Grimes' office: the semi-military environment complete with out-of-date medical information that Maggie is always trying to correct with the few patients allowed her—no, it is not necessary to scrub the breasts with a disinfectant before breastfeeding; no, one does not need to be strictly horizontal to deliver a baby, and so on. Another of our favorite subjects is going over what went wrong in our marriages.

"I just don't understand Ed," Maggie says, biting into an iced animal cookie. "Umm, I'd forgotten how good these are. Do you like the pink or white best?" She pushes the open bag across the table to me.

"I can't tell the difference, can you?" I say, reaching into the bag, only about a dozen left.

"Pink," she says, chewing. "Pink is best."

That's the other thing we do—eat. We eat Dylan and Willy's cookies and graham crackers and kid yogurts and we've both rediscovered macaroni and cheese. We eat bags of baby carrots and sliced up-apples with the skin peeled off. Vegetables and dip. We also eat a lot of cheese—cheese with crackers, cheese sticks, melted cheese on tortillas or toast—and milk, jugs of it. For dinner we eat whatever the kids are having, scrambled eggs, peas with butter and salt, pizza cut up into little squares, chicken nuggets and ketchup. Better this than adult junk food, we figure, as we munch on Nilla wafers and tiny cookies shaped like teddy bears. A passing phase, we tell each other, this eating.

"The thing is, Ed really is a decent father," Maggie says, "though he's high most nights. He didn't mind reading the boys books. Book after book after book. He reads nice and slow. So I don't understand," she says, munching another animal cookie, "how Ed can be a pretty good father—"

"And be such a lousy husband," I fill in. She says this

frequently. It's either this or she switches the subject to me, almost in my third trimester of pregnancy now; what am I going to do once the baby's born? Have I talked to Jackson lately? She's fascinated by him, his dilemma as the biological father of this child, a fact I don't like to be reminded of.

What Maggie doesn't understand is how I've allowed myself to get into the mess I'm in now.

"Sooner or later," Maggie says, "actually, sooner rather than later, what with the baby coming, you and Gregg are going to have to decide—"

Dylan wanders in carrying a toy toolbox, followed by his brother. "What you say, Mommy?"

"We're talking about babies, sweetheart. What a big job they are. How some people have no idea."

"True," I say.

"Where my orange screwdriver?" Dylan asks.

"Chucks," Willy says. He's not big on talking, Maggie says. His other favorite words are 'ball,' and 'gaga' for dog.

"Your trucks are in your room, Willy," Maggie says. "Maybe Dylan will help you look for them. And the last time I saw your screwdriver, Dylan, it was in the living room. Under the chair."

"It *not* there. I look there."

"Are you sure?"

He takes a plastic wrench from his toolbox. "I fix you," he says, first going to Maggie, then me. "I a fix-it man."

"He's got the midwife and the fix-it man a little confused," Maggie explains.

Dylan touches the wrench to my belly. "First I wrench, then I plier. Then I hammer."

"'Atta boy, Dylan," Maggie says. "You're going to be a great midwife."

"Mommy, where my orange screwdriver?"

Dylan is almost three, Willy is one, and both are mostly unaffected by the absence of their father, Maggie's now officially ex-husband, Ed. Other than Saturday afternoons when he comes for the boys, they don't see him much. Dylan simply continues to pretend that Daddy is coming home soon—to this home, the new house, no matter what Maggie tells him. After work, he says. Daddy come home. After trip, Daddy come home, to new house.

Willy doesn't say anything about Ed, except "da."

When I say Dylan's unaffected, I mean he's not affected in the ways you'd expect. He doesn't cry any more than usual, Maggie says; he isn't sleeping poorly or showing signs of aggression. Just a peculiar doggedness: he will search for a toy and search for it until he finds it. Start at one end of the house and work his way across.

A more definite sign is that he refused to think of me as anything but a boy or a man when we first moved in. "But you know Theo's a girl, Dylan, a woman. You've never said she was a boy before."

"Where he living?" he asked, according to Maggie.

"In the little house out back, the pool house. Theo is a girl, Dylan. A woman. You know that. She's going to have a baby, in fact. Won't that be fun?"

"Why he not living here?"

"She *is* living here, but in the pool house."

"Why he not living in this house?"

And so on. Maybe in his mind there had to be a father somewhere, a male figure where there wasn't one in our co-joined households, so he happened upon me. Maggie said he'd never mixed up gender before and regularly assigned girl or boy status to people, places, and things, but he was insistent about this.

"You stand up go pee," he told me.

"No, Dylan. I sit down."

"No! No! You stand up!" On the verge of tears. I looked to Maggie for assistance, who only said, "Never mind, Dylan honey. We can talk about it later."

Even when Dylan happened to walk in on me sitting on the toilet one day, he wasn't convinced. "Sometime you sit down. You need go poop?"

"I'll explain later, Dylan. Would you mind if I went potty alone? Please?"

After some consideration, he backed out of the room. "You need private," he said. "That all right." He closed the door, without slamming it, but called out, as I knew he would, "You don't flush!"

"No, Dylan. I won't flush."

I learned about this the day we moved in, when I went down the hall to use the bathroom.

"Um, Theo?" Maggie said. "Would you mind not flushing?"

"To save water, right? No problem."

"It's partly that," she said.

Dylan followed me down the hall, as if he had a bead on me. Green-yellow eyes like a cat's. He has freckles and sandy hair that stands up on end. While I was in the bathroom, he stood sentry right outside the door. "Mommy, he won't flush?"

"I told her not to, sweetie. It's okay. You can relax, I think."

I could hear him breathing out there. "You done, man? Mommy, the man done?"

Automatically, without thinking, I flushed. Dylan broke into an instant wail. "He flushed! He flushed!"

"He's got this thing, you see. The flushing sound upsets him," Maggie tried to explain. "Oh, never mind, Theo. In about two-and-a-half years, you'll understand."

Dylan was sobbing, screaming on the floor. The ultimate betrayal.

It took a solid week for me to repair relations, and then I was his favorite person on the face of the earth. He followed me everywhere. The second he woke up at the crack of dawn, he tumbled out of his house and into mine, Willy trailing after him in a soggy diaper. "It morning time! Time to get up! Time to play! Get up get up get up man."

Three days a week I drive my father to and from his Spanish Conversation class at Pasadena Community College. A favor he detests. His other eye has developed a cataract, which often happens in these cases. We found this out when he had a wreck shortly after he began driving again, following the operation on his first cataract. The police officer ordered him to get a physical and that's when the second cataract was diagnosed, since Dad himself wouldn't pay attention to the signs.

Every time I pick him up he sits in my car with his notebook on his knees and tells me next time he'll take the bus, thank you. "It'll pick me up a block away from the house, no reason not to."

"Dad, no. What if you trip on the curb or don't see a car coming? I really don't mind, Dad. While you're at class, I get my errands done." I get his errands done as well, his grocery shopping too.

When I drop Dad off out in front of PCC and wait till he's safely inside the building, I'm like a mother dropping off her child. He wobbles away carrying his notebook with his homework. I try to picture him inside. What he says in class. Does he talk? I imagine he might, in stumbling Spanish, try to join in—which breaks my heart. Is it pregnancy that makes me so touched by him? He who has caused me so much difficulty?

The nights Gregg isn't working, I drive up, park around back in the carport, and walk inside. The door's never locked, although this is a crummy neighborhood. Usually Gregg is watching TV or doodling at the piano, and stands up suddenly when he sees me, stubbing out his cigarette, as if surprised. As if I just happen to be in the neighborhood, dropping by on a whim.

Since he mostly works nights, we can't leave too much to chance. We talk on the phone:

"So what are you up to?" I say.

"Tonight we've got a bar mitzvah, tomorrow a studio session—both should be over around eleven."

"Meaning you'll be home around midnight?"

"About. Earlier if I'm lucky. The night after, Tuesday, I don't have to work."

"Free all night?"

"Unless something comes up."

Often something does. Whenever I visit, Gregg turns off the ringer on the phone, letting the answering machine take the calls, which come all night. The next morning he plays back the messages. "Gregg—Dan. High school reunion, Monday the 26th, eight o'clock, set up at seven—the Bonaventure, downtown. Cocktail party, Tuesday the 27th, set up at five—1620 Jacon Way in Pacific Palisades. Formal." "Gregg—Andy. Session at After-hours Recording, Friday the 29th, nine. Same place next night, Afterhours, same time, nine."

Occasionally I go with him to weddings or cocktail parties. Gregg plays in five or six different bands and combos, jazz, classical, rock; sometimes he plays alone and sings, standards like "Witchcraft," "Lonely Avenue," "Smoke Gets in Your Eyes." He knows more songs than anyone, the result of working everywhere over the years—Caribbean cruise ships, Alaskan bars, Southwestern desert towns. As a teenager during summer vacations he worked a string of pizza parlors across the Midwest, banging out polka tunes such as "Beer Barrel Polka" and "I Don't Want Her, You Can Have Her, She's Too Fat for Me."

Now he drives a dented blue station wagon that only gets eight miles to the gallon, but he needs the space for his electric piano and can't afford to trade up just yet to something nicer, like a van, or even a better station wagon.

But things are improving for him economically. He's sold a few songs lately and has even been in a couple of music videos as part of a session band, a kind of musician "extra." In one he showed me he wore a black shirt, dark glasses, his hair slicked back—he looked terrific. He's gussied up his rental house, too, on my say-so, and kicked out his traveling musician roommates who were never around much anyway. No more dirty dishes in the sink or cans of cat food with the forks still in them; no longer does the bathroom resemble a gas station's. Together we've torn up the old linoleum throughout the house and put down carpeting. He's even bought a decent couch.

"We could get married," I said a couple of weeks ago, experimentally. "Then we'd have two incomes. But not until the baby's older," I add under my breath. We rarely talk about the baby.

Gregg shifted in the bed beside me. "Theo, you're already married."

"What, is bigamy a problem for you?"

Silence.

"Not funny," I said, "huh."

While at Gregg's, I try not to think of it, my marriage or my pregnancy, now in its twenty-seventh week; the ligaments in my belly stretch, my skin itches.

"Do you think we should get married?" Gregg asked the other night after we made love. It was dark and quiet in his room, except for the hum and glow of his old clock radio, John Lennon's head taped to its front.

"I guess we could," I said. "Later on maybe." After my divorce, I meant. After the baby's born.

"Okay," he said, holding me loosely in his arms. "It's settled then."

Maybe not the most romantic proposal but, as Gregg said, it was settled. Decided. Actually I've talked to a lawyer on the phone, Maggie's lawyer as a matter of fact, who says getting a divorce should be a snap in my case, provided I establish residency in California. The house in Stonewall Creek is not in my name, she pointed out, so Jackson and I have no community property to divide, other than our Blazer. Furthermore, she added, (I swear I could *hear* her smiling, crisply), I gather there are no children? "No," I said, rubbing my belly frantically as if I could make it speak for me and tell the truth.

Up until the other night, though, my future with Gregg was a subject he and I generally avoided—that and the word 'love.' We didn't define our relationship or say what we meant to each other; we didn't even declare the topic off-limits. Which probably has something to do with why we still don't discuss my pregnancy.

The thing is, I can picture marrying Gregg, our life together. We'd buy a house, an old bungalow in Pasadena or something closer to the coast, though we'd have to borrow from my father— everything is so expensive, five times what it is in Colorado. Practical matters aside, Gregg would have a room for composing music; me, an office. A king-sized bed in our bedroom with a dozen down pillows, 200-count cotton sheets with violets trailing across. Casement windows that open out into a courtyard with cactus, gardenia, white lilies, a magnolia tree with leathery petals, enormous seed pods like drumsticks . . .

Only one little problem. The baby. I try to picture a nursery—can't. Try to picture living in the house with Jackson instead—can't. Try to picture living there alone with the baby—can't. I close my eyes and try harder. Picture living in a house with Gregg and the baby. Next to the music room and my office is the baby's nursery, a white gauzy room with a wicker rocker, filmy curtains, a crib. Myself in a pinstriped bathrobe, lace lapels—no. Wrong detail. A robe of one hundred percent cotton velour. Yes. And the baby, ah, the baby; sweet round head dozing at my breast, sweet little sleepy fingers . . . .

A feeling of déjà vu: I once wrote copy for such a scene, for a catalog. Pima cotton baby blanket, the silkiest cotton there is; crib sheets of English flannel; a lamb's wool pad; a mobile with a music box made in Germany. All stuff I can't afford anyway.

"Gregg," I ask him one night in bed, "remember that woman you almost married?" We haven't seen each other in days, he's been working so much. "Your fiancée. What was her name again?"

"Marcy."

"What was she like?" I ask.

"Well, uhm." Character assessments, talking in general, is not Gregg's strong suit. "She was nice, I guess."

Nice, my father's favorite word, although on Gregg's lips it doesn't convey a whole value system as much as it does vagueness. That is one aspect of Jackson's character I miss—how the man could talk. We'd stay up all night talking about people we knew or had known, verbally dismantling their psyches like other people take apart cars.

"What do you mean, Gregg—nice?"

"Well, she was . . . smart."

Now he sounds wistful, which I like even less.

"What did she do?"

"She's an accountant."

"You're kidding." I actually snort.

"What's wrong with that?"

"I just can't picture you with an accountant." A part of me feels insulted—she should've been an artist or something sexier, a dancer or a cabaret singer. Red hair. Juicy lips. Marcy I imagined to be wearing a taupey 50-50 suit, no hips or bust, sensible shoes. Figuring out their monthly expenses on a solar calculator while trailing after Gregg, straightening up, setting to rights pillows she'd needle-pointed herself—hard little thrifty pillows with sayings like "A penny saved is a penny earned" and "Only fools part with their money."

I can't decide whether Marcy was quiet and dull but sweet, or no-nonsense and as organized as drill sergeant. "But what was she *like*?" I pester Gregg.

He sighs. "I don't know. She was . . . pretty."

I imagine a cute turned-up nose; sharp, white, rodent teeth.

Gregg can see I'm still not satisfied. "What does it matter, Theo? I haven't heard from her in two years! What do you have to be jealous about, it's not like she's in the picture anymore—like your ex. If it's anyone with something to worry about, it's me."

Jackson: he's always with us, annoyingly, even if his actual name doesn't come up. "I've spoken to a lawyer," I say. "A divorce lawyer. She's sending me some forms to fill out."

"So how long until you get the divorce?"

"She didn't really say. I'm just curious," I say, turning the subject back to Gregg and his old girlfriend. "Whether you loved her, for instance."

"Marcy? Look, will you quit asking me about her?" He flushes, as if I were angling for details about their sex life. Not that I wouldn't. At the beginning of my marriage with Jackson we talked about that stuff all the time, discussing old flames and what they did or did not do in bed. Maybe it even turned us on.

Gregg just likes to have sex, he doesn't want to talk about it.

"Was she good in bed?"

"God, Theo!" Gregg gets up and storms out of the room. "I need a smoke. I'll be outside."

I haul myself out of bed and follow him outside to the small flagstone patio. "Okay, I'm sorry. I got carried away."

He flicks a spent match down the steep hillside in front of the house, where I imagine a slight breeze sends it tripping and spinning past mustard weeds and paste-colored gravel.

"You shouldn't do that, Gregg. The drought. Everything's so dry."

He won't even look at me.

"I'm sorry I upset you," I continue. "Can't we forget all about it? Please?" I press up against him. My belly bows out to meet his pubic bone—how can he pretend to ignore my pregnancy? Soon I'll have to buy more maternity clothes, not to mention things for the baby.

"You're still mad," I say, "aren't you?" For being so clumsy sometimes, Gregg can be stiller than a rock when angry. "Why are you mad?"

"I don't know," he says.

"Is it because I'm pregnant?"

Whenever I dare to bring it up, he always looks at me as though I'm prevaricating. And what does he think of the subject? Who knows? Maybe it's because he's not the verbal type that the subject of my pregnancy seems more avoidable than unavoidable. Despite all the hints I've thrown his way of late:

"God, I miss lying on my stomach. I can't sleep on my back anymore either—so the books say."

Silence.

"Do you like this maternity top? It's new. Not bad for J.C. Penney's."

Silence.

Just the other day I mused out loud: "I wonder what it will be like, having a baby."

That one seemed to really throw him for a loop. He looked at me, alarmed, as though just hearing the news for the first time.

"Gregg," I say now.

"What?"

"I'm having a baby."

"I know."

"So what do you think? Are you happy? Are you sad? Mad? You never say anything."

He smashes out his cigarette on the side of the house. "I'm not sure what to say."

"Say what you feel."

"I'm not sure what I feel."

He isn't mean about it, Gregg is incapable of true meanness, but he won't respond, won't simply say, *I'm not the baby's father.* That's what's really bothering him, what's bothering us both. Meanwhile my hair grows thicker by the day, my complexion as creamy as when I was twenty. I sweat more and pee constantly and keep a stack of baby books in plain sight at the pool house, where Gregg drops by now and then. He doesn't notice. He does notice what's on the radio and asks if he can switch the station.

My belly is like a drum when I thump it, like a watermelon—there is something growing, something delicious. My nausea long over with, I feel incredibly sensual, my nipples constantly erect. I bought a nursing bra (this too Gregg didn't notice or maybe he thought it was some kind of erotic contraption), just so I can let down the flaps now and then.

Day in and day out I ask myself this: why don't I just confront Gregg? Maggie asks me this as well. At first she found the situation amusing, like a prank we might've cooked up as teenagers, but now she is worried. I have no idea what I'm getting into, she says, being a mother.

"A single mother no less," she says one morning, standing over me while I sit outside, where the pool used to be, my nursing flaps down, sunning my breasts.

"Maybe I'm not going to be a single mother."

"If you're referring to Gregg, isn't he having a little trouble accepting the fact you're pregnant? By another man? Not that I can blame him exactly." She stares down at me, her blue eyes iridescent.

"Stop hovering, Maggie. Don't you have to go deliver some babies or something?" I've volunteered to sit with the boys today while she's at work, since their babysitter is sick.

"Put your flaps up," she says, breaking into a laugh that sounds irritated nonetheless. "Here come the kids."

NINETEEN

After a night at Gregg's I stop at the grocery store on the way home and when I pull into the driveway, there's the Blazer with its Colorado plates parked in front with a trailer hitched to it. *Oh hell, he must've gotten a job.*

Trying to act unperturbed, I lift the bags of groceries from the trunk, prop them against the sides of my belly (figuring my hands can't shake this way) and start towards the pool house.

There's Jackson. Reclining in the chaise, in jeans and a T-shirt, sunglasses on so that I can't see if he's asleep or awake.

"I got the job," he says. "Here I am."

"Congratulations," I say stiffly. "You sure didn't waste any time moving out here, did you?"

"The job doesn't start till August but I wanted to get settled."

"Oh. Right," I say, the grocery bags still framing my belly. Jackson stares.

"Wow," he says. The baby stirs, lands a good kick to my ribs. Damn. How after all this time even I began to believe this baby wasn't his.

"Let me get those for you," he says, rising from the chaise and reaching for the bags. He follows me inside, sets the bags on the counter while I turn on lights, open the small window on the north side.

Jackson brings in more groceries—bread, milk, juice, fruit, cheese—and I put them away. Just as we did at Stonewall Creek. An entirely normal and domestic moment. We pick up where we left off, an everyday sort of feeling, as when we used to make our own breakfasts side by side in the kitchen, cereal for him, yogurt for me.

"I'll finish up," I say. "Have a seat." I gesture to the carpet; there are no chairs, only my futon on the other side of the room.

162

He remains standing and if he's knocked out by the sight of me this pregnant, he's careful not to show it.

Only a little. His eyes drop to my belly, as if he's waiting for me to remove it, like a jacket or a sweater.

"It doesn't come off, Jackson."

"What?"

"My stomach."

"I know." He sounds doubtful. I notice he's still wearing his wedding band, and wonder if he's noticed yet that mine is missing. "Does it hurt?" he asks. "Your stomach?"

"It feels good, like a good hard peach."

"Can you feel the baby move?"

"All the time."

So when are we going to get to it? The subject or subjects we're avoiding. Jackson takes me out for an early dinner. We drive in the Blazer—how many times did we drive to town in this car?—which I greet like an old friend (though I glare at the trailer), patting its road-ragged hood, splattered insects on the windshield, mud on its flanks: more warmth than I can show Jackson.

At Margaritas on Rosemead, I hold my breath to see what Jackson will order to drink.

"I'll have a—" Jackson pauses. "A Coke," he says. Casually.

"Still not drinking?" I say.

"Nope."

I gather there's more to say on the subject, but he's not going to enlighten me just yet. With some sadness I realize we're not close anymore; we're like former compatriots about to go our separate ways, or we would if not for the baby.

"So where are you going to live?" I ask.

"You sound so tired," he says.

"I *am* tired." I eat a tortilla chip, noisily.

"Theo, why shouldn't I move here? Thousands of people do each year."

"Don't you read the paper?" I say, my mouth full of chip. "Everybody's leaving California. They're moving to Colorado."

"Aren't you even going to ask who offered me the job?"

"Who?"

"Costa Mesa Junior College."

Down by the beach, Orange County. "Oh." I bite into my next chip, which shatters. I brush the shards into my hand, not knowing what to do with them. I arrange them into a little pile on the table. "Jackson, I'm happy for you that you got the job, congratulations and everything, but it's probably unrealistic to expect me to be ecstatic about your moving here, okay?"

"I'm not expecting anything, Theo. I figure we'll just— adjust. Over time."

Our food arrives and I lose myself in my chimichanga. I'm off baby carrots and macaroni and cheese these days and craving Mexican. At least every other day I get take-out from this place, chimichangas for Maggie and me, quesadillas for Dylan and Willy.

"You've got sauce on your belly," Jackson says.

I look down and sure enough, a red glob of salsa stares up at me with two chunks of green chile for eyes. "This keeps happening," I say. "No matter how I drape the napkin, no matter how careful I am."

"It's like a big shelf," Jackson sympathizes. "It just catches things." He tries to dab it with his napkin but I veer away from him. The baby starts kicking again, one-two, one-two; I wonder if my belly trembles, if Jackson can see.

"I wish you all the luck with your new job," I say in the car, "but your moving out here isn't going to change anything between us."

"You know, you keep making that speech," Jackson says. "Why? What are you really trying to say?"

I lift a hand in the air futilely: who knows? Then for some strange reason we both begin to laugh. For a moment, I think we're going to hug each other, the bad months between us gone, simply evaporated, the baby with its rightful father . . . but what about Gregg? No, too much has happened, I'm in too deep, I can't change my mind now just because of an impulse. And there's my lawyer to consider; when do I tell Jackson about her? The forms waiting on my desk, forms I must fill out and sign. The first step toward filing for divorce.

"Jackson, tell me again. Why do you want to move here?" And go and spoil everything, I'm thinking. "If it's because of the baby, there's so much traffic between here and the beach. It'd take you less time to fly in from Colorado."

"I've changed, Theo. Things have changed. I quit drinking, for one thing."

We're stalled at a light by the racetrack now, tall skinny palm trees and the mountains beyond that, suffocating in smog. A pounding behind my eyes, a smog headache.

"Doesn't it make any difference to you that I quit drinking?" he asks me.

"That you *say* you've quit drinking."

"I nearly killed myself in the car, you know, myself and some other people."

"What?"

"On 287, about a month after you left."

Highway 287, our main road to town, that stretch of it is one of the most dangerous roads in the state. Still, I find myself skeptical. "You had an accident?"

"Almost. The car in front of me was going too slow, I decided, and I was pissed. You were gone, you'd left me—I was pissed all the time, drunk all the time. So I passed him."

"In a passing lane?"

"Nope. Passed him on a double yellow line."

"God, Jackson."

"Just missed a head-on with a Safeway truck on its way to Laramie. By seconds. Inches. The Safeway truck swerved, then just kept on going. Probably thought, 'Just another crazy drunk fuck on the road.' It would've been a two-car, one-rig crash, four people dead including me."

I nod slowly, picturing the near-slaughter of it all, having seen it when other people had lost their lives on 287—the paramedics, the jaws of life, the medi-vac bearing its gory load to Poudre Valley Hospital. The white cross by the side of the road a couple of months later.

"After that I decided to drop in on an AA meeting." Jackson smiles wryly. AA, what he said he'd never do. "I've been sober 189 days now."

The light turns green and the stranglehold of traffic loosens its grip; one by one the cars creep onward, the majority peeling off into a turn lane for the racetrack. I expect my headache to ease up—the relief of Jackson's being alive, sober, *in recovery,* as it's called—but now my head threatens to burst. I seem to be stumped for words, shaken. "I can't quite think what to say, Jackson."

"Don't say anything. I wanted you to know."

We don't speak again until he parks in front of the house. He reaches behind him, grabbing his canvas bag from the backseat. That oddly titillating canvas bag of his, though I hardly recognize it. It's usually full of books, but now it's full of what appear to be clothes.

"Uh, Jackson, what are you doing?"

"Getting my stuff."

"Your stuff for what?"

We don't even make it past the front lawn before Jackson launches into questions about the baby.

"Is this where you plan to live with the baby?"

"Why, is something wrong?"

"Nothing wrong, I guess." From across the lawn a peacock spots us and unfurls his tail, turning this way and that, shaking the iridescent feathers violently. "What's with him?" Jackson says.

"I don't know. It's not mating season anymore, but this bird seems to have forgotten that."

The peacock approaches, eyeing my dun-colored shirt and strutting half-circles around me.

"Listen," I tell the bird, "you're confusing me with somebody else." I hurry up the driveway, only to be pursued by the peacock. And Jackson, who continues asking questions. Do I have a doctor? How often are the appointments? When's the due date again? What about an amnio? I explain over my shoulder why I decided against it—how at age thirty-five the risk of Down's goes up just slightly, whereas it rises more significantly at thirty-six. The peacock calls forlornly, *He-elp, He-elp,* before flapping off to the roof of Maggie's house.

"You should know something, Theo. I want this baby. I always wanted a baby with you."

"You did?"

We're standing at the sliding glass door of the pool house, the red sunset reflecting warmth on our faces, our skin, as when we said our vows. I invite Jackson inside.

I'm more attracted to him than I think I should be; then again, maybe this is normal. Maybe the attraction never quite goes away. I borrow an air mattress from Maggie, and Jackson and I bed down on opposite ends of the pool house, except I can't fall asleep.

At midnight I'm still awake. I get up to go pee, only a trickle comes out, as if the baby is standing on my bladder, pinching it. Back in bed I toss and turn, get up to pee again, then remember the phone. Gregg often calls late at night, between sets or after shows. I tiptoe over to my desk, where the phone is, to unplug it.

I jump when I hear Jackson's voice: "What are you doing?"

He's sleeping by the desk, and it occurs to me he thinks I'm about to get in bed with him. "Unplugging the phone," I say.

"Why?"

"So it won't wake us up."

Jackson rolls over, sits up, his white T-shirt blue in the moonlight, and I'm filled with sexual feeling, or perhaps it's only a memory of longing, of lust. Jackson always sleeps without underwear and I wonder if he's wearing any now, if he woke up with an erection.

"Or," he asks, "were you expecting a phone call?"

"No." My belly sticks out so far, so heavily, that I feel myself being pulled down, down toward him.

"I thought maybe your boyfriend would call." His voice is calm and matter-of-fact, almost friendly. "The musician."

"You've been following me—" I back away from him, stumbling.

"Your father told me, Theo."

"You *are* following me. My father doesn't even know!"

"A friend of his saw you at a gig with him, the musician—a wedding or something—and mentioned it to your father. The friend assumed it was your husband, naturally. Since you're so goddamned pregnant." There it is at last, the edge in his voice. The disappointment, the anger.

"I'm sorry, I'm really, really sorry."

"Oh Christ," he says, starting to cry, "do you ever think how this is for me? Shut out of this whole thing, some *jerk* taking my place. I don't even know why . . . what happened to us?"

"Why did you let me go!"

"Why did you leave!"

"I tried to tell you I thought I was pregnant, Jackson." My face feels cold and tight, my mouth hardly works. "The day I left. Do you know what you said? You said 'I don't want to talk about this now.'"

"I know what I said, Theo, and believe me, I'm living to regret it every day. At that point I couldn't bear to think—it seemed out of the realm of possibility—"

"You pushed me away," I say. "Right out the door. You pushed me away with a baby. Your black moods, your drinking . . . ."

"Just one thing," Jackson says. "Does *he* know I'm the father? Your *boyfriend?*" His voice is bitter.

"He knows."

"All right." Jackson rolls away from me, wrapping his blanket up over his shoulders. "I don't want to know any more."

"Jackson?" It must be several hours later.

"What?" He answers immediately.

"Were you awake?"

"I've *been* awake. Listening to you snore. You never used to snore."

"It's the pregnancy," I say, chastened because he knows about Gregg now. Gregg, who sleeps right through my snoring, snoring that even wakes me up sometimes. I sense, in Jackson's voice, that he's not going to punish me further about Gregg, for which I'm grateful. He'd even recognize Gregg's name if I told it to him; all those talks we used to have about each other's past relationships.

Half asleep, I'm thinking about the wedding vows Jackson and I made to each other, to honor, to love, to cherish, to respect— or is it protect? I mean to say something to this effect, wedding vows and how we kept some of them at least. But instead I say, "People can't change, Jackson, can they? Not really. Whatever marks are on them don't go away."

"People can change, Theo. But I think you're talking about your mother."

"She couldn't change," I say.

"No."

"She was trapped."

"Do you know," he says, "this is the first time you've ever talked to me about your mother, willingly?"

"Yeah," I say. I tell him about her hospital records, her death certificate, how I've learned more about her, but how, in a sense, I know less than ever.

"Maybe it's because you're having a baby," he says. "You'll be able to get some kind of perspective on all this."

"What about you?" I ask. "You're having a baby. Are you going to get a new perspective on *your* parents?"

I wait for his answer a long time. "Probably," he says. "Whether I want to or not."

"I know what you mean."

"I can't help asking this, Theo—"

"What?"

"Did you love me?"

"Yes. Of course." I almost say *always*.

He sighs. "I'm still in love with you, I think. Did you leave me because of sex?"

"Sex? Come on, Jackson. I can't believe you're asking me this," I say. "It's so male."

"Well?"

"Sex was great."

"Then why?"

"Why what?"

"Then why are you fucking somebody else?" His voice has gone hard again. "What's his name, Theo?"

"It's none of your business."

"*What's his name?*" At each word he slams his hand into the wood paneling and I jump.

"All right. It's Gregg."

"The musician? *That* Gregg? Your old boyfriend Gregg?"

"Yes."

"You went back to him! So it is the sex."

"No."

"You used to talk about how hot he was."

"Can we not talk about this anymore, please? It's not as if I left you for him."

"Isn't it?"

"No. I didn't leave you for him. It happened after."

"Okay," he says. "Okay, then. Just tell me what was wrong with us, besides the fact I pushed you away."

"Your drinking—"

"My drinking. Yes," he says. "A definite factor."

"Maybe the only factor," I say. "Maybe the other stuff was just linked to that."

"My drinking wasn't the only factor, Theo. The other factor was you."

"What do you mean?"

"That you're so wounded. You know what I mean, Theo. Your mother, your childhood. It screwed you up," he says. "Undoubtedly. I don't know if you're really capable of a long-term relationship."

It takes me a full minute. "What did you say? I'm wounded? I'm screwed up? What about you? *You're* not screwed up?" The room is so black, I can barely make out his shape. "Wait a minute. First, you want to know what was wrong with us, never mind that you completely pushed me away—then you tell me you love me. Still. Now I'm 'wounded,' 'screwed up!'" I imagine a bird, blighted wings, a missing beak, unable to take nourishment. I'm strangling the sheet between my hands. "I'm screwed up! Is that what you came all this way to tell me?"

"I came all this way, Theo, to take a job. To be a father to our baby. You I've given up on. What do you care? What with your *boyfriend* and all. Does he fuck you when you're this pregnant? How does that work anyway? Does it turn him on that you're carrying another man's child?"

"Get out."

"You're pretty messed up all on your own, Theo, with or without me." With that he's up, pulling on his pants in the dark, zipping them. I press my hands to my bloated belly, thinking of my infidelity, now and four years ago, only a year into our marriage, barely after our first anniversary; what was the matter with me? I felt driven to do it, not by Jackson and not by Gregg necessarily. By me. The problem was me. When Jackson proposed to me in Europe, my first thought was no, I couldn't marry him. I couldn't be faithful. Not to him, even him whom I loved; not to anyone.

Jackson is in the bathroom, peeing. Ridding himself of the body's poisons—how I wish I could do the same.

We are both dirty and flawed, irrevocably so, and there is nothing to be done about it.

"The reason you left me, Theo," Jackson says on his way out the sliding glass door, his canvas bag slung over his shoulder, "is this: you're a liar. A liar to yourself. You don't have a clue what the truth is."

TWENTY

I'm at my father's, after swearing to myself I'd avoid him forever-more—let him find his own way to PCC, let him take the bus. Let him be robbed. Let him freeze, let him starve.

"Dad, how could you?" He's sitting on his front steps ready for Spanish class, notebook on his knees. "How could you tell Jackson about that *friend* of yours seeing me at the wedding with—with—" I draw a deep and sudden breath, let it out. "What in the world happened, Dad? What exactly did you tell Jackson?"

"*I* didn't know." He stands up, nearly tripping.

"Didn't know what?"

"I didn't know what Mrs. Fracht was talking about."

"Mrs. Fracht?"

"You remember her, we used to see her at church. Anyway she called me because she'd seen you at a wedding reception—she thought it was you, she wasn't positive—"

"She could've introduced herself at least."

"Curly hair, *very* pregnant. The picture of your mother when she was pregnant, she said. She mentioned you were with your husband, that he was playing the piano. At first I thought when she said she'd seen you with your husband, I thought—you know—that maybe you and Jackson had reconciled . . . but she was talking about a musician. I went along with it. What else was I to do? You might've told me you were seeing someone."

"So you made it your business to go and tell Jackson."

"He asked me! He asked me how you were—"

"And you told him the latest. That I'm seeing someone."

"Well, yes."

"Maybe you thought Jackson ought to know," I say.

My father shrugs. "Maybe I did, I don't know."

I look at him with his pens clipped to the pocket of his sports shirt, one hand splayed defensively—a good boy doing his best. It isn't worth scolding him or hating him for anything.

"Okay, Dad, forget it. Come on." I shoo him toward the car.

Though I'm reluctant to introduce Gregg to my family quite yet, I'm reminded how well things are going between us. We're even discussing the baby of late, and the house we will rent together after it's born. A couple of times now Gregg's even patted my belly—a bit tentatively—asking me do I think it will be a boy or a girl, which do I prefer?

Either, I say. In fact I can't picture either. Lately I can't picture a baby at all. Not a human baby. Animal babies maybe, or aliens.

I ask him which does he want? A boy or a girl?

Either, he says. I'd be happy with either.

We are as shy as if this were our first date, then he jumps up to crank the volume on the radio, to catch a particular riff on a song. He continues to sell songs and has just been asked to co-write a score for a possible public broadcasting show, a task that will keep him up all hours composing.

I do think he'll be a good father, though, gentle and kind. Maybe a little preoccupied with his work, but who isn't? Perhaps this baby is just what he needs.

That the baby isn't his never comes up between us, of course, because what would be the point? We both know that to talk about it at this stage might destroy us. It's enough that we plan to get married someday.

"Have you filled out those forms yet?" he's taken to asking.

The forms to set my divorce in motion, he means. Whatever happened to the Gregg I knew? The musician who avoided commitment or any other move to settle down? I'm thrilled he wants to settle down with me, I really am, but—

"I'm working on it," I tell him. In truth, I can never seem to get past page one.

Within a week of Jackson's visit, I talk to him on the phone and we both apologize. What's important here, we agree, is the baby. Civility for the sake of the baby.

"How's the job going?" I ask in this new spirit of trying to get along.

"I haven't started yet, remember?"

"Oh, yeah."

"How about you, Theo? So are you taking childbirth classes? I forgot to ask when I was there."

"I've been to one class so far," I say uncomfortably.

"What type is it? Lamaze, Bradley—? I've been reading up."

"Lamaze."

There's a pause.

"Is *he* going with you?" he says.

"Gregg? Uh, when he can . . ."

"It doesn't seem fair," Jackson says.

"I thought we weren't going to—"

"Right, right. Sorry."

Quickly I change the subject. "How's your new place?"

"I haven't moved in yet. I'm holding out for this place nearer the beach, so I'm rooming with a guy till then."

"How're you swinging that, a place on the beach?"

"Near the beach, I said. Two blocks away. Come Labor Day, the season is over and they lower the rents for the winter. I'll send you the address when I move in."

Jackson and I say goodbye, all very pleasant, *nice,* as my father would say.

The new baby blankets I ordered have arrived, from the natural fibers catalog I used to work for. Pima cotton baby blankets, one in white, one in yellow. I drape them, silkily, across my naked bulging breasts, leaking with colostrum. A new development. Not the only new development. Suddenly, overnight, I'm huge. People defer to me noticeably, moving out of the way quickly, as you would before something large and rolling, a boulder.

Too, I'm breaking out in a web of stretch marks, no matter how much belly cream I use. Some marks I can't even see, they're down so low, first glimpsed by Gregg, much to my embarrassment. Down under, is how he put it, while applying the cream for me since I can barely reach. Down under. We might as well be talking about Australia; that's how swollen and foreign that part of me feels. Lately we don't always sleep together, as in sex. At last it's gotten to him, my shape, my condition, though as usual he doesn't mention it. As for me, overnight I'm just as happy *not* sleeping together, genital pleasure a distant valley in a large fleshy country.

Nor are my feet immune. Last week my feet grew out of my shoes. I bought a pair of T-strap sandals, like Mary Jane shoes, but boats. Wide. My fingers swell up; I couldn't wear a wedding band if I wanted to. Maggie says to drink more water so wherever I go I'm accompanied by one of those jumbo plastic cups with the lid and straw attached. Drink more water. Her solution to everything.

She was the one who referred me to childbirth classes.

Last night at the second class, like the first, all I felt was big and old, compared to the other mothers. One appeared to be barely in her twenties and hardly showing, in a sleeveless sailor top I could swear was from Land's End, except they don't carry maternity. She looked as though she didn't *need* maternity, but her due date was a week ahead of mine. In the first class we'd gone all through that, introducing ourselves and telling our due dates. While I couldn't remember the other mothers' names, I'd memorized their due dates. August 21st was the one in the sailor top. And as August 21st clung to her husband's hand during the birth movie, I couldn't help comparing myself to her. Us to them. Apples and oranges. Her husband was clean-shaven, or maybe he hadn't started shaving; Gregg, at my side, hadn't shaved all week, I knew, the bristles grown so long they'd be feathery when later on in bed he would kiss me. August 21st's husband wore a polo shirt, naturally, a real one from Ralph Lauren, not one of the rip-offs. Gregg had on something leftover from college, surely. When I leaned over to take his hand, motivated primarily by August 21st holding *her* husband's hand—I wanted to know how it felt, this certainty—that you were going to be a mother and here by your side was the baby's father—when I took hold of Gregg's hand, I had to grant him an intoxicating bohemian sort of handsomeness, unlike August 21st's husband, probably a stockbroker (had he even graduated from college yet?).

As for last night's movie of a real birth, I couldn't watch. Only snippets.

Get a grip, I told myself. This was a baby's birth, a baby who now lived in the world somewhere, a child: from this I gathered hope, forcing my sleepy eyelids open in time for the baby sliding out, bloody and miraculous, cord pulsing and it was me birthing a baby, my mother birthing me.

I began to cry. I wasn't the only one. There was a roomful of us, no matter our age or how we came to be here, palpitating wombs and moist membranes, some of us with our breasts oozing in happy, leaky anticipation. We could drop our babies right there, we wanted them so much. "My," the instructor said, "a lot of emotion in this room," as we all burst into helpless, teary laughter. Even August 21st and her husband, both of whom had watched the movie dry-eyed and frightened; they glanced at me through damp eyes as Gregg held and rocked me.

TWENTY-ONE

I'm still not ready to introduce Gregg to my family. This weekend would have been a great opportunity except that, as luck would have it, Gregg has to work.

So it's just Dad and me driving out to Palm Desert, to see Corb and Diane's new condo, bought on the spur. For the boys, they said, so the boys can experience a place less urban, but really I suspect the condo is for Corb and Diane. There is always that need in them for change on a small safe scale, by buying something new—a car, an appliance, a puppy, a computer. Maybe the things they buy don't make them any happier, but they don't make them unhappy, either. They aren't looking for happiness anyway; rather, they *are* happy, or believe themselves to be.

Their condo is blindingly white. Corb meets us in the parking lot, although Dad has dozed off in the car, and at first in the sun, the whiteness of the building, I can't see Corb's face. Then I do. He looks as though he's been in a fight. A black eye, stitches on his cheek.

"Corb, what happened?"

"I had a growth removed. Basal cell carcinoma—"

I hold my breath.

"It's not melanoma," he says, "by any stretch. Doesn't metastasize, grows very slowly. It began as a cyst, looked like a pimple. Didn't hurt. I just went in to have it removed and—" He shrugs. "It's no big deal, Theo. Lots of people have this nowadays. Really."

But one can never tell with Corb. I glance at Dad, who continues to sleep in air-conditioned comfort. The air conditioning I finally got fixed.

"How many stitches do you have?" I ask.

"Ten. Usually these things are smaller, but this one was on the big side."

177

A dust devil stirs. There aren't yards here, just open space. I keep looking at Corb's face. It appears smashed, as though somebody hit him, hard.

Most of the weekend I spend with Corb's boys, taking them to a Western history museum and then to the tram in Palm Springs. We go on hikes up the hill behind the condo, me trudging laboriously, yards behind my coltish nephews with their long bony legs and pale arms with clunky black digital watches—how did they grow so fast? Who are they now? A little uncomfortable around me, pre-adolescence, I think. If they were small, they would have crawled onto my lap and pointed, asked me why I was so fat; is there a baby in there, Aunty Tea-O? What they used to call me. Now that they know where babies come from, they keep their eyes strictly on my feet, my double-wide feet.

Once or twice Dad walks with us, reminiscing about what it was like here when he was a boy. Just desert and a couple of filling stations, and a lot of date farming. He has a knack for catching lizards, it turns out, which entertains the boys. One lizard, a horned toad, he keeps for a while, tying a string around its leg and attaching it to a tiny gold safety pin on his shirt, blotched with dark red spots, from the toad's eyes shooting blood, from fear.

Our last night there, Corb and I sit out on the tiny deck alone, trying to identify constellations. He's better at it than I, former Boy Scout that he is. All I know is the Big Dipper and the Little Dipper; the rest, to me, is confusion, not crabs, bulls, warriors and the like.

"Do you remember us finding our mother?" I ask Corb abruptly.

"The morning she died?" He slumps back into his deck chair. *Do we have to talk about this again?* No doubt he was hoping for a discussion of double-coupon bonds, or the varying capacities of laptop batteries. What I really mean to bring up is the subject of our mother's hospital records, but now doesn't seem the time. Besides, I'm thinking of us finding our mother that morning.

"Yeah," Corb says. "I remember. Vaguely."

"What do you remember?"

"We went in there and she was dead or close to it. Flat on her back. Blue. I remember the ambulance coming."

"Where were we then? When the ambulance came?"

"In our rooms. Me in my room, you in yours."

A door opens an inch. It's me peeking out. A low narrow bed on wheels clanks by in a hurry, knocking into straight-backed chairs, walls; navigating the turns of our hallway I call The Woods. My mother is on the bed. I close the door, the last time I ever see her.

A scene from before the ambulance comes, before her body is discovered: A brother and sister go to wake up their mother. The girl is carrying something, flowers from the yard. They fall from her hands when she sees her mother's face. She and the boy race to the bed screaming, rock the woman side to side, like fighting over a heavy water raft. She's wearing white, her sheets are white, her skin is blue.

In this phantasm of stars, Corb and I seek out each other's hands in the dark, as we did all those years ago; before we were sent to our rooms and told to wait; standing by our father as he called an ambulance, we gripped each other's hands in terror.

Inside Diane switches on a light and in its sudden axis I study Corb's black eye and the stitches on his cheek, like secretive webbing, a veil.

On the road back to Pasadena, Dad reads the map, a familiar sight from childhood, except now he must read the map very close up and with a magnifying glass.

"Dad?"

"Hmm."

"Dad, I need to talk to you." A talk that is long overdue. Outside it is parched, cholla rushing by. "Dad?"

Reluctantly, he lays the map on the dashboard. "What is it, Theo?"

"Daddy, we haven't talked about the baby much, but it's time we should."

His eyes dodge mine, flit now and then longingly to the map on the dashboard. "Oh," he says. A puzzled oh, a worried oh.

"It's a good thing, Dad. I want the baby, obviously. I'm happy." How come whenever I say this, particularly to my family, it sounds less true than it is? "You know Jackson and I are getting divorced."

"So you've told me." He says this distastefully.

"Dad?"

"Yes?" He looks at me, startled.

"I'm seeing somebody else, as apparently you were told by Mrs. Fracht."

He fidgets.

"His name is Gregg. You'll meet him soon." They met sixteen years ago, but never mind. I take a deep breath. "Gregg and I are moving in together after the baby's born."

"Oh," he says. "No."

Theo living with yet another boyfriend—where's the shock? The lecture? The attempt to reconcile me with Jackson? I don't even bother to mention that Gregg and I might get married.

"About the baby, Dad." I wait. Why doesn't he ever say anything? There is no joy, hardly any acknowledgment.

"I hope you're not doing this for me," he says.

"What? What are you talking about?" I feel relief; this is familiar, the father I know—this ridiculous remark.

"A lot of parents," he begins, "and I'm sorry to say I know some—pressure their children into having babies. So they can be grandparents. I hope *I* haven't—"

"Dad. Isn't it a little late to be talking about this?"

Another of his pet subjects, like husbands and wives being together every night of their lives. For years he told me he hoped I didn't feel any pressure, that it was fine with him, just fine, dandy, wonderful, if I didn't have children. There was nothing wrong with being childless. Nothing at all! He said it so many times Jackson and I suspected a different message—that if I conceived, he'd disapprove or, more accurately, worry. That *I* in particular should not have children. Something to do with my mother. I was too temperamental, too—what? You look like your mother, don't be like her: I'd wind up hospitalized, a suicide. Or perhaps he meant what he said, that he didn't want me to have children on his account. Absurd! Had the man ever given the slightest inkling, ever, that he wished to be a grandfather to my children? He pretty much ignored Corb's children, so why in the world would I get that impression?

"Do you think I'd have a baby just to please you?" I ask. "Under these conditions? Being separated from my husband? About to live with another man?"

"No, I just—"

I pull over to the side of the road.

"Do you think you ought to stop here?" He glances over his shoulder as though expecting a squadron of police cruisers.

"We're out in the middle of the desert, Dad. Parked on the shoulder of the highway. It's fine. It's legal."

"Yes, but I wouldn't think it safe."

"It's safe, Dad."

"But a car could come out of nowhere—"

"It's flat, I can see for miles."

"Come to think of it, I'm not sure it *is* legal. Do you think we ought to find a turnout?"

"Shut up! Shut up!" My belly is throbbing, the baby kicking excitedly; I'm trembling all over. "You can't say anything normal about this baby, you can't even say you're happy for me, just this business about pulling over—and, you hope I didn't get pregnant because of you. Are you trying to say you don't think I *can* be a mother? A good mother?" I grab my super sipper and drink from it; for once I am thirsty, dying of thirst.

"No, I—"

I bang the cup down. "Just because my own mother was unfit?"

"She was a good mother."

"A good mother! What kind of good mother kills herself?" A sudden blast of wind rocks the car.

"To be fair—"

"Oh please, not the death certificate. How it says suicide but really it wasn't. A little error on the part of the coroner. How can you say that? Believe that? After all her attempts?" Little does Dad know I have a copy of the death certificate right here in my pocket, where I keep it always.

He folds his hands in his lap, doesn't even ask how I know this information about all her suicide attempts because certainly we've never discussed it.

"She was a mother who cared about you," he says quietly. "In her own way."

I'm trying to take this in, maybe it's even true, my heart loosening in my chest, a flower bud opening itself up to the sun, when he continues. "She cared about your clothes and your education, she left long notes for the sitter about your food and medicines."

"Dad, I don't have a single good memory of her. Not one."

He seems unfazed by this, nor does he contradict me at first.

A weak contradiction at best: "Well," he says, "there were lots of times—"

"Lots of times *what*, Dad? Tell me. Tell me one single good memory. I don't have the memory, so you give it to me. You're my father, you were there. She was reading me a bedtime story, she held me in her arms; she played with me out in the yard—what? You must've seen something, a moment. Please, Dad. Please. Before you get really old and senile and forget for good."

"Well." There is a long pause. "She was very concerned about your schooling."

"My *schooling?*" How could I be so foolish as to even hope? That if such a moment ever existed, my father might recall it. He doesn't know what I'm talking about and never has. "My schooling," I say dully. I'll take anything I can get. "What about it."

"She wanted you to go to Westridge, she felt the public schools were, well, deficient. But I defied her wishes there, I felt public schools were fine, that you would be happier . . ."

"Did you sit around in advance of her death, her suicide, and discuss which school I would go to *after* she died?"

"She felt it important that I know. She told me in the hospital. Afterwards."

"After what?"

"One of her—one of her—attempts."

"Once she made this clear to you, the matter of my schooling, did you exit the room so that she could get started on the next attempt?" I slam my hands against the steering wheel. "God! I'm sorry, Dad. I don't mean that, I know it's painful for you, too."

"Oh, no," he demurs, staring at the map on the dashboard. But his hands clamp down on his knees, his fingers twitching.

"Yes, painful, Dad. The whole rest of your life, being accountable for this. Having to explain it to your children." Although Corb required no explanation, that was his role. And this was mine: to know, demand to know, and now I would have to explain it to my children too. My child. Someday. I take a deep breath, ready, finally, to ask one of the questions I've wondered all my life. "Did she leave a note, Dad?"

"A what?"

"A suicide note."

"I never found one."

Almost a comfort, then, my mother's death certificate resting in my pocket, this last part of her. I've touched it so much over the past months that one of its corners is bent, soft, torn. I slip it out of my pocket. "How about this, Dad?"

"What do you have there?"

"Her death certificate. I got it when I sent away for her hospital records." I say this almost gleefully, as though I've found something deliberately hidden from me, a game, Hot and Cold, you're hot, you're burning up; you're cold, you're freezing.

"You could've asked me," he says shortly. "I would've made copies and sent those things on to you. Saved you the trouble."

"You have these already?"

He nods. "In the safe at my office."

"Didn't you think I might like to see them?"

"I didn't want to hurt you, you've been hurt enough—"

There's a wetness in the corner of his eye: a tear? He doesn't wipe it and continues to talk to me. "All right, ask me. Ask me your questions."

"Did you love her?"

"Deeply. Less so at the end, she wasn't herself anymore."

"What was she like?"

"A picky housekeeper, too picky, overall too worried about the details in life, which, when you get to be my age, you'll see don't matter. She was tense, she was unhappy. I wish I had made her happier."

"Dad, that's not why she—"

"But had she been happier with me—"

"You couldn't have saved her, Dad. I don't know this, I just *feel* . . . Dad, there were other forces. Her drinking, her drug use, her childhood." He looks at me intently. We know next to nothing about her childhood, either of us, and Aunt Lyla won't talk. "You did the best you could under the circumstances," I say.

"Not enough," he says.

That he blames himself is not surprising, but that he blames himself so bitterly—this is news to me. I lean over to hug him and he meets me halfway. "You can hardly move, you're so pregnant—" He fumbles. "I remember your mother."

"What?" I leap on it, as I always do, any detail.

"Your mother was huge."

With me in particular? With Corb? My mother huge with child. I move my tongue around my mouth, tasting this. It tastes like something frozen solid, preserved for all time. Ice. I want to ask my father about Charlotte, but I can't. Can't even say her name.

"What did my mother like to do?" I ask.

"She enjoyed reading, she enjoyed playing bridge. For a while she knitted but she gave that up. Too frustrating."

"What were her favorite subjects in school?"

"Oh," he says, as if trying to recall. After all, he didn't know her then. "She was an excellent student, the president of the women at Stanford, graduated magna cum laude. But you know that. She was good in all her subjects, English, Math, History."

Your Dead Mother, like all the other dead mothers, beautiful, intelligent, and oh yes, she loved you.

"What was her last day like? Her last week?"

"Nothing out of the ordinary really. She seemed happy."

But just five minutes ago he said she wasn't happy.

"You had no idea?" I say.

"None."

Only that she attempted it before, I think. Twice. *(To my mother, wherever you are, in the heavens, in the constellations Corb and I named last night, or are you in a darker place, a place not lit by stars: What were you like at the dinner table? Did you unfold your napkin, take small bites? Tell me about the everyday things, cooking, dishes, laundry, gardening . . . the things you did with us, Corb and me. Did you take us to the playground? On errands? To the market?*

Tell me about a normal day. Was there a normal day?

What did you talk about?

What did your voice sound like?

How did you look at me across the room? With amusement, anger? Or did you look right through me?

What was it like for you in the hospital? Did you eat the food? What did you wear? Your own clothes or a hospital gown? What did you feel when they set the mouthpiece in wrong that time, your teeth nearly shattered in bolts of current transporting you up, up, you might have flown off that table had you not been strapped to it. What did you think about in the hospital? Charlotte. You grieved over Charlotte. Did you miss me too?

Do you miss me now?)

My father's voice. "I have something to talk to you about, too, Theo."

"What?"

My father is reaching into his briefcase. Oh no. His last will and testament again, or worse, his Living Will, but no, it's a brochure. A color photo of a resort on the front, in Pasadena, it would appear. There is Orange Grove Boulevard, there are magnolia trees, the San Gabriel mountains in the background.

"The Grove," the brochure says, "The Fine Art of Retirement Living."

"I've researched all the places in this area," Dad is saying, "and—"

"When?" I say. Quickly I'm figuring out his age. Seventy-three, seventy-four. No, almost seventy-five. "But," I say, "aren't you a little young yet?"

"I've already done it. Made the arrangements. You have to buy into these places, you see. I'm putting my house up for sale."

His house. I've never thought of it as his but Dorinne's. He brought little of his own to this house and, knowing him, he will leave the house, more than twenty years later, with nothing, a small suitcase and a bill of sale.

"When?" I say.

"The house goes on the market next week."

"So soon?" Although I've never liked that house, I'm sad. I flip through the brochure, reading the language, examining it for signs of a cult, a place that would steal my father's money or his soul. "Gracious living in a country estate setting," "Studio, One- and Two-Bedroom Suites," "Elegant Dining," "Security," "Independence," "Deep pile carpeting for your comfort and quietness," "Ample parking," "Chauffeur and housekeeping services," "On-site health services," "Assisted living and skilled nursing also available on campus."

Campus. Like a college.

"I guess I was expecting you to move into a townhouse first, Dad, or an apartment. This just seems so—" Final is the word that comes to mind. Final exit, death. "Does Corb know?"

"I sat down with him and Diane this weekend while you and the boys were at the museum."

"Corb and Diane already know?" All this weekend and nobody said anything to me, when all along there I was with my mother's death certificate in my pocket, her hospital records in my bags, just in case her name should come up—when it's my father I should be concerned about. "Do they approve?" I ask him.

"Yes. Do you?"

I feel myself wilting in the desert heat.

"Do you?" he persists.

He's asking for my blessing, just as so many times I've asked for his. "Dad, won't you please change your mind?"

"No."

"But why now? You're so healthy, well, there's the other cataract, but you've already been through that, it's no big deal."

"I'm waiting to have the operation," he says, "until I'm settled in at the new place. Then I can get help if I need it—"

"I'll help you!"

"You can help, if you want, but this way it won't be all on your shoulders."

"Like your other cataract operation was *such* an ordeal."

"You've got the baby to think about now, Theo. And then, as I get older, other things will crop up. There's my hypertension, for example, or maybe I'd have a heart attack. Then what?"

"It's not like you're about to keel over!" I say. "My God, you can swim farther than Corb." Over the weekend Corb had told me about swimming with Dad recently at the Valley Hunt Club, struggling to keep up. Our father could swim a mile, seventy-two laps; Corb had to quit halfway through.

"I can swim at The Grove too, Theo. There's an Olympic-sized pool. It's not a nursing home."

"It's just not *your* home," I say. From what I read in the brochure, it's a "facility with nursing home capability." Meaning there's a wing of the place reserved for those who have lost the battle with aging.

The Grove is where my father will die someday, and then I'll be all alone.

"Well," he says, "shouldn't we be getting on?"

He means the car. Get the car off the shoulder of the road, drive back to Pasadena. My father, always eager for the next destination.

TWENTY-TWO

It's dark in the cavern that is the warehouse at Pink's Transfer Moving and Storage, although it's morning, baking hot and smoggy already. A green truck with pink lettering ("Those Who Think Call Pink") backs into the warehouse. I ask somebody who walks by what time it is.

He takes one look at me and whistles. "You sure you got time to wait, lady? Want me to call a doctor?"

"Very funny."

"Five after nine," he says.

I pace back and forth among the pallets, waiting for ours to be brought forth by a forklift.

"We might as well get started," I say to one of the men milling around. Thirty dollars per man per hour, although I can charge it to Dad. His treat since he's not coming to help me; he's getting over a cold and we both agreed it would be better if he stayed at The Grove today.

"Let's start," I say. A man wrenches open the first wooden pallet, now in the driveway of Pink's, while I hold my breath—as though we're about to exhume a body.

Things are stacked, covered with sheets, encased in plywood and cardboard boxes.

"Anything you'd like to see first?" he asks, prying open another pallet, then another.

"Bring it all out," I say. "I need to see everything."

He calls to several men to help him and they load out the big items—our old dining room table and chairs, couches, chests, bureaus; I recognize my old vanity. Sell it, I think. But what if I'm having a daughter?

"Do you have the schedule?" I ask the guy.

"Oh yeah." Carefully he sets down some nesting end tables, from our old living room, disappears into the front office, and returns with a thick stack of paper. "Here you go." He wipes his nose, waiting for me to say something.

It's bewildering, the number of items, the number of pages. Household Goods Descriptive Inventory, at the top of each page. I pick one at random:

MIRROR CARTON	P, B, O, QU
SM TABLE, CORN FEET	10, paint marks, CH, G, SC
SM ARMCHAIR	6S, SC, 4, R
SM ROCKER CHAIR	7 wicker, BR, 6s SC, CH
MAG RACK	6s, SC, CH, 1, 6, LSC, R
GAME TABLE	10, SC, G, CH, 1, 5, LSC
4-DRAWER CHEST	10, G, CH, Z, 4, SC, R, G, 8, 9, SC

The numbers and letters are codes for condition at origin, all explained at the top of the sheet; there must be thirty different codes. The four-drawer chest, for example, is scratched, gouged, chipped and cracked on top (#10); the front of it (#4) is scratched, rubbed, gouged, and so on.

There are more codes: bent, broken, burned, faded, loose, marred, mildewed, moth-eaten, rusted, soiled, torn, badly worn, cracked.

"Just like me." Bewildered, I sit on one of our old dining room chairs, propping my feet up on another chair to ease my back. I close my eyes for a second.

"Want me to open these boxes?" A man, in a white shirt with PINKS on the front and back, is poised and ready with a utility knife.

"Okay," I say, heaving myself up and out of the chair, toward the front office where I hope to borrow the phone.

I call Corb on his cellular. "Corb, get over here right now. You're late!"

"Theo," he says. "I made a slight miscalculation. I'm really sorry."

"You're not coming?"

"The boys have a game, you know, the fast pitch league."

"Can't Diane take them?"

"I'm one of the coaches, remember?"

"What am I going to do?" I wail.

"If you can't decide, just put it all back into storage, like we said."

I call Gregg, waking him. "But how am I going to know what you might like?" I say. "Wouldn't you like a say in how we furnish our house?"

He mumbles something noncommittal. Gregg doesn't notice such things, domestic details. That will be my job, once we're living together. "But Gregg," I say.

"What?"

"Christ," I say, hanging up. It's supposed to reach 105°F today. Perspiration drips from my underarms to the waistband of my front-paneled shorts; I have to pee again. I slurp from my super sipper.

Outside, Maggie pulls up.

"Those who Think Call Pink," she says once she sees me, the desperation on my face. "Hey, I'd buy you a margarita if I thought you could drink it."

"Tell me what to do!" I plead. Presumably Maggie knows since she went through her mother's belongings not so long ago.

"It's simple," she says. "Go out there and look at the stuff, and decide whether or not you want it."

Meanwhile the guys from Pinks are unboxing more furniture—headboards, lamps, mirrors. I pass by a grouping of chairs that once lined the hallway in our house; according to the Pinks schedule I hold in my hand, they're made of mahogany, their backs carved in the shapes of swan's necks. Worth a lot of money.

"Those are nice," Maggie says.

"Want 'em?"

"Don't you?"

"Yeah, I guess. Sure. What the hell."

Displayed now on our old kitchen table is my sewing basket, my first typewriter, and a huge, plush, God-awful, rug-upholstered pillow from college. I bend over to sniff its blue mandala-covered front and wonder whatever happened to my old hookah; this pillow still smells faintly of pot and incense, right down to the fringe.

"Why did Dad save all this stuff? This pillow can go in the trash," I announce to no one in particular.

A Pinks man approaches, handing me different colored stick-on tags. "So we know what you want to do with things. Red is for the dump, green for removal from the premises, yellow for re-storage."

"Corb," I whisper, "I hate your yuppie Brooks Brothers guts."

Maggie sticks a red tag on the pillow. "Start tagging," she says. "Or we'll be here all day."

The men from Pinks are opening still more cartons, about a dozen of them. "Oh God," I say, remembering all the stuff that must be here. The Japanese flower-arranging equipment belonging to my mother and all her wedding presents—silver, china, crystal, linens. Persian rugs, assorted antiques, junk. My old diaries and stuffed animals. Pots and pans, kitchen utensils, moth-eaten blankets, hot water bottles, combs, brushes, the contents of drawers dumped into boxes. I gaze at my swelling, aching feet and try to calculate how much it would cost for another day of this.

I end up with a garage full of stuff, *i.e.*, our garage in Arcadia until Gregg and I can move into our own place. Pinks will deliver the big items; Gregg brings over a carload of stuff that night on his way to work, some of the smaller, more delicate or awkward items which I'll store in the poolhouse itself—my old dollhouse, a box of Umari china, yet another box of my mother's linens that I nearly forgot, a floor lamp because, I realized, the pool house is too dark. In the passenger seat of the Chevy Cavalier, I placed my mother's recipe box, having a sudden yen for cold fruit soup; if anyone had a recipe for this, she would. Also, I thought I would like to have something so intimately hers, all the recipes she typed up herself, notations in pen and pencil.

As soon as I get home I fall instantly to sleep, stretched out on the futon, on my side, waking up later with a start. I hear a TV. I get up and look out across the dark yard, into Maggie's living room, thinking it's hers. But no, her lights are off. It's 10:30 already. I consider calling Gregg, then remember he's working tonight. For a split second I consider calling Jackson, to see how he's doing now that the job has started and he's moved into his new place in Newport Beach, so his latest note said. I think of calling him, no doubt, because I'm lonely and can no longer call my father late at night (not at the Grove, not after nine), a ritual we'd fallen into of late. He came to appreciate my calls, I think, though I always needed an excuse—financial advice or the name of a good car mechanic. He began to ask about my pregnancy, how was I feeling, did I think it was a girl or a boy, it'd be nice to have a girl in the family, and every so often he'd tell me something. Such as the fact that my mother had never experienced morning sickness with Corb, me, or Charlotte; or that I looked like Bela Lugosi as a baby, all that hair, which soon fell out. Normal things such as a normal father might tell his daughter, but I was hearing them for the first time, many years too late. And he told me other things, not so normal. That my mother played bridge in the hospital, that he and a couple of orderlies would join her for a game around an everyday card table as if they were somewhere else, at home, and my mother would wear a gray woolen skirt and her loafers and a pale yellow sweater, her glasses on a chain around her neck, and if it weren't for having such a lousy bridge partner—my father—she would've beat the pants off everyone. She was brilliant at bridge, and competitive; the shock treatments might have made her forget the names of her children, but had left untouched her ability at bridge. Such memories slipped out of my father's mouth, almost as an afterthought, but if I asked him directly, he'd say he couldn't remember. Like Corb can't remember and I can't remember: the family amnesia.

I look at the items Gregg brought over from Pink's, still by the door—the tall gawky lamp, the box of linens, my old dollhouse, and next to them, my mother's recipe box, humble and plain. I bring it back to my futon and lie down again, turning the cards idly.

Her recipe box is a mess now. It didn't start out that way, back when it was strictly my mother's, each category alphabetized and typed up by her on dividers. Sandwiches, Preserves, Pastry-Pie, Cake, Bread, Fruits, Poultry, Meats, Casseroles, Soups, Sauces, Salads, Menu Ideas—long fallen out of alphabetical order once my mother died, once Evan got her hands on this box.

Here and there is a recipe I recognize. Corned Beef Hash (disgusting), Parsnips (ugh), Tongue (need I say more?).

There is a hesitation, a lack of confidence, in some of the recipes. Shish Kebab, for instance—why would you need to write the recipe down at all? *Steak—cut in 1" squares and marinate in barbecue sauce; Tomatoes—cut in good-sized wedges, do not skin . . . .*

Maybe this was from the beginning of her marriage, when she was first learning to cook. Yes, this 3 x 5 card is older, more yellowed. Similar to my own adolescent recipes, added to this box later on—in that this, my mother's recipe, contains the most simplistic directions. Instructions to shred the carrots for carrot raisin salad, for instance.

I can picture her as a young bride, flipping through her recipe box on a long hot afternoon, making notes here and there—her whole identity tied up in the success of a recipe.

On another card is a list of sandwich fillings:
Date & cream cheese
Pineapple, chicken & cream cheese
Cottage cheese, chopped celery & chives
Egg, celery & watercress (moisten w/ sour cream)
One thing Corb has said about our mother, when I've pressed him for memories: "She didn't know how to cook for kids."

Yes, I can see that. Steamed Persimmon Pudding. Rabbit Cacciatore. Potato Balls. No recipe for cold fruit soup, so far.

I remember, suddenly, those dinners of lamb croquettes and

tongue, parsnips, twice-baked potatoes—of my sitting and sitting at our dining room table, refusing to eat. The bowl of split pea soup I was offered for two days running once, breakfast, lunch, and dinner; of Corb gliding by on his way outside to play while I sat stubbornly before plates of vegetables cooked God-knows-how, of Corb whispering, "Pretend it's candy."

I come to some newer recipes in the box: from Evan's era. Normal foods like fried chicken, tacos, meatloaf, cookies. Although my mother had numerous recipes for cookies and desserts, they were for company; we didn't have desserts, she didn't bake cookies. Too fattening. Our family was among the first to drink skim milk. She served it to us in liqueur glasses, so we could sample it—thin, greenish, icebox cold, tasteless. From then on we drank it nonetheless, and when she wasn't around, I ransacked the cabinets for honey, sugar—something sweet. I drank vanilla extract, bit into squares of baking chocolate, gagged into the sink, and from then on contented myself with smelling, imagining sweetness.

Then came Evan, who baked cookies. We baked cookies with her, a first. While our mother was resting, I suppose, or during her stays at the hospital. What must she have thought? Her domestic power usurped, though for some reason I imagine she was not angry, but relieved, glad to hand the reins over to Evan. A little laughter in the house, some fun for the children, might be a good thing after all.

Once my mother died, the recipe box became Evan's, who added recipes haphazardly, not necessarily in alphabetical order, then dumped more recipes on top. Those torn out of magazines in doctors' waiting rooms, the jotted down notes for someone's chocolate cake she'd admired, recipes scribbled on scratch paper or on the back of a birthday card.

Evan didn't use my mother's recipes but cooked simple meals, and taught me to do the same. Meatloaf with frozen vegetables. Iceberg lettuce salads, the dressing out of a bottle. Broiled pork chops, fried chicken, pot roast. Jello. Pineapple upside-down cake. Corb and I were delighted—food we could eat, food like our friends ate. Evan's specialty, however, was Mexican food: I can still smell her enchiladas, how I used to flip the tortillas over in a frying pan of hot oil, with tongs, before smoothing on the red sauce; the oil was the secret, Evan claimed. Kept the enchiladas from drying out.

I loved her cooking. I loved her. Corb loved her too, although the stiff and proper man he became would never admit to it. She was our housekeeper, that was all. She used to chase him around the house with one of his sneakers as a joke and threaten to paddle him with it; he would let her catch him on purpose, a teenager, just so she would hug him, so somebody on this earth would touch him, since his father wouldn't and his mother was dead. This became for him merely a fond memory.

The last time I saw Evan, I was twenty-four years old and living in Boston with a guy with whom marriage had been discussed, a Boston native whose accent I couldn't understand any more than his values, which could only be described as blue collar, working class. Whenever he found me sleepless at night, sitting in the dark in the living room, what he said was, "You'll be tired for work." Never, *What's the matter, what's wrong?* I wrote ad copy for an upscale women's clothing company, was restless at work and at home, unhappy in this relationship as well as on the East Coast in general.

In the middle of this, I sent Evan a plane ticket for Mother's Day. A whim. A folly. I hadn't talked to her in years, not since we'd had lunch at Woody and Eddy's, where Evan had regaled me with one story after another about my mother's exploits—her drinking, her driving all over town, doctor to doctor until she would find one willing to write a prescription. How she slashed her wrists once, blood *everywhere* and Evan cleaning it up in the nick of time, just as Corb and I walked in the door from school.

In Evan's stories my mother seemed a cardboard character, present but somehow not there, similar to the memories I had. I remember her pushing the shopping cart I sat in, or taking me to the playground. That is, I remember myself sitting in the cart, nudging her stomach with my feet, or being perched on the slide at the playground, about to go down—but while I know my mother is there, I can't see her, she's just out of view, even when she's right in front of me.

So I sent Evan a plane ticket and a month later she came, brassy, full of advice for me and my boyfriend; red patent leather purse; pant suit; hair in a bouffant, which she still wrapped in toilet paper at night. "So I says to her, if you don't get that operation you're gonna die. I'm a nurse, I *know.*" Tales of abscessed legs and livers, the raving, incontinent old people she'd cared for over the years, how they didn't want her to leave, not for even an hour. "'But Mrs. Sparks,' I says, 'I got to go out. If I don't go out, we don't eat. We have nothing in the refrigerator, Mrs. Sparks,' I says. 'You can go with me, Mrs. Sparks,' I says. 'You can go with me, get some fresh air. It'd be good for you, Mrs. Sparks,' I says. But she says, 'Evan, no. *No!* I'm too afraid!'"

She stayed two weeks, the longest two weeks of my life. Every day she took the trolley with me to work, talking all the way. "Did you *see* that person over there?" A fat person, a thin person, a black person, a sick person. "That person has gall bladder problems"—or a thyroid problem, or diabetes. "I've seen these things, I know." While I worked, Evan went sightseeing or sat in Boston Common talking to people—often drunks, the only people who seemed to line the benches there during the day. On the way home on the trolley she'd tell me what this or that person had said, what she had said. At first she told them she was here in Boston visiting a close friend, well, the daughter of a family she'd worked for many years ago; well, you see, the girl's mother was sick and . . . . Then after a few days the story became this: though the daughter wasn't her own, she thought of her as such, and the girl thought of her, Evan, as her own mother; why, she'd even sent her a plane ticket for Mother's Day. Then she began telling them I *was* her daughter. She was visiting her daughter here in Boston. Her daughter had sent her a plane ticket for Mother's Day!

Once, when I met her in Boston Common after getting off work, she introduced me to her latest companion, Mabel, a woman in a dirty blouse and skirt. "This is Theo," she said, "my daughter."

Mabel adjusted her cockeyed glasses. "Why, a plane ticket for Mother's Day! Your mother was just telling me what a wonderful girl you are, how fine you turned out, and now you're going to be *married*!" Her magnified eyes swept up and down my figure.

"Come on, Mother," I said, grabbing Evan's purse and stuffing it under her arm.

One night we had some friends over to meet Evan, who, for the occasion, made her famous enchiladas. "This is how we eat in California," she told them. "I bet you people've never had enchiladas." She bustled about the kitchen, her feet squeezed into sandals so tight that her toes popped out the front, her thick, cracked toenails painted fire engine red.

I wasn't supposed to eat the enchiladas, since I was on a diet. I fixed myself a plate of ground beef, carrot and celery sticks, a skinny wedge of melon, and a large gin and tonic, not on my diet but I thought I'd go mad listening to Evan telling my friends her life story and how they ought to have yearly checkups, she was a nurse, she *knew*. . . .

She began talking about me, my family; how she'd worked for us for almost ten years. "You should have seen Theo, she wore those puffy sleeves and she was tiny, such curly hair! I thought of her as my own!"

I should have told her to stop, but I couldn't. Weak with gin and hunger, I hid in the kitchen stuffing my mouth with Evan's enchiladas, eating them right off the spatula. Then I heard her say, "Theo's mother was a lovely person, until she got sick."

I stuck my head in the freezer, looking for the ice cream, and then my boyfriend was beside me saying in his Boston accent don't worry, I got her to pipe down, I changed the subject, let's get dessert on the table before she starts up again. I kissed him in gratitude, having known for a while now that I didn't love him and never had and would leave him soon, but that I would always remember this moment.

I saw Evan off at Logan Airport, the last time I ever saw her, Evan who had taught me how to sew, how to shave my legs, how to keep track of my periods; how to keep house, how to cook.

At the gate I held her tightly, breathing in her hair that smelled like air freshener. I promised to see her soon. She would come to Boston again or I would come to California. When in Pasadena, oh yes, I would see her, absolutely. We'd have lunch at Woody and Eddy's. I'd stay the night. We'd never lose touch again.

The recipe box became mine eventually, once Evan stopped working for us. "Let go" is how everybody put it; Evan herself said she was retiring. I was thirteen; I piled my recipes right on top of the old ones. The cards wouldn't fit exactly so I had to fold them over and stuff them between my mother's recipes or stack them on top of Evan's torn-out magazine recipes.

I was never able to change anything about the recipe box, unable to cook from it, add to it, reorganize it, or throw it away. My own recipe box, given to me as a present, somehow disappeared, got lost or dropped in cake batter and ruined—so that my recipe cards ended up in this box.

Most of my cards are empty, I see now—lined, three-by-five cards. In fact, I can only find three recipes: oatmeal cookies, egg nog, and sherry pound cake, using Heinz yellow cake mix and Jello instant vanilla pudding. On each one I drew a smiley face with curly hair—my sad, desperate adolescent logo, as it were, for a girl who so wanted direction, her own mother to teach her to cook.

I have another memory associated with those pathetic smiley faces: being told I needed a bra.

Who was going to do it?

Evan, one would think. But it wasn't her. It ended up being my cousin Susan, Aunt Lyla's daughter, put up for the task. Was this in fact accomplished by family agreement? Was she told what to say? Or did she just blurt it out: "Theo, you know what, I think you need a bra."

I was humiliated. On the sly I had poked at them with my fingers, prodded them under my books on the way to school—the bumps on my chest that felt like the bottoms of sno-cones, covered over with fat. This was long before Evan started telling me about what boys might want to do to me. I didn't know what the bumps were—mistakes, abscesses, secrets.

Evan bought me my first bra. This must have been after my cousin's informing me that I needed one. Did Aunt Lyla then instruct Evan to take me out and buy me one? (For that matter, why didn't Aunt Lyla get me one, since she was in charge of my clothes?) I'm not sure how the logistics worked, but there I was at Shephard's one day, encased in a training bra, which within a week split right up the middle, whereupon I got something with cups, a tiny embroidered flower between them. When we had to go back the second time, Evan was mercifully subdued.

Layer by layer, I empty out the recipe box onto the carpet. My mother's era, Evan's, mine. There is no recipe for cold fruit soup—what started this in the first place— just zucchini patties, lists for hot sandwiches on English muffins: creamed egg and asparagus, or bubbling cheese with bacon and avocado; wine jelly, guava jelly. . . . At the very bottom of the box are half a dozen slips of paper detailing various jam- and jelly-making ventures—boysenberry, apricot, strawberry.

Strawberry Jam—May, 1952

Berries (1 lug)	*$1.50*
Sugar (15#)	*1.53*
Lemons (6#)	*.90*
Paraffin	*.18*

Seals   *.32*
                           $4.33

Yield: 35 jars @ 12 1/2 c. per jar

I'm not sure why my mother kept these records. To compare costs and yields year by year? For posterity? For me, someday?

There's a tiny corner of blue paper sticking out of the bottom of the recipe box's metal bottom. I fish it out with my fingernail, but it starts to rip; the paper is very thin, pastel. Some kind of origami paper, possibly—did my mother learn origami in addition to Japanese flower arranging? I grasp the small metal bar running up and down the length of the box, yank on it—nothing. I shake the box, imagining I hear the thin blue sheet of paper rattling inside, but it's not my imagination. I know the paper is there; I can see the half-ripped corner, I can see there is more. I turn the box over, wood on the bottom, no way to open it from there. Returning to the metal bar, I pull on it inch by inch, looking for a weak place.

Rising to my feet, I hold the box over my head, hurl it to the floor. The hinges break and the top begins to crack; I hesitate, as though something inside me is about to tear and be broken. Picking up the recipe box, I throw it to the floor once more, then try the bar again, shaking the box and slamming it against the floor again and again until the cracks deepen and the hinges fall out as easily as pushpins, and finally the false metal bottom gives way. Underneath it is crammed with pale blue sheets of tissuey paper, written on front and back, and I'm so frightened that I continue holding onto the box as the papers sail out and seesaw downward, weightlessly, soundlessly.

TWENTY-THREE

March 5, 1964

Dear Theodora,

There is not one secret or memory, but scores of them splintering into thousands, all wedged and nailed inside you row upon row in the dark, like pelts on a wall.

I know all your secrets, little duck. I share them, I am the cause of them, I have the wrists to prove it. Ragged scars disguised by tinkling bracelets, a gold watch. I have the throat as well, made sore from all the pills and the lies I've had to swallow.

There is no candle out here in the darkness.

Your mother,
Marian

Dear Theodora,

Little girls, smiling faintly, we were body parts to be used, borrowed, and returned, though no longer in mint condition. I was the dutiful daughter, so that Lyla wouldn't have to be. To spare her.

Our father didn't spare her.

Divide and conquer: whenever I think of that expression I imagine tall grass being parted, like hair with a comb. Brutality disguised as a civilizing gesture that everyone can agree upon. Lying down flat, prostrated before the conqueror.

Lyla planned her own escape (more successful than mine, it turned out)—who needed college? She scratched herself to pieces to cover up the bruises, the scratching diagnosed as eczema. Sent to the Arizona desert to recuperate, whereupon every time they tried to send her home, she developed more symptoms. Wheezing, hives, welts. Congestion so bad I didn't recognize her voice on the rare occasions she was allowed to call home.

She was not spared, not any more than you have been, from me.

There is a look on your face I know well, Theodora. The gaze of a deer before it is hit by a truck on the road at night: a knowing look, a sixth sense. You know you are about to die. Do not feel what is happening around you, do not feel your body handled and twisted and forced. Your jaw aches, you nearly vomit; why would God let this happen to a girl, to anyone? Don't think about the details. Your body is a detail, demolished in most respects. Afterwards you are bruised, bruises that float away in the sunlight; you can make everything, your body, your smile, your bruises, float.

Marian

Dear Theodora,

Sometimes I experimented. I don't remember, I was drunk, fed by pills. I experimented on you. A pop bottle or an envelope rolled up small like a finger, or a lipstick, the canister made of chipped painted metal. Lipsticks I didn't want anymore, I used on you. I pretended to need to know how deep you went inside. I didn't pretend exactly. I was drunk; it was a blur.

Sometimes I was gentle, sometimes not. You stared at the ceiling, hardly moving, your eyes open but unseeing—I know this so well, how one can be in a twilight, how one does not feel physical pain. *My arm does not exist from the shoulder down. I am dead below the waist.* How the body is broken into parts, disassembled for the occasion, painlessly blown across the room as if by mortar. *It's just a body, somebody's body. I might know her.* How one can watch from another point in the room, the ceiling perhaps; how one can actually float above the scene and watch, because somebody has to witness this.

What he did to me, I did to you, and I might have done to Charlotte, had she lived.

I don't remember very clearly what my father did to me, only that over the years I became aware of a loathing whenever he entered a room. I came to hate him. Naturally the possibility arose in sessions with my psychiatrist: the fantasy of sleeping with my father. I would picture a small girl who happened to look like me, staring up at the ceiling in a bedroom that happened to resemble mine—or else she is face down in the pillows. Something horrible is taking place on top of her, she is numb from the waist down; something vile and rasping and painful. Sometimes there is a pillow over her head, so that she won't scream, or is it for him, so that *he* won't have to see and be reminded?

This was fantasy, my psychiatrist offered, and of course I was quick to agree.

Marian

Dear Theodora,

One time I came into your room, during one of your naps. Not long after Charlotte's death. I'm not sure what brought me there—if I'd come simply to stare at you, or to harm you, but I found myself at your bedside. As always your eyes were open, and somehow you'd gotten hold of a straight pin, which you jabbed and pierced into your fingers, stopping now and then to suck the blood or wipe it off on the sheets. Those stiff white muslin sheets, do you remember? I sank to the floor and watched you, because in my blurry trance, from drunkenness or insanity, this seemed an enactment of the truth: you were venting the poison from within. I could see it rising in wisps above your small child's body—

Marian

For my daughter, Theodora—

The dead must rely on the living for their vengeance, Theodora. As I am counting on you.

A gun is small, fits into your purse. It's sure and reliable, unlike poison or a knife.

A gun is definite, violent, bloody—as opposed to what was done to us, which was often indefinite, secretive, not always violent. Bruises are but blood under the skin, easy to hide from others and yourself. If you don't look, you won't see; no lingering in the bathtub, no lifting your blouse; no dressing or undressing in front of others, no gazing into mirrors—you know the rules we set for ourselves.

Our father taught us to shoot. Marian and Lyla, lying down on the cool, cool mat.

A shooting range out in the desert, but one could never tell. Appearances were usually deceiving with him, and we were understandably nervous lying on our stomachs; what might he do next? Everything was a surprise with him. Sometimes lovely surprises, grownup necklaces and bottles of perfume, or candy or stuffed animals, new dresses—sometimes the other kind of surprise. This time he deposited a rifle into our arms and told us to shoot. How? we asked. Shoot what? *The target, silly.*

A girl should know how to shoot, he said later on, after we had dutifully discharged our bullets, after we had walked thirty paces to retrieve our targets; we couldn't help noticing the spent bullets lying about in the sand; we couldn't help noticing his eyes upon us, the rifle cocked in his arms.

There is the matter of the gun I bought to use on you, on me, on us. One didn't need a permit or the permission of one's husband; I simply walked into a gun shop and pointed to what I wanted, a small black automatic pistol that fit into my handbag. I picked it for its smallness, its simplicity: it seemed like an answer. "Can you show me how to load this, please?" It was as easy as loading staples into a stapler and made nearly the same sound, the sliding of metal against metal, a click.

"Lady," the man said, "do you know how to use this?"

"Certainly." I'd learned on a rifle, but one could extrapolate.

I wasn't really sure why I was doing this. It wasn't a thought-out plan as it would seem, but a need. A need to have this answer in my possession, a say in my destiny at last—in our destiny. But never, never did I think the words: I am going to kill myself, I am going to kill my daughters. The gun was a weapon I kept in my handbag, a comfort, unattached to any action.

When the moment arrived, I walked to my handbag, stored

on the top shelf of my closet, next to my hatboxes, as if in a trance; you were napping in your room. Your father was at work, Corb at school—this didn't concern them, only us. Your sister. You. Myself. Our femaleness, the cleft between our legs, a matter of honor and self-loathing. Insanity. Yes, an insanity forced upon us. In another life there would have been no need for this. Of course, in another life none of this would have happened at all, we would have simply carried on as mother and daughters, shopping trips, shared intimacies—an experience of looking into a mirror that was whole and smooth, reflective, unshattered. In this life, however, the mirror was shattered at the moment of your birth. Never could you look into my eyes and see love reflected there. Although, and I know you question this, the love *was* there. I loved you. But what you saw reflected in my eyes was clouded, murky, and all I had to offer: the love of a troubled person.

I held the gun to your head. I ordered you to pray. All I could hear after that was the sound of my breathing. *His* breathing, what I'd had to listen to every time he touched me.

This was after I placed the pillow over little Charlotte and pressed down with all my weight, until she stopped moving. Then I put the pillow back on my bed.

I realized I couldn't hold a pillow over your head. You were bigger than Charlotte, you would struggle more, call out my name—

Not anymore than I could shoot Charlotte with a gun. So I discovered.

Why? you wonder. Why would a mother do this? Kill her own children?

My God, he had ruined us. Had ruined me and he would ruin you and Charlotte. Better to take you with me than to let my father turn you into monsters, misfits—

Already he had started with you. Twice in the past month I'd found you sitting on my father's lap, him pulling his hand away suddenly, the look of my entire childhood upon your face.

So I held the gun to your head and ordered you to pray. You

just sat there, a lamb, an innocent, swinging your legs against the bed frame. Clunk, clunk. Then you stopped. Silence, as if you knew it was time now to prepare for death. You stared straight ahead, your eyes crystalline like a doll's; never had I loved you more!

My finger on the trigger (my hand didn't even shake!), I listened for the last time to that terrible breathing, my breathing and his—how he had infected me.

Then there was a noise in the house, a scraping, a sigh. I halted, in a panic. Your father back early? Your brother home from school? Evan? When I'd told her not to come today? I set down the gun—on a ledge where you couldn't reach it, ironically, so you wouldn't hurt yourself. I listened hard, heard nothing further, then went to the toilet to vomit.

I was never positive what caused the noise. *If* there was a noise. Was it my imagination? Some last vestige of sanity distracting me, calling me off you? Or was it, as I came to believe, my Charlotte's soul leaving this earth, beginning its restless search?

In any case I couldn't pick up the gun again. Not even to shoot myself.

I nudged it off the ledge and into a hatbox, put the hatbox in my closet, and waited. Waited with you on the edge of your bed for your brother to come home from school, for your father to come home from work and peek into your sister's crib. When he did, I carried on like any bereaved mother, which I was. I fell to my knees, wailing uncontrollably, remembering how still Charlotte had lain afterward, how sweet; my distress wasn't faked and through it all nobody questioned me, not your father, not Lyla, not Evan. Not the doctor or the coroner.

You were sent to your room.

My psychiatrist made a house call and the order given: I was sedated.

As soon as I could manage—days later, a week later—I threw the hatbox into a dumpster in an alleyway and drove off, and within the month I'd landed in the hospital for the first time, never telling anyone what I'd done to Charlotte, what I'd almost done to you. While there, I hoarded the pills they gave me, first under my tongue, then in the little velvet bag I kept with my things, a jewelry bag. In it I always put my rings, my wedding band. I didn't like to wear them in that place. One night I swallowed all the pills at once; such a lot of work to swallow so many pills, the tongue dry and uncooperative, the throat sore and constricted. To no avail, that time. Only to have my stomach pumped and be sent back eventually to the life I hated, a life in which I hated myself.

At least I never touched you again, not in a way that was indecent. The gun put an end to that, mysteriously; made me come to my senses, such as they were. Nor, however, did I touch you as a mother should—no stroking your hair, or upsy-daisy onto my lap, no clutching you to me. Frankly, I've never touched you that way, although now I long to, before my death—I long to be the mother you deserve. Smartly, you won't allow it. Won't allow the hands of a murderer to touch you; you cleave to Evan, you look right through me. Although I cry and hurl myself on my bed and dig my nails into my sorry, misbegotten hands, I can't blame you. How can I? Inside, I'm even a little glad: this means you'll survive me. You'll *survive*. You aren't desperate as I am for love; you're full of judgment and disdain. You aren't foolish—this will see you through.

It's nearly one in the morning and I can't wait any longer.

I loved you.

TWENTY-FOUR

At first I am calm.

My mother's letters spread out on the carpet before me, her handwriting exact and neat, nothing erased or crossed out.

They're written in pen, they're written in pencil, they're written in red ink. They're written on blue sheets of her personal stationary, monogrammed MGM for Marian Greer Mapes; one is dated, the rest aren't. None are paginated.

I don't know what else to do, so I lie down right where I am, easing myself down sideways, my belly not a part of me but an obstacle I must curl up around. My nose winds up near her letters and recipe cards. A musty odor, chalky to the touch, decomposing and turning to dust.

Then: the sound of breathing, in and out, in and out, all around me, as if I'm standing in a lung—as if somebody else is breathing, but it's me and I can't stop. I try. I cut off my air halfway through a breath, hold it, start up again, more softly. No use.

Somebody breathing in my ear. My mother?

Must call somebody. I start for my phone, crawling and creeping, my belly slung low, the baby kicking *let me out of this madhouse,* I can't seem to stand up and walk, why bother getting up anyway, the phone's just across the room—

The goddamned dollhouse in my way. Why'd I ever bring this back here? Did I think for a minute I'd want to give this to a baby? My baby?

I flounder on the floor like a helpless insect, a roly poly. I brush my foot against the house. It's painted vanilla with green shutters and a red chimney. My mother gave it to me, my father said, painting and fixing it up for me late in the night, working in the basement so I wouldn't see. The dollhouse had been hers as a child; I fancied it resembled the house *she'd* grown up in, although I never visited there that I could recall. Icebox in the kitchen, claw-footed bathtub, grandfather clock under the stairwell, an old black phone with a horn for your ear and a horn for your mouth and the whole town shared a party line.

I lug myself upright to open the doors on the side of the house. Stuffed inside are three plastic bags; I know what's in them since I packed them myself as a teenager when Dad married Dorinne, each bag filled with debris from the house.

This house I destroyed as a child.

I empty out the first bag, that awful sound of breathing in my ear. A number of tiny painted wood bed frames, a green couch with ripped upholstery, an oval rug, a highboy bureau, its drawers with their pulls made from straight pins; a cracked mirror the size of my thumb, a miniature vase with the flowers torn from it, the black phone—the cord cut; bathtub, toilet, sink, kitchen table, coffee table, all in surprisingly fine shape; the grandfather clock, its face scribbled over; several broken straight-backed chairs, rungs cracked, legs missing—I used to break them over the head of the doll without any hair, just as I used to run over her legs with the tiny metal vacuum cleaner, painted red and chipped, also here.

I feel as I've always felt about this dollhouse: fear and hate.

In the second smaller plastic bag are plump striped mattresses, teeny pillows still in their cases, towels with fringe, sheets with hems, quilted bedspreads and blankets with satin bindings, all of which my mother sewed herself to give to me.

Such a dollhouse should be a little girl's dream come true—why did I hate it so?

I try making a bed from the dollhouse: first one tiny, hemmed sheet goes onto the mattress, then another sheet on top of that, *then* a blanket, the bedspread, oh, and the pillow. Like making a real bed in miniature, but with no room to tuck anything in. In my mind—did my mother tell me this?—there is only one way to make this bed. You are not allowed to cut corners.

Making beds was the job of the doll with no hair.

My mother standing at my bedroom door, arms crossed,

watching me play with my dollhouse. It must've taken me all day just to make the beds alone. Then there were the towels to be folded and hung properly over the towel racks, chairs to be arranged around the tables, dishes to be put away—I forgot about those.

They're in with the dolls themselves, in the last plastic bag. Most of the plates are broken; a vague memory of throwing them against the walls of my room, or chiseling away at them with a ballpoint pen.

The dolls. I spread them out before me. The mother doll in her clingy red dress, platinum blond hair pulled back severely, black metal shoes. No father doll—was there ever a father doll? Six children dolls, one missing a leg. Instead she has a cutout piece of cardboard stuck to her torso with a Band-aid. Another pretty doll is missing a foot. There are two boy dolls, unscathed, one in a plaid shirt, the other in a green felt sweater. Then, the doll that hurts me most to see: the doll without any hair. In her pink shorty dress and no underwear, she is bald, except for the miraculous presence of two teeny felt bows. You can still see the glue on her head, where the hair used to be. There's a seam there, where her head is joined together, as though she's survived brain surgery or chemotherapy. A lumpy fabric face. She's ugly, I think, though she might've been pretty.

Her head always hurt and she worked all the time and tried to stay clear of the other dolls, the pretty two-faced girls who were maimed nonetheless and the two boys who were perfect-looking and not always mean to her, but who never stuck up for her either.

The mother doll—my stomach still churns at the sight of her. Sometimes she was nice, or pretended to be. Then she stood up straight, dipped her fabric head kindly. What would a nice doll say? I didn't know. So she said very little. Then she'd leave and come back, her chest bent out, legs splayed, metal shoes clacking, her head twisted and contorted.

At the mere sight of the doll without any hair she would fly into a rage, destroy the house, beat her with the vacuum cleaner, break a chair over her head, stick her head down the toilet, kick her with her hard metal shoes. Only her for some reason: the other dolls were too attractive and clever to incite her rage, and besides, they only lived in the house sometimes, they could get away—

She is a prisoner, the doll without any hair. Not forever, though. In her painted-on blue eyes is a kind of lumpen determination, despite the glue on her head and the seam up its back. Oh yes, here is her cardboard suitcase and her rocking chair. She rocks in her chair, faster and faster, suitcase on her lap, until she imagines she is somewhere else.

When I think of her head, my head hurts, a pain that erupts in her stomach, my stomach. *She can make the pain go away. She twists her fingers around each other and stares at them until they aren't connected to her body anymore, and she feels nothing, no pain. It's really miraculous, this trick she has, and things are soft and distant, as though she were wrapped in flannel. . . .*

That sound of breathing in my ear, still. I make it over to my desk, to search for some scissors, where the hell did I leave them? Here are the nail clippers I left out earlier, they'll do. I swivel out the nail file, stab it deep into the legs of the platinum-haired doll.

Bitch.

I laugh aloud, a howl. A doll, for God's sake, what am I doing? I force her chest outward, contort her head, yes, like this she looks monstrous. Flesh-colored string goes round and round her legs; I unravel it, tear at it, rip out the batting inside her legs, attempt to hack off the black metal feet—where are my goddamn scissors?

I spot them, on the counter from cutting the twine off the carton of my mother's linens—

I snip off her feet, right, left, then throw them at the walls. I cut her body in half, then into segments. I turn what's left of her dress into a messy red fringe, tatters, then it's off with her head.

I giggle. Inside I feel vile. Relief. Nausea. Guilt like an avocado pit in my stomach.

The other dolls I leave alone. The one without any hair I set upon her rocking chair, place her suitcase at her feet.

I finish what I began as a child. A rampage, a riot—I carry out furniture and smash it to the ground, stamp it with my feet. Getting out my X-acto knife from my desk drawer, I carve my initials everywhere, on the walls of the dollhouse, the floors, inside the tiny bathtub, the icebox. I scratch the finish off the tables, slash the face of the grandfather clock—

I stop. The breathing in my ear, loud and venomous.

Those fucking little beds with their sheets and blankets. I grab one of the sheets, skewer it with the X-acto knife and let 'er rip, along with another sheet, a bedspread, then a tiny towel. I get to thinking about my mother's linens, how they sat unused in the sideboard in our dining room for all those years after she died. Irish linens, filmy organdy, embroidered edges, the finest cloth. How, as a child, I would open the sideboard with the skeleton key just to read her handwriting on the clear plastic-wrapped packages. *A dozen placemats, dozen monogrammed napkins, one runner.* She had written this, she had held the pen in her hand: it seemed astonishing. I'd search for more words, a message to me, to no avail. *Two dozen doilies. Round tablecloth, 5 ft. diameter.* Her wedding presents, no doubt, and now they are mine. Sitting complacently on the pool house floor, protected by plastic wrapping; the linens are white, lace-edged, themselves the virgins my mother and I never were.

The urge is irresistible. How can I not?

Slashing them out of their casings, I cut a couple of the napkins to get them started—snip and rip, a snarling sound.

Scissors are too civilized. I bite a tablecloth to get it started and I'm about to rip it in half, when I stop. I feel my mother's presence, as when she comes to me in my sleep, kneeling in the corner. Only now she's bent over completely, her head turned away in shame. My mother with her dowry of wounds and sorrows and orifices, bands of metal on her teeth. She wants to be freed and only I can free her. She's watches me now as I'm about to rend this tablecloth in two, which I will do again and again until the tablecloth is in shreds, and she's glad. She doesn't ask to be forgiven, that's not what's important. What's important is the truth. That I tell the truth. She's waiting, as the doll with no hair is waiting. It's like attending a hanging. I think maybe the doll with no hair wouldn't like a hanging, so I turn her to the wall. My mother continues to watch.

As I destroy her linens set by set, in my head I begin a dialogue with her:
Me: He raped you.
Her: I don't know what you're talking about.
Me: He raped you. Why don't you admit it?
We're sitting on a low garden wall. We're girls, the same age. We've not reached puberty, who knows how long this has been going on? Forever. For as long as we've known.
Me: He would have raped me, Charlotte too.
Her: (she sighs) Yes.
She demonstrates what she does on such occasions. She lies on her side, drinks milk from a wineglass. Then she asks me what I do.
Me: You know what I do. You've seen me do it.
Her: Show me.
Me: The trick with the fingers. Numb from the waist down. You know. You were the one who taught me. When you raped me.
I want her to admit what she did to me, face to face. Maybe I want an apology. We're grownups now, around the same age or perhaps I'm older than her. We're talking in a basement and it's summer, hot outside, cool down here. She's perched on a step stool and I stand before her.
Me: But that's just the beginning. That's nothing in comparison. Don't you remember?
Her: Remember what?
Me: What you did to Charlotte.
Her: I didn't mean to.
Me: But you did. You murdered her. You would've murdered me. How could you do that? Murder a baby.

Her: I suppose. You're right.
Me: You say so yourself in your letters.
Her: (in a tired voice) It's true.
She's like a child. Her eyes won't meet mine.
Me: It's because of him that you did it. Isn't that right?
Her: I suppose.
We're getting nowhere. She doesn't mean to be elusive; it's that her mind is damaged beyond repair and she is counting on me now. I have to be the mother. Her mother, my own mother, my baby's mother.

"Charlotte!" I cry. My sister. The thin white arm I'll never touch again. I kneel like my mother, bent over at the waist, and weep.

A peacock screeches, waking me.

I've fallen asleep, for a moment, for an hour, I'm not sure, my head resting on a stack of tea towels. All about me are doilies hacked to bits, torn up placemats, napkins, tablecloths, reduced to ragged strips, threads. My arms ache from driving in the scissors, the nail file, the X-acto knife; my palms are blistered pink. The baby in my belly is asleep so I remain very still, surveying the wreckage, the recipes and little bitty plates, tiny ransacked furniture, dolls with their legs up in the air, blind eyes staring up into the blazing lights of the pool house.

Outside it's pitch black still, though it feels close to dawn.

I must've been asleep because now I remember a dream. It's about my mother, so I savor it, as I always do. My mother in Nordic dress, a dagger upheld in her hand. I'm afraid to look in her eyes. Somebody tells me to look, *look*. When I do horrible things spew forth—snakes, blackened metal, wet trash, clods of dirt, slime, vomit; my stomach churns, now as in the dream.

Then the dream is gone and I remember my haircut from when I was thirteen years old.

I don't want to think about this and shut my eyes and hold my breath, to keep the image away. I'm thirsty, terribly thirsty. The X-acto knife is near my thigh and I hurl it across the room, not a good idea to have it so close. I'm thirsty and my bladder hurts but I'm pinned to the floor—

My hair is cut badly, unevenly, as though with a butter knife. I do it myself in front of the mirror every day, every time I'm in front of the mirror, in fact, shorter and shorter, I can't stop, shaving it up the back of my neck with my father's electric shaver, bristles of hair inside my clothes, scratching me, annoying me. It's supposed to be a pixie cut, but my hair is too curly so I tape it down at night, snipping off anything that curls or offends—

I've taken to shaving my arms as well, not just under my arms. Any single hair that stands out, doesn't lie down straight: first I trim it with the scissors, then I go after it with Daddy's shaver, hovering just over the skin at first so that the hair is almost sucked into the shaver, then I move in closer and closer until I'm shaving my arms, wrist to elbow—

Until somebody says at school one day, eyeing me in gym class—we have to wear sleeveless shirts, she must see the bristles on my arms like five o'clock shadow—"Do you shave your arms?"

I glance at them as if for the first time. "Yes."

"Why?"

"I don't know."

The doll with no hair.

A baby.

Charlotte.

I vomit and vomit, there's no end to it. I hold my belly as if to keep the baby in, and vomit again, but for once I'm not frightened, the toilet is just a toilet.

I've crawled to the bathroom and now I crawl back, my fingers alternately twitching and claw-like. I'm worried about the baby—what if I miscarry? Too late for that, but what if I have the baby early? Is three-and-a-half-weeks early too early? This is what drives me to the phone. I have to call someone. Maggie, my friend and midwife, but what will I say? I'm not contracting, I'm not cramping, I don't hurt, I'm just having a nervous breakdown.

That must be what this is: look at this room, wall-to-wall destruction and a toilet filled with vomit. People have been committed for less.

My mother's words: *Why would God let this happen to a girl? To anyone?* As I crawl across the room I'm listening inside myself, for the baby. *Are you all right, little one? Are you all right?*

I pick up the phone.

It's still dark out, must be earlier than I think. Maggie is here now, shoving debris out of the way, laying me down on the futon, pressing pillows to me and a blanket, cool cloths to my forehead and wrists. She lifts my shirt, pressing the Doppler to my belly.

"Good heartbeat, perfect. Not too fast, not too slow. As for you, your pulse is racing." She pumps the blood pressure cuff. "Blood pressure on the low side. I suspect it's the shock. We'll check it again in a while."

She pulls off my pants, my underwear—I'm a rag doll, limp—and checks me inside. "Everything is as it should be. Cervix ripening a bit, nothing abnormal about that. As far as the baby is concerned, as far as I can tell, everything is fine, Theo. You're a good mother."

"I doubt that." My voice is hoarse, as though I've been screaming all night. For all I know I have been screaming. In any case I can't talk in a normal tone of voice; my words evaporate halfway out of my mouth and I gaze at the ceiling as if expecting to find them there. "Not possible to be a good mother," I say.

"You're taking good care of your baby," Maggie says firmly. "Now drink your water. Rest."

Water. Maggie's cure-all. She's poured me a pitcher of it and expects me to drink every last drop. I sip the water, let my eyes close for a moment. An image of my mother rising from her knees, walking toward me, her hand extended. Suddenly I'm very, very cold. Shaking.

A blanket appears, is tucked around me.

"It's the blood pressure," Maggie says.

"Will I have to go to the hospital?"

"I doubt it. Unless you want to."

Panic. Which hospital are we talking about—the mental kind? "No hospitals," I say.

"If that's the way you feel, then, drink." She lifts me to a half-reclining position, fits the glass to my mouth. "Come on, a little more." I feel like a whale, my bladder pinches and aches, like somebody's standing on it.

"I have to pee."

"Good," she says. "That's wonderful news." She helps me to the bathroom, ignoring the stench. She flushes down the vomit before I sit. It takes a long time to even start, my bladder is so swollen. Maggie turns on the faucet at the sink, fetches me a cup of warm water to splash on myself. When finally I do go, it's one drip at a time for a while, then it's a torrent, endless.

Maggie walks me back to the room; I'm leaning on her hard. "I feel like I'm in labor."

"What?"

"No, no. Not labor. I meant, you escorting me around like this." A feeble attempt at a joke. "Like the husbands in birth movies." Oh, husbands. Let's not think about that.

Then Maggie is scooping up armfuls of torn linens, recipe cards, papers, bits of splintered dollhouse furniture and other wreckage, and without really looking at any of it, thank God, she dumps them in mounds against the wall and covers them with sheets and towels from my closet, so I won't have to be reminded, I guess, only now the mounds resemble corpses, exhumed bodies.

I turn my head away, toward Maggie and my nest of blankets and pillows. "I'm so ashamed."

Maggie says, while feeding me bites of yogurt, "Never mind, Theo. We'll talk about it tomorrow."

All this attention—Maggie moving about so efficiently, like women do. Women at feasts, women at funerals, lifting, carrying, wiping up the juices of food, of death.

"Maggie," I say. She's by my side, holding my hand.

"What, honey?"

"I was looking for my mother's recipe for cold fruit soup. Can you believe it?" I gesture at all the crap piled against the walls. "That's how this all began. You know, I feel awfully sleepy," I tell Maggie. "How come I'm shaking so much?"

"Low blood pressure. Shock. Have you eaten lately?"

"Is this what it's like to have a nervous breakdown?"

"I wouldn't know," Maggie says, "but you seem lucid. Even if you weren't, the last place you'd want to go is a hospital. Now let's stop talking. I want you to drink. Rest. In five minutes we'll check your pressure."

I lay there breathing in and out, trying to ignore the sound of my own breathing. I feel utterly like a child. A child in the nurse's office at school. Somebody come and pick me up. An adult. My father can't, he's beyond hope, always was. He stammers, he hesitates; who knows what he really feels or believes? Well, then, there's Evan, who talks too much and says all the wrong things— and who is probably dead now anyway. Aunt Lyla, she would come in a pinch, in her stiletto heels and Lana Turner sunglasses. Too glamorous to fill the shoes of my parents, but she would try. The Aunt Lyla of old, that is. And my mother, where is she? I'm lying on my side pregnant as a cow, I'm going to be a mother myself; where is she? Who is she? Swathed in scarves, a mystery, a casualty. A suicide, a victim, a sadist, a murderer, the murdered, a savior, an angel, a ghost. She is good, she loves me. She is bad, she hurts me. And I will never really know who she is or why she had to die. Why she had to kill my sister. Charlotte's death. My mother's suicide. The stones I would have to push uphill all my life. But now I've reached the crest, the other side; the stones are about to roll downhill, a rockslide, and I'm standing on top of the mountain, unscathed. Mostly. I'm alive, aren't I? Sane, or so they say. A slightly dented but improved specimen about to release her genes into the next generation.

TWENTY-FIVE

Maggie brings her sleeping boys over for the rest of the night. Come morning, I throw everybody out, insist I'm fine. No, I don't want to talk about what happened. Not now. Maybe later. Yes, I'll drop by Maggie's office around two this afternoon so she can check me again.

They leave and I call Corb. His business line, I don't want to talk to his wife. He answers on the first ring, "This is Corb Mapes. Hello?" he says. "Hello, hello—" Impatiently.

An imagined sound like a helicopter in my ears, or maybe it's my heart pounding. "It's me."

"Hi, what's up? How did Pinks go?" I picture him dressed in a shirt with a soft collar, the hair on his arms curling at the base of his black watch. Like our father, so much hair. Men. A wave of revulsion rides over me until I'm flat. I see I'm lying on the floor again, mirrored in the sliding glass door of the poolhouse. Mirrors—no wonder I fear them so. In them I see my mother's face, beckoning, whispering, solutions that are chemical, lethal.

"Theo?" Corb says, cautiously.

"I was going through our mother's recipe box yesterday and I found some letters from her."

"Oh." Said so casually, as if I'd announced I'd gotten a bill in the mail. "And what did they say?"

"Letters from our mother, Corb. Awful stuff. Insane." I stare at my reflection, hateful and bulbous, like a snake that has eaten a cow.

"Well, she *was*, Theo. Mentally ill. I don't like to use that term, but yes, she was out of touch."

"Are you stating that from memory? What do you mean she was out of touch?"

"She used to weep and weep at the dinner table."

"That's crazy?"

"We were all supposed to act like we didn't notice."

"*That's* crazy."

"This was after she'd gotten all over us about our table manners and why didn't we like the dinner she served. Lamb croquettes and other dishes kids would never touch in a million years."

"I thought Evan cooked the meals."

"At the end maybe. I remember Mom cooking." Strange to hear her called Mom. "Anyway, Theo, why are we talking about this? There's no point in going over it."

"Don't you want to know about her letters?" My voice is cracking. "I feel so alone—"

Silence. I guess that means he's listening.

"She hid them in her recipe box, it's—horrible. Like a long, long suicide note. One of them *is* a suicide note."

Still he doesn't say anything. I hear a sound—is he crying silently? I realize we've never said that word between us, suicide. Never. Not once. We say death, our voices drop an octave. We say she passed away—never, never suicide.

"There's something else," I say. My voice is so much lower, hoarser. "Something far worse than our mother's suicide."

I wait for Corb to say *what*. He doesn't.

"Corb, don't you want to know what it is? Corb, it's about Charlotte. Don't you want to know?"

His voice quavers. I am sure he's crying. "I don't know that I do."

"You don't want me to tell you?" I say.

"No." His voice turns very cold, very bitter. His answer is a rebuke.

"Well, then, goodbye, Corb."

"Don't you dare hang up—"

I punch the off button, hurl the phone across the room. The cheap paneled wall quakes.

Maggie is back at my door with Dylan and Willy. "Honey, do you need anything?"

"My brother's an asshole."

"Do you want to talk about it? Should I come in?" The boys peek out from behind her legs.

"No!"

The boys duck.

"All right, then, I'm going to the store. What can I get you?"

"Ice cream." Nausea like the first trimester again. I've eaten nothing since the yogurt. "No, Maggie, forget it, nothing. Thanks. And sorry. I just can't . . . talk yet."

"Later, then."

I hear her walk away, sandals slapping and echoing on the cement, Dylan asking a question, her murmured answer.

The baby moves rhythmically in my womb, not a kick, it's down too low and there's no room anymore. Elbows beating like confined wings, fingers drumming in impatience.

I picture Corb hopping into his car, driving down Huntington Drive at ninety miles an hour. An emergency; for the first time in his life he understands my distress, as I understand his. I retrieve the phone, hit the redial button.

"This is Corb Mapes."

I hang up. Business as usual, the jerk. If the next earthquake hit his house dead center, he would continue to work. My belly feels unusually heavy; it tightens up, Braxton Hicks, but it doesn't release. I lie down for a minute to rest, then get up, find myself some orange juice in my tiny refrigerator, and a hunk of French bread. Eat it dry. Margarine is too much of an effort.

"Take it easy, baby," I say, stroking my belly, trying to get the Braxton Hicks to release. "Hang in there."

Throwing the sheets and towels off the mounds of debris, I pick around for my mother's letters, heartlessly throwing aside the platinum blond doll's feet and head in my search. Recipes, torn linens—this is taking too long. I go to the garage and get a rake, raking everything out into the center of the floor.

At the Sierra Madre post office, I insure the package I'm sending to my brother. I wonder why I don't just drop it by his house, but I know why. I can't see him now.

"How much do you want to insure it for?" the clerk says.

"What's the limit?"

"Five hundred dollars."

"Good. I'll do that."

She looks at me strangely; a black woman. I look back with what I hope is an impassive gaze as she slips the packet of Xeroxed letters into the overnight delivery package addressed to Corb. A confession of murder, of infanticide, I'm thinking: here I am mailing my mother's murder confession to my brother. His inaudible sorrow.

"Will that be all?" she asks.

I imagine my mother sitting on the barstool by our kitchen phone, near the cabinet where the recipe box was kept; writing late at night, after my father has gone to bed, one small light on. Writing what she could, when she could, a tumbler of crème de menthe beside her, then hurriedly folding the letter, not dating it, lifting the metal bar of the recipe box and shoving the letter inside.

"Yes," I say, "that will be all." Earlier I stood at the little office supply shop around the corner, Xeroxing these letters, three of everything so there's a set of letters for Corb, for my father, and for Aunt Lyla. Every so often I had to pause, one hand on the copier for balance, the other on my belly. It doesn't hurt exactly, it's as though I've got a snake wrapped around me, a python squeezing gently. Walking is a challenge. Now, as I make my way to the car, my belly tightens up all over again, the snake feeling.

This is where I have to go today:

—my appointment with Maggie to make absolutely sure I'm okay

—a stop at Fedco, I hardly have anything for the baby

—the bank, I'm low on money

Just a normal day of errands. Should I stop at the police station, show them the letters? How does one turn in a dead person for murder?

It occurs to me again that I didn't tell Maggie what my mother said in her letters. Can't say the words out loud yet.

Nor can I do these errands. I drive past the bank, keep going, drive past Fedco. Can't go back to the pool house either; it's like a husk I've discarded and suddenly I know for a fact that I won't have my baby there. I can't. A fine time to decide this, what am I supposed to do about it now, mere weeks before my due date? It's the wrong place, I'm thinking frantically. Too dark, too small, all wrong, and now with all that crap in there. Ripped-up tablecloths and a trashed dollhouse and my mother's recipes all over the place. Even if I could clean it out, which I can't summon the energy to do, I still don't want the baby there. No. Out of the question.

Instead I imagine a freshly painted white room, wood floors swept clean.

The house I will rent with Gregg. Gregg. I haven't talked to him in more than twelve hours, when he brought over the stuff from Pink's; he has no idea what's happened to me and I don't know how to explain to him, where to begin.

No, it's all too exhausting. Everything.

Never mind about Gregg. I feel a lifting in my heart at the thought of those wooden floors and the white-painted walls. I almost stop for a paper so I can look for a new place, *that* place, but it's futile now, too late. I don't even have any baby stuff, only the two blankets I ordered. No crib, no baby clothes, although Maggie and Diane have offered to take me shopping.

I'll be lucky if I manage to pick up a package of diapers in time for the birth.

Lightheaded, I drive around aimlessly, the baby very still. Space is too tight, especially when I'm sitting upright like this; the baby's feet are hooked over the bottom of my ribcage. Periodically I pull over and readjust the seat, trying to get some relief. My feet and ankles are swelling again. Look at them! Pickled logs. I know what Maggie would say to that: drink water. Which doesn't make any sense. Aren't I just swimming in fluids already?

It's then that I remember my appointment with her. I'm more than an hour late. Why go now? Nor can I seem to will myself to find a phone booth, call Maggie, try to explain, drive over there.

Just go. Now. But I keep driving aimlessly, what difference does it make? Down Lake, across California Boulevard, cut over toward the Huntington Museum, circle around to that hilly part of San Marino we used to call Disneyland: Tudor homes with small turrets or the occasional waterless water wheel, lots of Spanish-style mansions with red clay roofs, olive trees, ersatz Mission Bells. I ride the brake down Shenandoah, then it's back up to Pasadena, to the Grove, my father's new home.

Because I know I have to face him.

No place to park in front, so I park in back, then wind my way backwards through the building, down hallways with handrails and peach vinyl wallpaper—a home for old people despite the advertised plush "apartments," the Olympic-sized swimming pool, the meticulously landscaped "campus." There is still the just-banished odor of day-old pudding, incontinence, loneliness. I choke up every time I come here, at the prospect of my father spending the rest of his days here.

But today when I enter his apartment, to my surprise, I momentarily regain the part of myself I lost since going to Pink's yesterday. After all, nothing here has changed. In his small living room my father sits in a chair reading with his magnifying glass, exactly as before; as always, he acts slightly disappointed to see me.

"Weren't you just here?"

"That was two days ago, Dad."

I expect him to notice: to see what's on my face and ask me what is wrong. At the very least notice the folder in my hand and ask what it is.

But he doesn't.

I pull up a chair, our legs almost touching, and think of my usual topics: funny stories about Dylan and Willy, or that I talked to Corb.

"I went through the stuff at Pink's," I say. "It's all sorted."

"Oh?"

"Only some of it's destroyed now. Never mind, Dad." His face contorts in confusion. "I'm joking. Sort of. I'm having a lot of Braxton Hicks. I don't suppose you know what those are."

"No."

Weeks ago, I asked him if he wanted to be present when the baby was born.

"Why would I want to do *that*?" he said.

"You've never seen it before. I thought you might be curious."

"I know where babies come from, thank you," he said.

No getting around it, he's himself, a product of his generation. And he's going to be a negligent grandfather, the same as he's been with Corb's boys.

"Why was I so frightened as a child, Dad?"

"Why?"

"Yes, why. All those nights I woke up screaming, so loud the neighbors could hear me."

"I don't know."

"You didn't ever ask yourself why I was frightened?"

Silence.

"Why did my mother kill herself?"

He looks at his TV expectantly, as if anticipating it will go on automatically and enlighten him.

"Dad. How did Charlotte die?" My tears spill over, my fingers pressed to my eyeballs so tightly I can feel the round gelatinous shape of them.

Dad's knee shakes so hard, it shudders.

I get up to close the door, then I stand before the TV and prepare to him tell everything.

But I find that I can't. He's not the person to tell. He's too old now, too fragile. Too broken by loss—his own father, his wife, his infant daughter.

Instead I ask him, "What was it like when your father died?" I sit on the floor beside him. I rest my cheek on his knee.

"He died right in front of me, you know. There was nothing I could do. It was the middle of the Depression," he says. "I never got over it. He was a good man, a good father. He loved me and I loved him."

He strokes my hair with trembling fingers. If he was so loved by his father, I'm thinking, he must be strong enough to take my mother's letters. Perhaps he already suspects the truth, perhaps not. But I know I will never show those letters to him.

TWENTY-SIX

I let myself in the back door calling out, "Yoo hoo! Aunt Lyla!"

No answer, but of course she's here. Sure enough, there's something in the oven, foil-wrapped, and sun tea in the refrigerator, and her car keys and cigarettes on the kitchen counter.

I stand at the bottom of the stairs. "Aunt Lyla, it's me! Theo!"

A slight sound: pen on paper, a stamp being licked, a foot emerging from a bathtub.

"Aunt Lyla, I'm coming up." (My father's voice harping, Don't you think you should've called first? Don't make her fix you lunch! You don't just barge into somebody's bedroom—)

That's exactly what I do. She's standing in her closet in her bra and panties figuring out what to wear, as I've seen her do thousands of times, and as always I study the diminutive hips, the potbelly, the nimble legs, trying to see my mother in her, what my mother might've looked like at this age, had she lived.

"Aunt Lyla."

"Hello. My, look at you! You're huge!" She busses my cheek, then goes back to scrutinizing a red sleeveless blouse on a hanger, no doubt thinking about accessories—a scarf or necklace, earrings. "Won't you stay for lunch? Nothing fancy, just some leftover ham and cantaloupe, a little salad, some rolls."

"I'll stay. Thanks." I'm clasping the folder of letters to my chest, waiting for her to notice. I'm breathing hard, partly from climbing her stairs, partly nerves.

She turns away to dress. "Is it warm out?"

"Broiling."

"And being pregnant, I suppose, only makes it worse." She sighs as though she hadn't been through this herself. Twins, no less. "When is your due date again? In a couple of weeks, isn't it?"

"Three and a half weeks."

"It'll be over before you know it, dear. Next thing you know, you'll be seeing him or her off to college."

"Aunt Lyla."

"Yes, dear?" In tiny bare feet, she pads right past me toward her shoe closet.

"Can we talk?"

"Why, of course." She slips on white high-heeled sandals and stands before me, her scarf like a flag fluttering. Red, white, and dark violet—an almost patriotic ensemble. "Shall we sit?" she asks.

"I think I'll stand."

She perches on the edge of her bed, crossing a leg, one sandal clacking pertly against the bottom of her foot. "Do you want to take off your sunglasses, Theo?"

"Oh." I remove them, squinting. I wait another moment before speaking. "You see what I have here." I slap the folder against my leg a couple of times.

"What is it?"

"Aunt Lyla, they're letters my mother wrote. I found them in her recipe box."

"The letters she wrote before she died."

I'm so stunned I nearly sink to the floor.

"You knew about these letters?" I say.

"I knew about their existence. She told me about them. I didn't know where they were or whether they'd been destroyed. I assumed they *had* been destroyed."

"She told you about them? Wait. I have to make sure we're talking about the same letters." I open the folder and flip through, to find the letter about her, Aunt Lyla. "'I was the dutiful daughter, so that she wouldn't have to be. To spare her. He didn't spare her.' She means you, Aunt Lyla."

I skip ahead. "'Lyla planned her own escape (more successful than mine, it turns out)—who needed college? She scratched herself to pieces to cover up the bruises, the scratching then diagnosed as eczema.'"

"Yes," she says, "my allergies."

"But bruises, Aunt Lyla?"

She shrugs, unperturbed. I read from another letter, at random, rapidly, "'I know all your secrets—I share them, I am the cause of them, I have the wrists to prove it. Ragged scars disguised by tinkling bracelets, a gold watch. I have the throat as well, made sore from all the pills and the lies I've had to swallow.'"

Aunt Lyla interrupts. "Those sound like the letters. The ones explaining why she . . . killed herself, basically."

I try to draw a breath, compose myself. "What exactly did my mother say to you about these letters?"

"She called me up one day and told me."

My face flushes, followed by a wash of perspiration, almost pleasurable. An actual story about my mother, my mother picking up a real phone and speaking into it, words that someone remembers—a story truer, it seems, than the letters themselves. "Go on," I say.

"I was in the middle of something, a luncheon or a meeting, ladies in the house and children running everywhere, so I might've seemed a little impatient. I never knew what she wanted from me, Theo. What I should do."

"What did she say?"

"She said she was on her way to the hospital. I asked her if this was her idea or Hal's. She said it was her wish. She was checking herself in that day. I asked her if Hal knew and she said yes, he was taking her over there in a few minutes. Her voice was—breathless, strange, and I wondered if she were drunk or had taken something, were they going to have to pump her stomach again.

"You have to understand the times, Theo. Nobody talked about such things then. Maybe it was a fear that word would leak out, that it might make things worse for you children. Everybody in town would know then, so it was better not to talk about it. It was 'Marian's going to the hospital.' That was all. We never said the words 'suicide attempt,' or 'breakdown.' And when she died, we didn't say she killed herself. When Mother called me to tell me the news she said, 'Marian is gone.'"

She tilts her head to look at me unceremoniously, one eyebrow raised. No tears. It occurs to me I've never seen Aunt Lyla cry, not about this, not about anything.

"But about the letters," I say. "What did she tell you?"

"She told Hal to put her bag in the car, she'd be out in a moment. She seemed awfully lucid for somebody having a breakdown, but she always seemed that way, around me at least. She never let her guard down, not even when we were girls. Anyway, Hal went out to the car, I guess—which, if it had been me, I would've never done, who knows what she was capable of? She might slit her wrists again or cut her throat. . . . But he knew her better than I did, I guess, in that way. So she told me, 'Lyla, I've written some letters. They're for Theo. For Corb too, if he's interested some day.' I said, 'Fine, fine. You'd better go along now, Marian. Go to the hospital, please. Hal is waiting.' I rushed her along because I was scared she was going to kill herself right then and there. Her voice was so strange, like a part of her had died already. I kept picturing a gun in her lap."

"There was a gun," I say.

Aunt Lyla turns her head sharply, taken aback, but not as shocked as I would think.

I still can't tell her what happened to Charlotte, so I go about it backwards, sideways. "My mother did know how to shoot," I continue. "Her father taught her, and you, she said. He did teach you how to shoot, didn't he, Aunt Lyla?"

"When we were younger, yes. That was years ago." She's threading her scarf in and out of her fingers, an eel swimming to and fro.

"He raped her, apparently." How to talk about this? "My grandfather raped my mother, his daughter. Did he rape you, too, Aunt Lyla?"

Her mouth is just—open.

Sitting on my grandfather's lap. My mother sees me there, but I don't see myself. I'm four, shouldn't I remember? I don't remem-

*ber sitting there or his hand beneath my dress. I don't remember
his hand. His face. Nothing. Just evil. Just fear.*

"Anyway," I continue. I can hardly breathe. "My mother was
afraid. Afraid he'd harm her children. That's why she bought the
gun, that and the fact she was crazy. That's why she killed Charlotte. She meant to kill me and herself too."

Aunt Lyla stands up so quickly, she knocks the phone off the
bedside table. "What are you talking about? *What in the world are
you talking about?*"

My hands shaking, I flip through the letters. I pull out that
one. "She says so. Right here."

I hold up the letter but she waves me away, placing the phone
back in its cradle.

"She put a pillow over Charlotte's head because she couldn't
bear to shoot her with the gun."

Aunt Lyla just stares, at me, as though *I'm* the one who
committed murder. "Please, please, stop. Why do we have to talk
about this?" She opens a drawer, takes out a pack of Carltons,
tamps one out. Click, click with the lighter.

"Didn't you ever wonder how Charlotte died?" I say. "Last
night I—"

"Never mind, dear. You'd best get some counseling. If that's
truly what happened, your mother . . ."

"But you don't deny that she killed Charlotte."

"I'm saying I don't know."

"Did your father rape my mother?"

"I said *I don't know.*"

She rushes from the bedroom, sandals clacking, scarf trailing.
By the time I lumber downstairs, there is a roast on the counter
and she's peeling off foil. "Will you hand me the baster, please?"

I'm bumbling around in various drawers but before I can find
it, she's gotten it herself. She squirts drippings all over the meat
and rewraps it in foil.

"I heard what you said up there and I just have one question,"
Aunt Lyla says.

"Yes?"

"It doesn't matter what I think. You know I spent my whole life going against my father, and Mother too, when she was alive. But the question is, what do you think, do *you* believe he did that to us? To Marian and me? Do *you* believe your mother killed your sister? That she meant to kill you?" She's taken my hands in hers, and I'm a child again with an ache in my throat, my heart, needing her.

It's like talking to my mother in my fantasies last night. Evasions, but of a different sort.

"Oh, why don't you let it go, dear? Get on with your life? Your mother and sister are dead. You are alive." On her tiptoes, she stretches up and over my belly to kiss my cheek. I incline my head to receive her kiss, my head remaining bowed afterward as though I'm asking for forgiveness.

"And you're going to have a baby," she says. "Isn't that what you ought to be concentrating on? On the new life inside you?" I'm nodding in agreement, exhausted suddenly. "Theo, where are you going?"

I've broken away from her and I'm hurrying, waddling, back upstairs to get my purse and my mother's letters so I can leave.

"Theo?" I hear her muttering to herself as I lug myself up step after step, my fingers laced under my belly like a sling. "Theo?" I hear the faint click-click of her lighter.

In her bedroom, panting, I pick up the folder of letters from the bureau where I left it. Uncle Morgan's bureau, I know, from various snooping excursions when I was a child. I snooped here as much as at home, in search of something having to do with my mother.

I close my eyes tight, then open them again. Everything looks cockeyed and bulging, cartoon colors. That breathing sound in my ears again, relentless now, and the snake feeling in my belly. I open Uncle Morgan's narrow top drawer, left exactly the same; Aunt Lyla hasn't disturbed it since his death, apparently. Shoelaces, spare change, cufflinks, a few nuts and bolts, an envelope of paper money from other countries. In the center of this drawer, in the midst of all the clutter, is what I'm really looking for—a small silver ivory-handled pistol. It fits in the palm of my hand, like a toy, the silver tarnished, the ivory yellowed.

The first time I saw it, probably when I was about ten, fright made me slam the drawer shut. What was it doing here? Was it loaded? Then each time I snooped after that, it was the gun I most wanted to see. Would it still be there? *Why* was it there? It didn't seem big enough to hurt anyone, perhaps it really was a toy. Did bullets even come that size?

I hurl the folder with my mother's letters across the room, scattering them everywhere so Lyla will be forced to see them in order to pick them up.

"Theo, are you all right?" She's in the doorway. "Theo! My God! What are you doing!"

I aim the gun at my head.

TWENTY-SEVEN

*Paper bag rustling. Something black, hard. Click click. A sound
like when my mother works at her desk and puts new staples into
the stapler. Click click. My eyes shut, I can't open them. Click
click. I open them, wait. Outside green branches catch each
other's arms and they sway back and forth, but what I see is
brown. The nubby brown folds of my curtains, closed to the sun.
I sit and don't move. Feet propped on the bed frame, hands in my
lap, knees pointed out into the room, my scalp tingling click click
numb. Sometimes by the side of my eye the black hard thing, then
it's gone. Click click. Click click. My mother or the person who
looks like her drinks from a bottle. She jams it in my mouth burning until I cough.*

Driving up San Gabriel Boulevard, I'm going sixty, seventy,
eighty, cars swerving out of my way; I almost hope for a cop. To
stop me, chase me down. Shoot me. The ivory-handled pistol
rests on the seat beside me, so slender and tiny it might be a joke,
but judging from Aunt Lyla's reaction, it must be real enough.

She had walked toward me carefully, talking gently. "Theo,
honey, think of the baby. Theo, put the gun down now. Theo—"

I started to do as she asked, then at high speed I rushed toward
her; instinctively she jumped aside. I ran past her downstairs and
out the back door, clumsily, like a duck. In the pocket of my
maternity dress was the pistol. Absurdly, I worried it would go
off, shoot me in the foot, if it was even loaded.

I'm flying down the 605, radio playing, baby kicking dully.
Every time there's a commercial, it seems, I feel a twinge. A
contraction? Can't be, I'm three-and-a-half-weeks early, but at the
next commercial I step on the gas, my hand tightens on the wheel,
and I moan—just a little, I'll save the screaming for later, as the

Chevy Cavalier eats up the miles between Aunt Lyla's and Newport Beach, where I'm headed. To Jackson's, though I haven't the foggiest notion where he lives, the address back at the pool house. He lives off the main drag, he wrote, on a street called—what?—in a two-story building, stuccoed and sparkly.

Great. Only a few hundred of those in Newport Beach.

In homage to Maggie, whom I have yet to call, I'm sipping from a bottle of Evian I found rolling around in the back seat, bought several days ago. Plenty of time, I tell myself as what must be another contraction starts: women giving birth in cars and taxi cabs are rare once-every-three-year occurrences, aren't they? Myths to boost the morales of taxi cab drivers, bus drivers, husbands. I mean, how many people has this *really* happened to? Instead, I think of every story I've ever heard of about women going to the hospital too early, their labors halting the minute they hit the maternity ward, their pacing the corridors, sitting in the hot tub, nothing. Their membranes being stripped, punctured, still nothing. Nothing for hours, days, Pitocin finally being administered.

Of all the drugs and interventions, Pitocin scares me the most, being trapped in a terrorizing, chemically-induced labor, a needle in my arm. Like the abuse itself. Already I'm thinking of it that way, whatever it was that happened to me as a child: "the abuse," an ugly friend I have to take with me everywhere. The doll with no hair, humiliated and wet between the legs. Which reminds me. I am. A slick feeling between my legs. The plug, I'm losing my plug. Or else it's sweat. I'm sweating buckets, after all; it's over a hundred degrees today.

"All the time in the world," I say out loud, to the din of the freeway, my eyes burning, lungs bursting from smog. Very carefully, I place the gun into the glove compartment, then concentrate on positive imagery: streams gushing down a mountain— no, wait, no gushing, no water. A dry hot desert. No, too hot. Fevers, infections. No, no. A big bowl of ice cream, frozen and inert—yes. I tell myself it's just nerves, I'm not really in labor. Everybody knows you don't have your first baby early. First babies are *always* late. I picture Jackson's face when he sees me at his door: joy, then panic. Me giving birth in the hallway, no time to make it inside even. Or what if he's not home? Giving birth with strangers on a litter of dishtowels, people speaking foreign languages.

The next contraction sends me across three lanes of freeway to the shoulder of the road.

By the time I reach the 405, I'm dripping like a faucet between the legs. By the Pacific Coast Highway, I'm timing contractions, about every six minutes or so. Every time one comes on, I pull into a side street, hoping it's Jackson's street. Two blocks from the beach, he wrote ("I've arranged to move in after Labor Day, once the season's over")—but the beach, Newport Beach, goes on for miles and miles; I'd forgotten. *Thousands* of stuccoed apartment buildings in pale blue, pastel yellow, mint green, white, and every one of them sparkling like sugared candy.

I wail, "Jackson, you idiot, what color, what color?"

The next contraction's so bad, I'm lucky I make it to a phone booth afterwards, with three minutes to spare until the next contraction. Four dimes: one call. Who will it be? Maggie. Jackson. Gregg. 911. 411.

411 it is, figuring I'll get my dimes back. Shakily, I retrieve the coins from the pocket of my maternity dress—change I had to scrape from the floor of the Chevy while everything inside me ached and shuddered.

The phone, in this booth that reeks of urine, eats my dimes before I even get directory assistance. I slam my hand against the receiver. "Shit!" I'm crying, in the middle of another contraction, pounding my fists against the glass. Why don't I just scream for help? A couple strolls by with beach chairs under their arms, then a man with a dog, but no one notices me.

When I can stand up straight, I scan the instructions on the pay phone frantically.

Is it possible to make a local collect call? My eyes fall on a boy sitting in a camaro parked across the street, a Chicano guy, fourteen, fifteen years old. He's sucking on a pacifier of all things and I involuntarily smile. He sees me and smiles back, and then I'm doubled over with the next contraction.

"You need help?" It's him, speaking through the crack of the door of the pay phone. "You having your baby?"

I manage to grunt out a "Yeah."

"Where's your husband?"

"Trying to find him. Long story."

He walks me to his camaro and everything is spinning. He's taller than I expected so I come up to about his shoulder; I find myself staring at his pacifier, on a string around his neck. It's illuminated in the hard tones of sunset, orange, red, cerulean, but the pacifier is clear and plastic. Suddenly I've got my arms around his waist and I look down and see streaks of blood on my dress.

"Sorry." So good to hold someone, it keeps the pain at bay. I'm starting to lose track of everything, up, down, sideways, time, night, day; it's just as likely right now to be sunrise, dawn. It doesn't matter where I am, who he is.

"We better get you to a hospital," he says.

Hit with another contraction. He breathes with me while I hunch over the hood of the car. "How do you know about breathing?" I say afterwards.

"My sister's baby."

"Good," I gasp, afraid he was going to say his own.

His muffler is so loud it hurts my ears.

"Are you old enough to drive?" I shout over the roar. He's doing sixty at least, running stoplights, and I realize all this time I've been waiting for someone older to show up, his brother or a cousin. A grownup.

"Turned sixteen last week," he says. In a trance I'm watching the pacifier glisten around his neck. He's wearing a huge T-shirt on his skinny frame, a baseball cap on backwards, and when he turns toward me, I'm amazed by the beauty of his eyes, deep and black and still, like something I remember from a dream, a good dream, the bottom of a well or the top of a lake. Then I remember: the swimming hole at Stonewall Creek, round and scattered with red rocks glowing like this boy's skin.

"Got my license last week," the boy says. "Like I told you, my sister had a baby, two, three months ago. I got to watch her being born, it was cool."

He pops the pacifier back into his mouth. Swinging from the rearview mirror are a dozen more, all different colors catching one last ray of light.

I stare at my hands in desperation as the next contraction slams through me. My fingers inches from my face, I twist them round and round, willing them to go numb. For my whole body to go numb. I'm in tears because it doesn't work, I can't go numb anymore. I'm human like anybody else.

"A favor," I say to the kid running alongside the gurney as I'm being rushed to delivery. He's given me his pacifier to hold, which is sticky and clammy and sweet in my hand. "Call my husband for me. Call information. Jackson Zander, with a Z, he works at Costa Mesa Junior College and he lives in Newport Beach."

The boy is racing down the hall.

"Tell him to hurry!"

Then I'm in a white room screaming with the best of them, a doctor's hand up me, some guy with a paper mask. "Okay," he says. "I'm Dr. Frank. Now push!"

"I am! Jesus!"

"Push, push!"

I've got a nurse on either side, their arms under my knees, pushing my legs up and back.

"Good! Would you like to touch your baby's head?"

Hard and warm, it's almost hot—a shock that it's not myself I'm touching but another being.

"Let's get this baby out now! Push!"

The nurse I begged and pleaded with to go buy one of those insta-cameras from the gift shop is back now, taking pictures of the baby's head coming out, its mouth being suctioned.

The next push just about rips me in two. "What is this!"

"You're birthing the baby's shoulders."

"They hurt . . . worse than the head."

"Just one more push! Push! We're almost through."

To push, I concentrate on babies, children. Images of Dylan and Willy, and my nephews when they were small, such as the day I held my nephew Bruce for the first time—how his parents and I joked that he resembled Queen Victoria, round and formidable, an eyebrow that went all the way across. And how I changed my other nephew's diaper once, Gabe like a frog on his back, legs bowed, belly out, delicate and pulsing, the wondrous mother-of-pearl skin. Then I feel this baby leave me, slithering out, now placed in my arms, this baby with red skin and smushed face, swollen genitals, her eyes focused on mine, her beating waxy cord, her warmth and bloody dank smell.

Part Three:
The Milk

TWENTY-EIGHT

Theo's Letter

Dear Gena,

Three days after your birth when my milk came in, my breasts became puffy, swollen, practically suffocating you; when you nursed I had to make a space for you with my fingers. I leaked milk for months, long after the books said. At night I slept with a towel pressed to me and in the morning it was soaked.

So insistent was this milk, that if you began to nurse and stopped for even a second, milk would squirt you in the face. The first time this happened I was so surprised I just stared. So did you. I couldn't stop the milk shooting from my breasts and had to put you down for a moment while I marched around the room with my arms pressed hard against my chest.

Our whole lives revolved around the milk. First, in the hospital, it was learning how to breastfeed you, each nurse demonstrating a different method until the only way I could do it was to hunch over and stuff my nipple into your mouth. I kept thinking about what I'd read: that in our species, breastfeeding an infant is no longer instinctual behavior. It is learned behavior.

We left the hospital before my milk came in, while you were still getting colostrum. I think of how your father's bedroom looked after the first few nights, littered from one end to the other with the items I'd sent him running to the store for: diapers, blankets, pacifiers (rejected by you who preferred to suck on our little fingers); wrung-out tea bags and moist, flattened cotton balls we'd put in the freezer; washcloths wet from melted ice cubes—all those little tricks gotten out of baby books, none of which helped my poor cracked nipples—an open tube of A&D ointment, the only thing that did help; baby clothes fed-exed to us from Maggie, my own discarded clothes. . . . I could only nurse you stripped down to my underwear: shirts, bras, pants were just that much more interference and confusion.

I knew I had it down when on day six I was able to walk and nurse you at the same time, one arm free no less, holding it out for balance and dramatic effect, *voilà*. Your father was suitably impressed though bleary-eyed, watching us ascend the staircase from his bed on the couch, this mother-daughter duo like some two-headed beauty queen hybrid, me in maternity underwear (I was to look pregnant for months afterwards), you in a diaper.

It was four in the morning. You didn't see any difference yet between night and day, a condition that took months to change. Those first two weeks your father slept on the couch half the night so he could spell me in the morning, since I was up the rest of the night with you, either attached to my nipple or to my little finger. This is how we went to sleep those first few weeks: we swaddled you, laid you between us, taking turns on little finger duty (it isn't easy trying to fall asleep with your finger in somebody else's mouth). Even in the dark we could see your eyes were wide open, your mouth with one of our fingers in it bobbing up and down. Sucking, you'd observe us sleeping. Until feeding time. Anytime was feeding time. An hour, two hours after the last time, half an hour, forty-five minutes: you would scream and we'd scamper around like fools trying to please you. "The chair," I'd tell your father. "No, wait, the couch, it's more comfortable. Get the pillows!"

He'd race, collecting pillows on the way: one for under my arm, two for my back, another for my other arm, several beneath my feet like a footrest. Meanwhile I'd strip off my clothes (soon I got smart and skipped wearing them altogether), panic-crooning, "It's all right Gena baby, Mama will be there, Mama's hurrying—" and carry you football-style to the next nursing destination, milk squirting every which way. The screams! Like you'd turn yourself inside out. Like your head would pop off your neck and hit the ceiling. Like you'd die it hurt so much, this hunger. You'd attach yourself fiercely, sucking so hard you practically knocked yourself out breathing through those tiny nostrils. The squeaking wheel, we called you.

During pregnancy I'd imagined gauzy scenes of me all in white, my baby plump and content, the two of us gently swaying in a rocking chair, pink booties on the baby's feet that I'd knitted myself. I wasn't prepared for a baby who sounded like she needed WD-40, a baby with bowed skinny legs who needed me desperately; I wasn't prepared to feel so in love; I wasn't prepared for bucketfuls of sweat pouring off my face so that in all the early pictures of me holding you, I look like I'm crying, about to drip away.

That was something else no one had told me: that some women sweat the extra water weight strictly through their faces. Another thing: very suddenly, my hair grew two inches, thick, wild in the humidity of my face.

The milk.

Mornings, after the six o'clock feeding—or thereabouts—your father would take you and pack you in the snugly. Up and down the beach he would walk, or over to Balboa Island; he was practically a local landmark, the town greeter. He'd walk to the pier, to the post office, to the store to buy milk, ironically, for me. He planned his trips to the minute, making sure he never went so far that he couldn't hurry back in a quarter of an hour or less. In case you needed to nurse. You'd begin by squirming, smacking your lips; within moments you'd be up to your full-tilt, heart-wrenching cry.

Sometimes I heard you proceeding up the boardwalk, my drenched towel held to my breasts; sometimes, in a dead sleep, I didn't wake up until you were beside the bed. That was the reason for these walks—so that I could sleep, so that my milk supply would build. As soon as I tied the snugly in back for your father, I'd down a glass of juice or milk or water, then fall on the bed asleep. An hour might pass, or two, but it seemed you were back in minutes, wanting me, screaming. Exhausted as I was, I was as glad to see you as you were me, my breasts engorged and hard as bricks.

You'd drink until you were stuffed, milk dribbling down your chin, then you'd sink into slumber, me beside you, and beside me, your father. All of us like rabbits in a hutch, curled around each other, helpless in sleep.

Colicky evenings your father took to walking you, too. In his arms facing front ways, cradled sideways, or held against his chest; over his shoulder as he did what we called the 'horsy walk,' a bouncy, slip-gaited stride that seemed to calm you. Or he walked you swaddled in blankets we'd warmed in the dryer, or pushed you in your pram back and forth across the apartment until he scratched out a path in the hardwood floor. Walking you was his equivalent of nursing. Colicky evenings were the only times you didn't like to nurse, and your father became an expert.

Bedtimes he racked up another five miles at least. First I nursed you, then changed you, dressing you in your nightie with the drawstring at the bottom; next we eased you into the snugly and turned off the lights. Your father did laps around the apartment until we were sure you were asleep. Both of us holding our breaths, this was the tricky part—getting you out of the snugly and into your cradle without your waking up. Which happened about half the time anyway, meaning another five miles for your father.

By ten weeks you were as plump as you see in magazine pictures, your bowed legs rounding out, wrists like sausages. You nursed a little more regularly, more predictably; you went to sleep a little more willingly. You smiled and showed your gums, your eyes were bright, focused. I exchanged my maternity underwear for the other kind, although it was a tight fit; your father was a little more awake at work. I could change diapers with the best of them now and on good days life was smooth, easy, sleek, and I felt filled with the milk of life itself.

Other days I had my doubts, a sense of loss as never before.

Beginning with the simple immutable fact that my own mother no longer walked the earth; she could not be there for me. She *hadn't* been there, not to break the news of my pregnancy to, or to offer advice and annoy me with phone calls about whether I was eating right, and had I thought about baby names.

She wasn't there for the birth, or there to knit booties and sweaters. Or to tell us from whom you had inherited your nose, or that you hated the sun in your eyes, just as I had. She wasn't there to argue with, to tell us we were burping the baby wrong, or to inform us that in her day there wasn't so much pampering of babies.

She wasn't there, not to soothe us, care for us, or cook us supper when we were exhausted. But that sort of mother wasn't *my* mother anyway.

What remained of her, my real mother? Her tortured letters, her terrible deeds against Charlotte and myself. I couldn't think about this when you were first born.

For your father and me, then, there was no sense of family history or continuity, no rituals. It was freeing in a sense, but lonely, like being settlers in a new world. So we would tell each other, standing at the ocean's edge at sunset, your father's arm around me, and you against my shoulder or attached at my breast, the undertow sucking our feet down into the sand, deeper and deeper, as if trying to root us that way.

So for me, mothering wasn't something handed down, from generation to generation, mother to daughter; like nursing, it was learned behavior. If I liked the way somebody talked to her baby, I copied it. Whatever made sense to me in books and magazines, I adopted, developing my own philosophies along the way. I became a student of mothering, from the very basics to ideology. Not that I treated you like a project, but I listened to your cries, tried to read them. When I didn't know what to do, I looked into your eyes and watched and listened.

There were some things I just plain didn't know that had nothing to do with philosophies or ideology. Giving you a bath, for instance. The first time, your father and I actually followed instructions from a book. We had two books, in fact, that weren't always in agreement.

"Step one," I read out loud. "Start at the head. Wipe each eye from the inside out with two separate corners of the washcloth or two cotton balls." It had been a week and we hadn't given you a bath yet, terrified we'd do something wrong. "Use cotton balls," I said, "all right?"

"It said we could use a washcloth."

"Yes, but the other book specifically says cotton balls. They're sterilized. We're talking about Gena's eyes, Jackson."

Step two: ears. The books didn't agree on this either.

"Theo? Would you mind using a washcloth instead of Q-tips? I'm afraid you'll puncture her eardrum."

"She's asleep, how can I possibly miss?"

"What if she wakes up?"

"Okay, you have a point. God this is nerve-wracking!" My face was perspiring even more than usual, rivulets of sweat rolling down my hot cheeks. I proceeded to wash your face, step three, with plain water, no soap (although this was optional in one book, a no-no in the other). You stirred for a moment, grimaced, then fell back to sleep. At step four we reached an impasse: my book said to wash your hair next, your father's said to wash your body first *then* your hair.

"I vote we wash her hair first," I said.

"Won't she get chilled?"

"But Jackson, she has on a tee shirt."

To our surprise you seemed to enjoy your shampoo, completely relaxing into my hands. Washing your body was another story. Just as I suspected, you hated it, first squirming, then stiffening up into a loud wail. "Hurry," I told your father. "Get the towel. Get two of them! One for now, and one to put her in after she's dry."

"Do you think she's hungry?" he asked.

"Who knows," I said, opening my shirt that was drenched with milk, sweat, water. "All right, all right. Here I am, Gena. Have at me."

From sponge baths we graduated to tub baths, once your umbilical cord fell off. You slept during the shampoos, screamed through the rest, so that I took to nursing you *before* the bath to make sure you didn't get hungry *during*. I nursed you right after, too, to soothe you from the bath itself, and I nursed you again after you were dressed, which also seemed to upset you. It was instinct, nothing I'd read in a book and anyway, it worked.

We thought of ourselves as birds. Parent birds with a baby bird. Division of labor. Some things your father did: kept the nest warm and dry and clean (more or less), went out and got food (take out), filled the car with gas, and put baby equipment together.

I nursed.

We shared the bathing, traded off on diaper changing, me taking over for your father when he felt especially over-whelmed—when poop had gone up the back of your shirt, gotten into your hair, landed on the walls somehow, not to mention our own clothes. Sometimes when you pooped we all needed chang-ing.

Spit-up was something else. There was the bad kind, which also necessitated a full change of clothes all around, or the medium kind, which required a simple change of shirts. Then there was the kind we hardly noticed anymore, just a line of white stuff down our backs.

Birds didn't have extended family. Neither did we. We tried not to think about it, the fact that we were doing this all alone. The fact that we had to get instructions out of a book on how to give our baby a bath. Later we wondered why we hadn't at least hired a nurse for a few days, to help us make the adjustment. But a nurse, I think, would've only reminded me that I didn't have a mother of my own: I had to hire one. I preferred to pretend—not that I had a mother, but that not having one didn't bother me.

It did and it didn't. Having you made me feel rooted to the ground and for the first time in my life, I could cast off my mother, not be haunted by her shadow. I was free of her at last.

Yet I felt a blackness lurking around the edges, as if I'd better not stray from the center of this life I was building. I stood here, the blackness there, not two feet away. Better not run my hand, not even my little finger, through that blackness on the other side, the blackness that was my mother. All of this—my daughter, my husband and I newly returned to each other—all of this—could be ripped from me in an instant. Gone.

TWENTY-NINE

EPILOGUE

The thirtieth anniversary of my mother's suicide and we're about to have a party. Not a party exactly—friends over for dinner. I didn't plan it this way, the date creeping up on me as it always does, or maybe unconsciously I *did* plan it this way, but here we are, Jackson throwing tortilla chips into a bowl and setting out his homemade salsa, while I take our daughter onto my hip and head upstairs to dress. Though I showered earlier today, I'm barefoot and wearing a Rockies T-shirt down to my knees, my hair up in a knot coming loose. Gena's still in her pajamas.

She's two and we're back in Colorado where we belong, where we moved after the riots, the earthquakes, the drought, the flooding.

But that was after Gena was born. For a while Jackson and I lived in separate rooms in his apartment, though we spent every minute together—a newborn to care for. No time to talk, not about us, not at first. Maybe it was better that way. Jackson had continued to attend AA meetings and was thoughtful, edgy, emotional. He tended to his business, I tended to mine, and together we tended our daughter, and if we learned anything, it was that we sometimes talk too much, picking at our wounds unnecessarily.

My own wounds: that was a different matter. I'd wake up kicking, thrashing in bed, and couldn't talk enough—to Jackson, to Maggie, and especially to my therapist in Pasadena, whom I began to see a few months after Gena was born, driving up there once a week, with Gena of course, who was lulled by freeways and hysterical on surface streets. At stoplights I had to keep the car in motion, in forward and reverse, a few inches up, a few inches back, because once she started screaming, there was no end. To have her along was soothing to me, screams or not: no matter what happened in therapy—and it was hard work, like dredging up a corpse from a lake, a slow and reluctant process with ugly results—at the end of it was Gena, waiting for me at Maggie's house, hungry to nurse and be with me.

I'd see my therapist for an hour, followed by lunch with Maggie. Then I'd check in on Dad at the Grove. Never exactly overjoyed to see his granddaughter, or me, he always assumed we had better things to do than visit him and seemed eager for us to be on our way to do those things, whatever they were. As a grandfather he was inattentive, as I knew he would be, but I also knew he loved us, if mostly in theory.

Corb and I didn't see much of each other during that time, only now and then so that he and Diane wouldn't be total strangers to Gena. His only response to our mother's letters had been to eventually mail them back to me, no comment. I pictured him drying up in the Southern California heat, and I came to believe that the cancerous growth in his cheek had been a rotten fruit that nonetheless bore the seeds of possibility. A missed chance, the chance all survivors have—survivors of near-fatal accidents, illness or tragedy. One should walk away from the wreckage radiating life in the open palm of one's hand, and much as I loved Corb, for the simple yet elusive reason that he was my brother, his fist was closed tight.

Aunt Lyla I saw only once during those months, admittedly out of curiosity as much as to show off the baby. More nervous than usual, she frittered about serving me yogurt and juice and did the baby want anything, she kept repeating. Rice cereal, a little mashed banana? She's nursing, I said, too young for solid foods. "Whatever, dear," she said, but I got the impression she thought I was a little too devoted to Gena, that I coddled her. She asked if I wanted to put her down. She's not sleepy, I said. But you can put her down, she said. In the other room. Why would I want to do that? I asked. Oh, she said, I don't know. When Gena pooped, she whisked her out of my arms in order to change her for me, the same efficiency with which she kept house, cooked, wrote thank-you notes and accessorized her outfits. "Children have to be managed," Aunt Lyla advised me. In her day—my mother's day—babies were trained, is how I saw it. Trained not to cry by being left to cry, trained to go to sleep when they weren't tired. Trained to entertain themselves. Trained to be good. Trained not to need.

"There, now," Aunt Lyla said, handing Gena back to me; I could smell the powder beneath her diaper.

"Did you ever read my mother's letters, Aunt Lyla?"

She startled, as I knew she would, stopping in the tracks of her stiletto heels, about to light a cigarette.

"Well, did you?"

"I read them and then I burned them. I suggest you do the same."

"I'm not about to burn my mother's letters!"

"Oh stop being such a warrior, dear. All I meant is that it might give you some closure, as it gave me." She smiled obliquely, adjusting her earring for a brief vulnerable moment, before crushing out her cigarette.

Good old Aunt Lyla. Still capable of a vogue word now and then. Closure: *I* saw a closed door. I saw my mother's ashes and the tiny decayed body of my infant sister. I saw my mother's sister, my aunt, glancing at me furtively with all the love she was capable of. She was at peace. Not a peace I would choose for myself, it seemed to me a compromise of sorts. What peace wasn't? Hammered-out agreements and concessions and everybody walking away from the table with a scrap of paper, a bit of land. When would I achieve peace, the palm of my hand radiating life?

I had more than a scrap of paper, a bit of land. I had my daughter. But I'd made a pact with myself the day she was born, that she was here for herself, not me.

The day after she was born, Gregg came to the hospital. His face was drawn. *Why didn't you call me?* He couldn't say it out loud, anymore than I could say, *You know why.*

He wasn't good around the baby, his hands knotted in his pockets. "She's pretty," he ventured.

It broke the tension at least and we both started laughing: tiny Gena—so gorgeous to me—squashed face and pointy-headed, her diaper at that moment filled with black tar.

It was a test, I realized, calling Gregg here. How would he act toward the baby, toward me? Here was my answer: absolutely wooden. He looked at her as if confronted by an animated melon. *What is this? What do I do with it?* He kept his hands in his pockets, not offering to hold her, and I knew it was over between us. She wasn't his, even Gena seemed to sense this. I nearly ordered him out of my room, I was so disappointed. Instead, I closed my eyes, and through my tears, told him I was sorry. He said he was sorry too, and kissed my forehead. We parted as we had begun, romantic friends.

An hour later Jackson visited, his second visit since Gena's birth the previous night. Thrilled with her, gently jogging the bundle that was Gena, he'd remember me, his smile fading. What were we going to do? Tears in his eyes, in mine.

What would we do?

I was beginning to think I knew, swabbing at Gena's sticky black, prolific bottom (I had just changed her!) until it was clean. A bottom that could fit in the palm of my hand, with room to spare. I got her into a diaper, a new tee shirt, and rolled her up in her blankets somehow. She was slightly premature but at six-and-a-half pounds, not a preemie.

I sat down on the bed and flung open my hospital gown. With Jackson watching, I nursed our daughter.

The thirtieth anniversary of my mother's suicide . . .

I tried a support group for incest survivors, since something of the sort had apparently happened to me. I disliked the women, some of whom seemed bona fide crazy: in and out of hospitals, off and on antidepressants and tranquilizers; obese, alcoholic.

One had been imprisoned for prostitution and another, a teenager, was still living in the same house as her perpetrator.

The facilitator listened to the women's stories, all the while playing with her thin, limp hair, single strands of it, and I had the unnerving feeling that had we not been there she would have plucked the hair out, storing it under her seat for safekeeping.

Where were the normal ones, I kept wondering, the normal women who had experienced the word I still couldn't accept, much less say aloud? And who but me in this group had had this word enacted on them by their own mother? Normal I was not, not even by this group's standards. But I was alive, thriving for reasons I couldn't fathom: a husband by my side, milk staining my blouse, a baby daughter; life itself.

I stuck with therapy but joined another support group instead, La Leche for breastfeeding mothers. I loved their humdrum talk of cloth diapers and natural foods and homeopathy. I loved holding Gena in my arms and everybody in the room nursing.

All that milk would heal me.

The thirtieth anniversary of my mother's suicide and my daughter and I are dressing.

"New tights?" Gena asks. "New shoes?"

New: her favorite word, her voice rising at the end, as though she can barely contain herself. New-*ooo*?

"New tights, new shoes," I answer, helping her into them, then her dress.

"Not new dress," she says.

"No, but new tights, new shoes." Shoes and tights I got through my latest catalog, in fact. "Polka dot tights," I add for emphasis.

Her eyes that look exactly like mine grow wide. "*Poke* a dot?"

I nod.

"New shoes?" Gena repeats, pointing to mine.

"Sort of." Not wanting to disappoint her. I realize she wants us to match, the way all mothers and daughters should. When the daughter is two, that is.

She watches me intently as I gaze at my reflection in the mirror and I'm aware we're engaged in a ritual, though I know not where it comes from—a ritual from before the time of mirrors.

"New earrings?" she says.

"Yes," I say forcefully. "New."

The thirtieth anniversary of my mother's suicide and we're nearly downstairs to greet our guests, my daughter and I almost to the last step, slowly because she is small and we are holding hands, me in new earrings, Gena in her new shoes and polka dot tights, chapstick (to match my lipstick) smeared on her mouth and cheeks so that she smells like grape soda.

Tonight I feel my mother's presence, though she no longer kneels, no longer haunts my dreams. She waits at the end of a room, her face illuminated by moonlight, in her arms a child; I can't see her, but she's there—she's there—

With us now as our feet leave the step.